W9-BNN-535

A WYATT
BOOK for
W
ST.
MARTIN'S
PRESS

A Wyatt Book *for* St. Martin's Press
New York

# Cowkind

A Novel by

Ray Petersen

*This is a work of fiction. Names, characters, places, and incidents either are the product of the author's imagination or are used fictitiously. Any resemblance to events or persons, living or dead, is entirely coincidental.*

 For information, address A Wyatt Book for St. Martin's Press, 175 Fifth Avenue, New York, N.Y. 10010.

*Book Design by Gretchen Achilles*

Library of Congress Cataloging-in Publication Data

Petersen, Ray.
Cowkind / by Ray Petersen. — 1st ed.
p. cm.
ISBN 0-312-14302-8
1. Human-animal relationships—United States—Fiction. 2. Vietnamese Conflict, 1961–1975—United States—Fiction. 3. Dairy farmers—United States—Fiction. 4. Farm life—United States—Fiction. 5. Family—United States—Fiction. 6. Cattle—United States—Fiction. I. Title.
PS3566.E7638C6 1996
813'.54—dc20 95-53352
CIP

First Edition: June 1996

10 9 8 7 6 5 4 3 2 1

# Contents

BOSSY (1971)
*1*

SMITTY (1968)
*10*

CALVIN (1968)
*21*

PEANUT (1968)
*34*

JOHN (1969)
*45*

ARETHA (1969)
*56*

KING (1969)
*76*

RENEE (1969)
*99*

GERRY (1970)
*112*

EDNA (1971)
*130*

THUNDER (1971)
*149*

BOB (1971)
*178*

# Acknowledgments

Whether they realized it or not, the following people helped with this book: Dean Anthony, Iris Bass, Alice Booth, Lee Booth, Pat Chatman, Jim Ciment, Peter Corodimas, Bruce Coville, Mark Fischweicher, Chris Foster, Dr. Albert Fritz, Joanne Hebert, Tom Kriger, Karen Lizon, Rob Morrow, Bill Petersen, Carole Petersen, George Petersen, Keitha Petersen, Laurie Lind Petersen, Louie Petersen, Ralph Petersen, Craig Reicke, Dave Reid, Corin See, Ted Silverhand, Suzanne Thiessen, Nancy White, Bob Wyatt, and Andrea Wyman.

# Cowkind

## Chapter One

# Bossy

(1971)

"Moo," she said derisively.

She couldn't get herself to care. She felt used. He was just another man, like all men. Only interested in what was in it for them.

She'd be damned if she'd come to his call.

He persisted. "Come, Bossy. Ca-boss, ca-bo-oss." His voice, which once had warmed her, now felt like a razor.

It hadn't always been that way, but something had changed. It had started back when the old man stopped coming around. He had been Bossy's first favorite, after her own father. It pained her even now to think of White John. He had been handsome and strong, and all the cows loved him—none more than her mother. But it was his job to pay attention to all the cows, and Bossy's mother could not let go of her special affection for him. Could not allow him to do his work.

When Bossy was young, before she had even seen her first winter, her mother was frantic with White John's unfaithfulness. The problem was, he enjoyed his vocation too much. He took too seriously the responsibility of being the herd's protector. Often it got him in trouble with the humans on the farm.

Bossy's mother didn't care about White John's troubles with the humans. It was his playing around with other cows that bothered her. She went to Bedelia, who was the oldest cow in the herd at that time and knew something about the traditions of the Old Ones, to ask if there was anything that could be done.

"I don't know, Marianne. Of course, the stories tell of a time when each cow would be mated with one bull, and only one bull, for life. But that was so long ago."

"But which is more important, Bedelia?" Marianne pressed. "Is it more important that we do what humans want, or that we live according to our beliefs?"

Bedelia waited a long time, reflecting. "There's nothing in ancient law that allows for the kind of family we have today. The humans have taken that away. I know why you're asking about this—I know about your feelings for White John. But you've got to understand that we had to make this compromise a long time ago, and if you don't allow White John to do what the humans want, then they won't let him stay here anymore. Do you understand what I'm saying?"

Bossy's mother nodded and turned slowly away. *I don't care,* she thought. *If I can't have him, nobody's going to have him. I can't bear to watch him whoring around with all the others.*

She resolved herself to be distant, cold. She decided that she would spurn White John, not allow him to have her, and certainly not to do the dance the next time it was her turn.

But her resolve crumbled as soon as she got back to the rest of the herd and saw that Daisy was in her time, and that her love was nearby. She looked at John, and the frozen lake of her passion thawed instantly. She hurried over and began to rear up onto Daisy's back, to show that Daisy was bulling, that she was in need.

She did the same when Smitty went into heat, and Dutchess, and Wings, and Brownie. Bossy couldn't understand what was happening to her mother. She was hearing things from the other cows that were hurtful, but she was afraid to say anything about them. Marianne was lost in her pimping, in complete denial. In her mind she had become the Priestess of Old, the Matchmaker.

So Bossy grew up hearing whispers about her mother. But when she had grown so that it was close to her own time, her first time, her mother's sanity began to unravel. She could not bring herself to arrange the mating of her husband—her faithful lover—and her daughter.

Whenever John came around to test Bossy's progress, her mother was there, always placing herself physically between her daughter and her husband. It started to make White John testy. He'd never had to pay attention to the offspring of his conjugal visits. All this talk from

Marianne of the Old Ones and the Old Ways, the ways Before Dominion, made no sense to him. They didn't live in that world now.

It made him start to take to apples, eating more and more green and fermented apples, so their juices would fill his head with the ooze of unconcern. That made him even rougher with the other cows, the ones with whom Marianne would let him do what he wished.

But it made him meaner also with the humans, and the humans grew more and more unsure of him. The cows were uneasy, whispering. Still, Marianne stood between him and the necessary union with her daughter.

Bossy couldn't understand what was going on. Her father always smelled like silage that had been put in too early, like the breath of the hired man, Merle, when he came down to the barn acting loud and rough. Her father, whom her mother had cherished, was getting angry and distant. She wanted somehow to save him, and to save her mother, who was slipping further into the past.

"No," her mother said, "you can't do that, dear. It's just not right." Bossy had told her mother that she was going to her father, because it was wrong for her not to know him.

She had to know him.

"I won't let you. I'll fight him if I have to. I'll kill him, or I'll kill you if I must. It's blasphemy, a betrayal of all that is sacred. I'll fight you, I'll fight," her mother ranted in the stall next to her.

"No, Mother, you're wrong. It can't be your way anymore. The Old Bond is broken."

Merle pulled the bolt free and slid the sideboard away so Bossy could back out of her stanchion, while her mother hung her head. She turned and strode out the barn door as her mother was unstanchioned, trying to get as much distance between them as possible.

From a safe distance on top of the hill that gradually sloped off into the river meadow, she turned back toward the barn to catch a glimpse of her father as he came through the door. Forty was just clearing the barn, followed by Wings and Brownie. White John had to be coming soon.

But he didn't come.

Bossy heard only after it was all over. Her mother had turned to attack White John once he was unstanchioned. The fighting was so vicious that her mother was chased out of the barn and her father was locked up again. Later that day the truck came to pick him up and take him away to the auction.

She never saw him again.

Her mother became even more unhinged, went dry months before normal, and also was sold for beef.

So Bossy grew up abhorring violence and all manner of excess, and with a hunger to save her father, some father, any man. The new John never captured her interest, because he lacked her father's strength and despotism; and while she had loved the old man, Russell Scott, their relationship had been limited to his scratching a favorite itchy spot behind her ear and below the tuft of black hair that was always sticking up from the crown of her head. And even he had disappeared mysteriously four harvest seasons ago. She would not listen to the other cows' whispering about him, not after what had happened to her parents.

She had fixed her love upon Bob Scott, the old man's son. By ancient practice he was called Farmer Bob by the cows, a title recognizing that he had the power to name, and thus decide life and death. The utter impossibility of her love's being reciprocated had helped to ensnare her at first into the savior role. Then Farmer Bob's early gentleness and care completed the infatuation.

When she was young he had taken the care during milking to warm his hands before he cleaned her bag and her teats. There was a time when he would tenderly, gently massage each quarter as it was done giving its milk.

When her bag was relaxed and emptied, he would unhook the air hose from the vacuum line, carry the milking machine to the dumping station, and make a grunting sound as he lifted the pail—it was so full.

Sometimes in the winter, steam from the fresh milk she had produced would rise and lightly fog his glasses. She knew he didn't mind because she had given her best.

Each time he grunted when he lifted that pail filled with milk, she knew.

Bob was a traditional farmer, one who had lived through the Depression. Survival, especially in this mean part of the country, always had depended on being close to the land. His farm was on the southeastern curve of Lake Ontario, on the lake plain that gave way to the even meaner land of Tug Hill.

He was just as traditional about how the house should be run. Men worked outside and women worked inside, except when the men needed help. Inside, men were waited on, served their three square meals—breakfast, dinner, and supper. Breakfast was always at the kitchen table. At dinner and supper, the men's meals were sometimes brought into the living room on trays, as if they were visiting royalty—or paraplegics.

Bob knew that there were cycles, and you had to get through the winter the best you could, and not go crazy in the spring when things were flush.

He had cared for his cows.

In the winter when they were cooped up inside the barn, had little space to be dainty, to maintain their cow dignity, Farmer Bob would make sure that their hindquarters and tails were groomed, clipped, brushed. Even though it was a hard metal brush used to scrape off the deposits from Bossy's toilet, the brushing meant he cared.

The younger cows didn't seem to see it that way. Not Charlotte, nor White Brat, nor Thunder, nor Killer, nor Billie. During clipping, Bossy would shuffle back and forth on her back hooves, and sigh a little. The others made fun of her.

They didn't know what Bossy knew. She had heard on the music box, in between the country songs and the weather reports, that there was something called TV.

There were soap operas and game shows set in exciting places, where the weather was nice and people were glamorous. Farmer Bob could be up in the house on winter days, watching those shows. He was in the barn instead.

It had to be an expression of his love.

Now Farmer Bob had lost his love. He had become more and more distant after the strangers came to install a newfangled milking machine. The dumping station was gone. Now the teat cups would still hang from her, but her milk wasn't going into any bucket underneath the pulsators. It was going straight from the teat cups into a vacuum line, and it was whisked away up into that room she knew only as the milkhouse.

The milkhouse. What was it? There was a narrow doorway that led there from the barn. It was wide enough for Bossy to have gone through to see what was in there, but it was hinged to swing closed whenever the human walked through. All any of them knew about the milkhouse was what the sisters stanchioned right in front of the doorway reported.

The stories from those cows had changed. Bossy remembered hearing that in the old days Farmer Bob's son, Gerry, used to carry buckets of milk up through that doorway, because there was no dumping station then. At first he would carry one bucket at a time, then later two, one in each hand, once he was older and stronger. He would turn around and push the door open with his backside and then swing each pail through and disappear.

Daisy had said that those were even better times. She could crane around and catch Gerry out of the corner of her eye, scooping up froth from the top of the milk. He would suck it off his fingers, savoring its warmth and sweet richness.

And then he would carry the buckets up, and of course disappear through the door. But she would hear the sounds of metal things being skidded and rolled around, and she heard what Farmer Bob and Gerry and the hired man would say about the vat: "Putting the cans in the vat."

So they learned that there were cans of some kind in there that you could see occasionally as the door swung back. They had figured out that these must be the milk cans.

And once Daisy had reported seeing them load the cans into the back of the pickup truck, rolling them until they clanged together, then putting the tailgate up. The pickup truck always pulled up out of the circular driveway and in the direction of town. (They never knew what "town" meant, but they'd heard enough of the humans' conversation to know which turn out of the driveway headed toward town and which one headed elsewhere.)

Those were the old days. Now the new cow that had been moved into Daisy's place, Pet, said it was untrue—there were no cans there, there never had been. All you needed to do was turn around and look at what happened after the milk was dumped into the station to know that there were no cans in there. Nobody was carrying pails of milk up through that door into the milkhouse. Nobody loaded cans onto any pickup truck.

And just look at the small vat for the dumping station. You could dump milking-machine bucket after milking-machine bucket of milk into that small dumping-station vat, and it would never fill up—only when it was running too slowly because of dirt or a problem with the milk.

No, there was something new up in that milkhouse. And this new cow, Pet, said, "This is now a military operation."

"A military operation?" Bossy craned her head around. She couldn't believe what she'd heard. She was standing almost cheek-to-hindquarter with Pet, whose cheek was also next to Bossy's hindquarter. Pet was sleek dark, cool-appearing but overwarm, steam close to rising from her even when it wasn't cold. They stood in the pasture chewing cuds, swishing flies off each other's face, in the muggy heat of summer.

"A military operation?"

"Well—that's all I can make of it. I see some huge metal thing in there, shining. And I know from what I've heard on the radio, when they were reporting on the war, that they use the same kind of equipment."

"What are you talking about?" Bossy demanded.

"It's a tank," Pet said. "That's what our milk is going into now."

Bossy gulped, half-swallowed her cud, and then managed to belch it out. "What? A tank? I can't believe that. Farmer Bob would never do that—he'd never let it happen."

Pet looked at Bossy consolingly. "It's true. You know you've heard it. You've heard Gerry talk about it. You've heard Farmer Bob. You've heard Merle."

"That just *can't* be true." Bossy moved off by herself, restlessly. She needed to go down toward the woods, to sit in the shade, maybe to get a drink of water from the river. She knew what she had heard on the radio about the war, about how many people had gone off to fight and die already.

"Nixon will end the war," Merle had said. But that was three grass seasons ago, and, if anything, the war sounded worse. And she knew from the arguments, during the tense evening milkings especially, that something might be happening with Gerry, that he might have to go off to that war.

But she could never imagine that Farmer Bob would allow it to happen. Now she knew it was even worse, that they were being used to support the war. He was sending their milk up into a tank.

*It just doesn't make sense.*

She hadn't made it halfway to the edge of the woods before she had to sit down again and think. *Our milk is going into a tank. Farmer Bob doesn't really care for us anymore, or for what we produce. It's not going to babies—it's going off to that war.*

She had heard the war stories Farmer Bob told Gerry and Merle during milking. She knew that he had fought in the Big War, yet despite his experience and being proud of his part, Farmer Bob didn't like the army. He didn't like officers; he couldn't abide being told what to do. And she couldn't imagine that he would let his own son go to fight in this war that so many people were against.

The shock of Pet's news was making her wobbly.

She had been upset before with Farmer Bob. And now she was not hearing any appreciation from him about the amount of milk she made. Because of this new vacuum line she would never hear again that special grunt. Her milk went straight up into the milkhouse, with all the other cows' milk, with Thunder's and Lightning's and Wings', with White Brat's and Billie's.

So he didn't know how much they were holding out. That had been bad enough. But now—their milk was going into a tank. And—she just knew it now—it was being used for that war.

What had happened to the Farmer Bob she had known, who appreciated his animals, kept them much longer than any other farmer would, and knew about each one's special needs?

She lay there in that same spot in the pasture, her legs tucked under her, without the appetite to graze or the thirst to bring her to the riverside. But her mind was racing, trying to redefine her purpose in this changed life.

Something she had seen recently swirled sharply into focus.

She had caught a glimpse two days ago of Farmer Bob's daughter, Renee, when she was near the barn for haying late one afternoon. Bossy recognized the look in Renee's eyes—a combination of hurt, anger, and yearning—that she remembered once before from a reflection in the water at the river, shortly after her father and mother had been sent away. *What was happening to Farmer Bob?*

The sun arced toward its last quarter, and the air changed ever so slightly toward dampness. Evening milking was going to come soon. Just when she was about to get up to go to the river, Bossy saw Gerry and Merle head out into the pasture. Most of the other cows were up close by the gate, waiting impatiently to get into the barn to gobble up feed and drink from the water buckets. But she didn't budge; she couldn't get herself to move. Then off in the distance, up by the barn door, she heard Farmer Bob's voice, calling: "Ca-boss, ca-boss, come Bossy, ca-boss."

It had always given her pride to be the one he was calling, the one who would hear his voice and go toward the barn, to be the one to lead the rest of the herd.

Now she hated the name she had been given. Now that voice cut.

No, she wouldn't go first. She didn't even get up onto her feet until Gerry made it out into the pasture and came over and kicked her rump with his tall black Wellington boots. She still wouldn't have moved, would not have let herself be moved, if she hadn't swung her head around and looked into Gerry's eyes and seen his confusion and disappointment staring back at her.

"Come on, Bossy. What's wrong with you today? You're usually the first one up there," Gerry said. "Come on. Get up, girl. Let's get some of that milk of yours into the machine. With your bag you'll be leaking all over the place, you've got so much more milk than the rest of these cows."

Bossy thought, *He knows. He understands. He appreciates me.*

"Come on, Bossy."

She didn't get up for Farmer Bob, but she did struggle to her feet and turn to face the barnyard for Gerry. And as she walked along with Gerry behind her, distractedly tapping her rump with a stick, she sneaked a look backward. She could see that he wasn't there in that pasture, he wasn't even there on the farm; not in his mind. He was troubled. He didn't know what he would do.

She found herself plodding toward the barn for Gerry, and resolved to give her milk for him, from that day on.

## Chapter Two

# Smitty

(1968)

Smitty had been at the farm since before time.

One of the last of the veterans of the Long March, she had memories that even preceded the stone farm. She had known of bulls, the seasons, humans, and even the theft of her babies before she had been transported to the stone farm. There she learned one more important thing about humans: they had the power to heal.

She was in a fever when they delivered her to the stone farm, in part because of the chill wind that blew through the sides of the stake rack, but also because her second calf, and first daughter, was bouncing around in the back of the truck with her. The farmer at her birthplace had been pleasant enough, having raised her and sent her daughter along in the truck with her, but ever since her first baby was pulled away by that rough driver, while the farmer watched, she never had been able to trust him fully again.

This baby was barely four cuds old and had not been able to keep her milk, so Smitty was anxious as the truck slowed, inched into the mud of the barnyard, and finally stopped. Her calf was tied in the front right corner of the truck, shivering as she lay in frozen piss and dank straw.

The tailgate was lowered halfway and held level by a stooped old man as the truck was backed up to the barn door. When the truck motor died out completely, Smitty climbed to her feet. Then the old man achingly set the tailgate down, squinting at her bag.

"Thought you said this was a first-calf heifer," the old man said.

"Yeah, I did." The driver grinned malevolently.

"Well, what year were you talkin' about?"

"This year I'm talking about."

"When this year? Last January? Got her bred back real quick?"

"Listen, if you think two seventy-five is too much, I can take this heifer someplace else," the driver growled.

"No, no. That one quarter does look kinda hard, though." The old man stooped a little more, waiting for a new offer.

"Sure you don't want that calf, too?" the driver asked, ignoring the old man's baiting. But a tremble sheared through Smitty, so that she sagged back down to her knees. Her daughter, only understanding her own fever and discomfort, was watching her. Smitty kept one eye fixed on her daughter, buoying her spirits and calming her with a steady warm look. From the center of her other eye, panic radiated outward.

She did not know where the reassurance for her daughter came from, and did not believe in it herself. Though she kept that half-gaze fixed on her daughter's face, she would not look directly into her eyes.

"What makes you think you can pass that sick calf off on me, too? That calf's got scours, ya know. If you really knew anythin' about the animals you say are yers, you'd know this one's got the shits bad. Ain't a farmer up at the auction barn gonna buy that thing for veal, 'cuz they know it won't live that long."

"Well, it will live that long if it's taken care of."

" 'Zackly. I'll take the calf, too, to nurse that hard quarter back on the second-calf heifer."

"Now wait a minute. How much more?"

"What? Money? You think I'm gonna pay you more? Or do you mean how much more of this bullshit am I gonna listen to? Two seventy-five's good for a second-calf heifer with a bad quarter and a half-dead calf." Smitty could not stop herself from shuddering.

The driver sneered. "I think I'll just take both of these animals to the auction barn and see if I can't get more than two seventy-five for 'em."

"Ah, I'd . . ."

Smitty wheeled around and clomped down the tailgate, pushing right between the two men. The driver yelled, "Hey!" as he was knocked onto his behind. The old man grinned at Smitty while she bellered for her calf, still tied in the front corner of the truck. Her daughter thrashed and bellered back, eyes rolling completely white and frothing at the mouth against the twine around her throat. The calf pulled and fell on her knees and slammed into the sidewalls of the stake rack, growing ever more frantic as her mother retreated farther into the dim recesses of the old man's barn.

"This will get the sonuvabitch back in my truck," the driver yelled, waving an electric prod at the old man.

"Better think about whether you want to use that on a cow you're plannin' on takin' to the sale," the old man drawled. "That calf is gonna save ya the trouble of not sellin' at the auction—'s gonna die right there in your truck."

"I'll kill both of 'em first," the driver said.

"Okay, Fred, but then you won't get your two-fifty."

"*Two-fifty!*" the driver roared, turning on the old man.

"Well, look at that calf," the old man whispered.

Smitty's calf was on her side, stretched much too far away from her tether. The sliding knot had worked its way over the restraining knot into a garrote, bulging the eyes and purpling the tongue of her daughter. Smitty went mad, smashing through an empty stanchion in her frenzy.

"Jesus, no," the driver gasped.

"Don't you have a jackknife? Cut that thing loose," the old man said.

The driver quickly fished a knife from his pocket and cut the twine. The old man pulled the rope from around the calf's neck and pumped its front legs vigorously, to no effect.

"C'mon, Asa, give me a hand," the driver pleaded. He lifted the back end of the calf as the old man carried the front, down the tailgate and into the barn. Fred hoisted the back legs of the calf up over the planks of an empty stanchion and hooked them behind the galvanized vacuum line. Smitty's calf hung limply from the stanchion, eyes still bulging. Asa pried open the calf's mouth with both hands, then gently worked her tongue back and forth to clear the air passage. Fred held the calf's back legs with his right arm and pumped her front legs with his left. Almost imperceptibly at first, the calf's lungs began to take in air, then she spasmodically began to choke, cough, and wheeze. After a few minutes her breathing steadied, so the men lowered her to the ground.

They looked at each other, studying, waiting to see where the bidding had left off.

"Ya better get a new piece of twine for that calf," Asa offered. " 'S a long trip."

"Let's stick to the deal," Fred replied.

"Okay, two hundred forty." Asa winked slyly.

"Awright, let me get outta here before I owe you money."

Asa prodded the calf over to the manger of an empty stanchion and carefully tied her to one of the frame planks. Smitty followed her calf and allowed herself to be locked up. Mother and daughter nuzzled each other into contentment while Asa counted out the money.

Asa continued to feed the calf scalded milk stripped out by hand from Smitty's swelled quarter until the diarrhea went away. Smitty recovered from her infection and grew to feel safe and at home on the stone farm. After Asa's wife decided that they would raise Smitty's daughter, and gave her the name Daisy, Smitty decided to name her.

She chose Daisy as well.

Smitty had two calves for Asa on the stone farm—a bull sold for beef at two days old, then a heifer raised with the name Miss Jerome—before she moved to the mud farm. She was the source of seven more offspring there, earning the right to live out her natural life, from Bob Scott's point of view. She had become a fixture, but not all of the cows respected her: with each new addition to the herd and succeeding generation, Smitty's understanding of the farm and of the humans there became more out-of-touch. It would not be fair to say that she was senile. It was just that things changed too much, too quickly, for her to have a claim to wisdom.

In her last years, life for Smitty revolved around eating well and keeping out of the way of the other cows. She was thirteen years old, brittle and aching with every step. Her stanchion was the closest to the barn door, which gave her an advantage in moving out into the barnyard before the younger, heavier cows came through to get to the lane which led to the meadows across the road. Smitty was jostled regularly and pushed right up against the two rusty strands of barbed wire and held there as the rush of the herd passed by. And it seemed to her that a few of the cows went out of their way to ram her, even when there was room to go around. The problem was there was no way she could stop them, no way to get help.

But it wasn't all trouble for her, mainly because she had learned to enjoy simple pleasures, like ladino clover and good timothy to eat.

"Yes, that's all you really need in life, good grazing," Smitty said.

"Oh, why don't you tell us all about it," Dutchess replied, with a yawn.

"Well, I will, then. I mean really. You might not think so, but when I was your age, right on this very farm, not the stone farm, but this old mud farm—"

"There isn't any stone farm," Dutchess stated flatly. "I'm so tired of hearing that old lie."

"What?"

"You heard me. I said it's a lie."

"Well, I never."

"I can believe that."

"Why should I ever expect that you'd understand?" Smitty fretted. "You never had to live through it."

"Yes, that's right, so I don't believe you about not having enough hay, or only having bad hay. Your problem is, you hate Farmer Bob as much as Bossy loves him."

"I don't hate Farmer Bob. It's just that I really loved the old man, the one at the stone farm. He never made us eat hay that was so mildewed it had to be drenched in molasses. And that is the reason why I graze as much as I can, unlike some big-time milkers I could mention."

"I suppose you want us to believe those stories about being chased by horses, too, come from far away, from town."

"That did happen!" she insisted. "It did! Only you forgot that they were ponies. At least that's what your precious Farmer Bob said."

"Oh, please, don't go into that story again. It's worse than the stone farm. Oh, the stone farm," she trilled. "Ah can see you, Mammy. Take me back, back, oh please." Dutchess's voice fluttered into falsetto, her broad white face smirking, breaking Bossy and Charlotte and even Daisy into snorting giggles.

"Get away from me! Leave me alone!" Smitty demanded, with as much dignity as she could muster.

"Oh, Mother, Dutchess was only having some fun. Don't be so serious all the time," Daisy soothed. "I remember the stone farm."

"Then why do you act like you don't remember?" Smitty demanded. "You know how kind Asa—"

"Wasn't his name *Farmer* Asa?" Thunder demanded menacingly. She had just returned from the pond at the swamp, and looked and smelled like it. The swamp stench was almost worse than her own characteristic odor.

"Yes, but—"

"Oh, Mother, you can't. You can't call a master—"

"Of course she can, she's special. How much milk does she have? Why is she still here?" Wings asked. "And she doesn't like Farmer Bob."

"I never said I didn't like Farmer Bob. It's just that I . . . loved Farmer Asa," she finished quietly. She pretended to graze, but they all knew she was too embarrassed to meet their eyes.

"You'd better graze, but off somewhere else," Thunder said flatly, pushing her shoulder into Smitty's ribs.

"I'm going. I'll go, alone." She retreated, not even looking back to see if Daisy was concerned.

It was already early afternoon, and while there was nothing she would have enjoyed more than a chance to rest in the small maple grove in the middle of the meadow, or to soak her legs in the cool, muddy pond bottom, there would be no space for her in either of those places.

Smitty hobbled off toward the lower gateway to the pasture on the river side of the road. She knew there was not much good grazing in that corner of the meadow, especially since swale grass was mixed in with the regular stuff on two sides of that lot, by the swamp and along the drainage ditch on the side of the road. But on the far end away from the swamp there was a little hill where she could sometimes find timothy. Or by getting on her knees she could probably reach under the bottom strand of barbed wire to snag some roadside clover. If all else failed, she could just eat some June grass and show the others that she really did know what it was like to make do with rough grazing.

Her ribs ached and her right rear hoof was getting even sorer as she hobbled away from the rest of the herd. Three days ago in the mud at the head of the lane she had picked up a stone high in the cleft of that hoof, just as the mob started to push her ahead. Because she couldn't stop, the stone kept splaying the hoof until it split the flesh in front of that knuckle, slowing her so that they pushed her even more. Once she finally got to the end of the lane and could turn out and away from the herd, Smitty managed to get the stone out, but it had already done its damage. To make it even worse, when Merle pointed out that she was hobbling, Farmer Bob dismissed the seriousness of her injury, saying, "I can't afford to pay for a vet call for Ol' Smitty. She just doesn't give enough milk."

It seemed like hours before she made it to the lower gate, and the throbbing had crept all the way up to her haunch, but then she was content to rest and casually search out some interesting stuff to graze upon. By this time it was midafternoon, only a few hours before they would have to go to the barn to be milked, but Smitty felt pretty sure that whoever was bringing the cows in would walk down to the lower gate to let her across the road.

*Well, some timothy. I guess I'm not so dumb,* she thought to herself. All she had to do was pick around the thistle and puffballs and she would have a nice meal. It was even better that she was alone, because no one could take this away from her. Her solitude was even beginning to feel comforting until she recalled Daisy's betrayal. That thought stopped her short.

*But there really is nothing I can do to help Daisy, because she is reaching the time herself. The next time she freshens she'll have even less milk than before, and that means that Farmer Bob might have to call the driver to get Daisy . . . and her calf.*

Smitty's hurt was so great that for a time she could only sit in a frenzied calm, not even chewing her cud. The recollection of her mortality, through Daisy, put Smitty completely off her feed. Suddenly she felt all of her ninety-five-odd human years in every particle of her being, and in no place more sharply than in her loins—the definition of her life and of its betrayal.

Gerry came to let the cows across the road for milking, later than usual because he had been baling hay all afternoon. After swinging back the barbed-wire gate he started calling out "Ca-boss" and pelting the cows near the fence with rocks. Most of the herd were already there, anticipating the grain waiting for them in the barn, but there were always a few that needed to be called or chased from the far reaches of the meadow. King was not around, and if Gerry had to go off into the meadow to chase any of the obstinate cows, there would be some wandering off up the road. He just kept calling and calling until all of the cows, save Smitty, had crossed the road.

"Why don't you come up here, you stupid animal?" Gerry fumed. Then he remembered that Smitty's leg had been hurt, so he closed the gate and trotted down the road to the lower gate. It didn't make sense for Smitty just to be sitting there. It didn't look like she had been eating all day. Her eyes were blank, staring straight ahead through him and everything else. He had to go out into the lot and slap her on the rump with his bare hand before she jumped to her feet as if she had been startled.

She moved slowly but steadily, sleepwalking in pain through the gate and up the short stretch of pasture to the lane. Its mud slowed her to a snail's pace, adding a reflexive wince to her grim visage. Hobbling over the gutter and into her stanchion, she fell into a stare at the flyspecks on the whitewashed wall directly in front of her.

Gerry swung by to lock the stanchion, noticing that she had not touched her grain. He aimed a vicious kick at Dutchess's snout; she had been reaching over to lap up Smitty's portion. He looked into Smitty's eyes and saw nothing.

"Dad, Smitty's sick. She ain't eatin' nothin', and she's just starin' straight ahead," Gerry yelled as soon as Bob came into the barn.

"Jesus. I've got enough trouble already—the baler's not tyin' right," Bob complained. "She eat any grain?"

"Nope."

"Not even her grain?" Bob was incredulous. He walked down to the end of the barn and around in front of her stanchion. "What's the matter, old girl?"

Smitty stared ahead.

"Was she reaching under the fence again?"

"Not when I went down to get her. She was just sittin' there," Gerry replied defensively.

"Looks like she's got hardware."

"Can't the vet fix that?"

"Maybe, but they might have to cut her open to find the staple or nail, and it would be real expensive." Gerry's father chewed on his lower lip, an expression Gerry recognized as meaning that getting a vet would cost too much.

"Run up to the house 'n' tell your mother to go get two quarts of beer from town," Bob said.

"Beer? What kind? What for?"

"To see if she's just off her feed. Any kind. Black Label."

"Okay." Gerry ran across the two stretches of circular driveway up to the house and gave his mother the message, then ran back down to the barn. Smitty was still unconscious on her feet. In fifteen minutes Gerry's sister, Renee, ran into the barn, breathless, carrying a brown paper bag.

"Bring that down here so we can give it to Smitty, honey," her father said.

"Okay, Dad." Renee poured each bottle down Smitty's throat while her dad lifted the cow's head. Smitty took both quarts, apparently without being affected. Then her right eye, which always looked a little rheumy, rolled back into her head. Smitty drooped her head down even farther and arched her back, then let out an enormous belch. She looked at Farmer Bob as if for the first time, with warm love-for-the-world eyes. As she ravenously dived into the grain in front of her, Gerry, Renee, and their father grinned at each other.

*Come on, come on, let me out,* Smitty thought as Gerry rinsed out the milking machines for the night. She had finished what was left of her grain and then had gotten onto her knees to slurp up the last fine bits of meal and husks left in front of Dutchess. When Dutchess had swung her head to butt Smitty away, the old lady had tilted her head to stab a blunt-edged horn into Dutchess's neck.

"Ow! Why did you have to do that? You old biddy," Dutchess complained.

"That's right. Not much left in me. But at least you'll find out what it's like to be pushed around for once."

"Don't threaten me."

"It's no threat. Just wait till they let me out."

Dutchess shuddered without even knowing why.

After all of the milking machines were rinsed out, Gerry picked his way across the barnyard to the high end to open the gate for the night pasture. But before he could let any of the cows out, his father yelled to him to put the cows in the mill piece for the night, since the river meadow had been grazed too low. Gerry grumbled about having to change the gates again. Smitty rejoiced.

*Good. Now I can get into that lane,* she plotted.

Gerry recognized something new as soon as he pulled the bolt and the stanchion board fell open. Instead of backing straight out, slowly and gingerly, creaking out the side of the big door, Smitty jerked her head back and turned to her left, raking Dutchess's side with the point of her right horn before stepping spryly over the gutter and out the center of the barn door.

She strode across the barnyard without betraying any evidence of pain in her leg, turned left, and picked up the pace, trotting down the lane before any of the other cows had even gotten across the barnyard. Gerry and his father were standing in the doorway now, admiring the way she carried her new lease on life. Smitty turned around to face the mob, eyes narrowed into a focus of ferocity. Then she started back up the lane, shouldering cows on either side of her, head up and shoulders square, moving with a purpose.

Every slight she had suffered, every brutish blow, every torment of her long twilight at the mud farm, was avenged in that one trip back through the gauntlet. She would be the one to deal out the punishment, she would be the source of the pain. She encountered Daisy almost at the very end of the gauntlet. Daisy's head and eyes were averted; she was pretending this was not happening. Smitty aimed a blow from the center of her forehead directly beneath Daisy's chin, lifting Daisy's front legs off the ground for a moment. Thunder closed in on Smitty from her left flank, grinding that one straight murderous horn of hers into the socket of Smitty's left front leg.

With an air of calm, of nonchalance, of pure unfeeling logic, Smitty dropped on her right knee, secured her skull into Thunder's breastbone, and then rose again, pushing Thunder straight back against the barbed wire. Thunder peeled off to her right and retreated back up the lane all the way around behind the barn. Smitty turned back upon Daisy, slamming her skull into her daughter's with a resounding crash that stopped the whole herd in its tracks.

Daisy groaned softly, afraid to actually speak to her mother. Gerry and Farmer Bob ran across the barnyard to chase Smitty and the rest of the herd down the lane. Smitty, who had been so violent a moment before, walked meekly, quietly, down the lane.

"Don't forget. Don't ever forget," Smitty said under her breath to Daisy, acting as if they were not being herded.

"Mother, why did you do this?" Daisy gasped.

"Just don't forget it. Promise me."

"All right. But I don't understand, Mother."

"Shhh, don't let the others hear," Smitty warned, then horned Daisy again for good measure. Thunder had just stolen a glance at them, returned fiercely by Smitty. Thunder moved away hurriedly.

The night of Smitty's mean drunk passed uneventfully after she turned the gauntlet on itself. The next morning she was moving more slowly and with greater pain than ever before. Farmer Bob had watched Smitty's revenge admiringly, even though her fight with Thunder ended up with a broken corner fence post. When Gerry started to go out to break up the fight, Bob had stopped him. "Let the old girl have her moment," he'd said.

Smitty's appetite was back, and she seemed to have gained a grudging appreciation for the healing powers and medicine of Farmer Bob. But her hoof wasn't healing and the soreness was moving up her haunch. After three weeks of hobbling, Farmer Bob still wasn't willing to get a veterinarian to treat Smitty, even though it troubled him to see her in such pain.

But by the time Daisy had delivered a smallish heifer calf, about six weeks after Smitty's drunk, not only was there an extra stanchion open for a heifer to grow up into, but Farmer Bob had a little extra cash from Smitty's sale to use to raise a scrawny, yet tough calf.

Now Daisy was the elder.

Now Smitty's sacrifice was real to her, and profound.

## Chapter Three

# Calvin

(1968)

As soon as he was born, Calvin was asking questions.

"Why are you trying to make me get up, Mama?" he inquired politely, as she nudged him to his feet. "It seems that the temperature is fine and there is more than sufficient food for us to eat right here in this meadow, Mama. Why are you leading me off into the woods?"

"You don't know about men, dear. They are not to be trusted," she worried.

"But wait a minute—are we hiding?" he asked, incredulous.

"Of course we are. If you lie here in this orchard grass without making a sound, they will never know you were born and then you can grow up wild." She looked at her young calf hopefully, yet not totally concealing her panic at his being taken away from her. He looked so sweet, and vulnerable, with his hair just dried from the bath she had given him after freshening. She had given him an extra going-over because the dusting of white hair on his back, like chalk residue on a blackboard, looked as if it should come off.

The look he returned to her was dispassionate and scientific. In a word, he was disdainful.

"Mother, I cannot believe that you could possibly want us to run off and hide. That's so silly. No, it's worse, it's bestial. It's archaic, uncivilized. People just don't do—"

"But we're not people. Don't you understand? Our lives are all about doing whatever they want. There's no chance for us to live the way we want to live."

"No chance for what? I don't get it. It seems so beautiful here. I'll bet you're just trying to scare me," he concluded.

"Just be perfectly quiet," she begged. "That's all I ask. Especially when they come looking for you. If you hear the tractor, be absolutely still. I'll be back in plenty of time to feed you before it gets dark, so don't worry about that. I'll be back. You just stay quiet."

"Okay," he agreed, with a patronizing roll of his eyes. Once she was back in the meadow grazing with the rest of the herd, he fell to examining his mother's paranoia.

*It's probably a hormonal thing. Wanting to run off into the woods. Huh. What a crazy idea.* Calvin proceeded to inspect the orchard grass all around him, noting that it was coarse and that the tassel was awfully full. He sniffed at a few ants, giggling as they scurried away. Lazily, he extended his tongue toward the grass, selected a stem, and wrapped his tongue around it. He wasn't ready to digest the grass, not being more than three hours old, but he did want to test it, to feel what it would be like to graze.

There no longer was any sound of cows grazing in the nearby meadow. They had all gone off toward the barn. Calvin waited a few moments in the silence of the woods, then climbed to his hooves to see if he could find out where his mother had gone. Once up, he had only reached eye level with the orchard grass, and was unable to see beyond a few feet in front of him.

Listening for the sound of the river to recede behind him, he picked his way carefully through the grass in an attempt to trace his mother's trail through the woods to the meadow. When he reached the edge of the woods he could not contain himself from snorting at how easily he had tracked his mother, how quickly he could have been found by anyone following her trail.

It wasn't hunger that made him venture out into the meadow, or fear, or loneliness. It was pure curiosity. And also, it was because he had been warned not to move, to stay hidden in the woods, so the forbiddenness of the meadow beckoned him all the more.

Gerry was doing the milking alone, because his father and Merle and his cousins were still putting in hay. He didn't notice that Forty had freshened until he had milked half the length of the barn and was about to climb in between Forty and Miss Jerome. Forty had cast her afterbirth in the meadow, but there was telltale blood and mucus on her tail.

"Darn it. She's freshened already and hidden the calf, and I gotta go back to the mow. Man, how am I gonna get the calf?" Gerry was fifteen, and it was the first summer he had been allowed to milk alone when haying was going on, so he took the responsibility very seriously. He also really prized the break from the sweaty heat and dust of the haymow, and the chance to listen to whatever he wanted to on the radio. Right now, "Nowhere Man" was on.

Gerry put the milking machine on Miss Jerome, then quickly checked the ones on Daisy and Peanut before running up to the house to get his sister.

"Ruh-nay! Ruh-*nay!*" he bellowed, as the screen door slammed behind him.

"What?"

*"C'mere!"*

"Why?"

"Because I need help!"

Renee descended the stairs from her room slowly, with obvious disdain. "What do you want?"

"Forty freshened, and I can't go get the calf because I have to finish milking and then go back and put hay in, so you've gotta go find the calf."

"Why?"

"I just told you! C'mon, Renee, I've gotta go back down to the barn. I can't go through the whole story over again." Gerry couldn't stand Renee's attitude since she had gone away to college for a year and come home to sit upstairs in her room while all the work was being done. Plus, she always acted so superior it made him sick, looking up at him through her nose like he was some kind of idiot.

"Just come down to the barn to talk to me while I'm doing the milking if you need me to explain it again," he said with a sigh, summoning as much haughtiness as he could manage while retreating out the kitchen door, which he had to slam four times before the latch would stick.

Gerry ran down to the barn as fast as he could, finding that Thunder had kicked her machine off and no milk was flowing through the line from the machine on Daisy. *Oh, man,* he thought, *she'll have mastitis tomorrow and I'll get in trouble for it. Renee!*

She entered the barn five minutes later, an unexplained delay that made Gerry fume even more. Renee picked her way carefully past the splashes of urine and manure that would not dry in the humidity of July. Gerry rolled his eyes.

"Why can't you just go after the calf when you finish what you're doing?"

"I've gotta go back over to the new barn to put hay in. I told you."

"Well, who's putting it in now?"

"Dad and Merle."

"Then why do they need you?"

Gerry's mouth fell open. He was losing his patience, and Renee could see it. If she could push him into fighting with her, she could go back up to the house.

Slowly, in a clipped tone, Gerry explained, "Dad cannot unload and bale at the same time. I am supposed to go back over to help as soon as I am finished with my task of milking the cows." Gerry smiled to himself, pleased with his composure.

"As a matter of fact, I was doing something for Mom," Renee intoned sweetly.

"I am sure that she will understand and agree that you should help us, *dear.*" Gerry was in danger of losing it again. Then suddenly he had an inspiration.

"As a matter of fact, you could go over to the new barn and put the hay in instead of me, Renee. Then I could go look for the calf." The thought of staying out of the haymow for the rest of the day brought Gerry's inner smile out.

Renee immediately understood the source of the smile. "Which pasture is the calf in?"

Gerry looked at his sister silently from his vantage point, wedged in between the sweaty flanks of Wings and Miss Jerome. He hated her. But he knew that she had him, so he shook his head slightly and frowned. "Most of the cows were down by the Old Homestead, but I'll bet she hid the calf in the woods by the river."

Gerry would not have thought to look at Forty, but if he had he would have seen a wild, frightened look consume her when he gave Renee the directions to her calf. She craned around to see Renee gingerly picking her way across the barnyard toward the gate leading to the pasture where Calvin was hidden.

Calvin was in the ruins of the Old Homestead, sniffing among the dried remains of the wild roses, when Renee came across the field on a bee-line toward the swimming hole. The Sand family farm had been abandoned more than forty years, after there was no third generation to take it over.

Gerry would have known to enter the woods just past the fence-line, but Renee was loath to search through all of the woods, especially when the cows, and bull, were going to be let back out soon. She looked around the swimming hole, and where they fished for bullheads in the first warm nights of the spring, but not in the taller grass in the rest of the narrow strips of woods along the river.

After checking out the clearings in the woods, she quickly headed due east across the pasture to get to the back road, so that she would be on the opposite side of the fence when the bull was let out. On her way she passed within twenty feet of Calvin, nestled smirking in a patch of heavy grass among the wild roses in the Old Homestead.

"Hello, Mother. I've had the most interesting adventure since you were gone," Calvin blurted out.

"Adventure? Where have you been? You were supposed to stay right here where I left you!"

"I know. But when you all left, I found a better place to hide. Didn't you think they would be able to follow your tracks through this tall grass right to me? That human came right to the woods first. If I hadn't moved, it might have found me."

Forty looked worried, instinctively nudging Calvin to follow her farther into the woods. She found a spot near the bank of a small run that fed into the river and let Calvin suckle her until he was full. Then she helped him to settle into hiding before going out to graze.

There was no break in the heat and mugginess, so the herd grazed lazily near the woods and river. A crescent of moon had become visible while they still were in the barn, but now the unforgiving heat hazed it over. Dew was indistinguishable from sweat when it finally came, and the setting of the sun offered no relief.

Just as the first flickering of fireflies began and before Forty headed off to rejoin Calvin, Dutchess and Daisy approached her and whispered, "Gathering." Forty nodded in reply, grateful that the other cows wished to celebrate Calvin's birth and continued survival with a prayer meeting.

Ritual was not possible very often for these cows. The purpose of the Gathering was to relate the folklore of their race. It was a celebration reserved for newborns who were still wild, with no experience of confinement in the world of humans. As such, it was a rare summer ritual on the mud farm, because Farmer Bob kept his cows in the barn from late September through early May.

This summer night was so brutal in its oppressive heat that Dutchess, Forty, and the elders did not expect the Gathering to begin until very late, but minutes after dark all of the cows were in the clearing near the swimming hole, awaiting the start of the proceeding. They were gathered in irregular groups, yet all facing toward the center of the clearing, within which Forty and Calvin appeared suddenly.

One might expect murmurs of approval at the sight of a child that still was wild, the first time they had had a Gathering in two years. But there were none. There was only silence, absolute stillness filled with awe, and respect, and the anticipation of grief. Forty was extremely shy, blushing deeply under her summer coat in the hazy moonlight. Calvin was excited, curious to learn all about this event and his people.

"What once was wild will be again wild. What once was sacred will be again sacred. What once was ours will be again ours." Daisy chanted the words slowly, carefully, with reverence. "In the time before wire, before barns, when we ate the grain wild, humans were our children, and we were their children. There were no walls, no divisions, no beliefs other than One."

Daisy's eyes were closed, and her voice was taking on an unearthly quality. Calvin looked all around him at the rest of the herd, everyone with a dreamy expression, no cud-chewing, no licking out of nostrils, all merged into the energy of the moment. The warmth and hazy moonlight of this night, punctuated by fireflies and the distant flash of heat lightning, lent an even eerier quality to the ceremony. Calvin found himself transfixed, sinking into an ooze of rapture.

Only Forty was not entranced. All through the ceremony she sat twitching, growing more nervous as it proceeded. Calvin reasoned that it was the residue fever from giving him birth, but the warmth of her body next to his was not appreciably greater than his own. Why was she so nervous?

"Mmmmmmmmmmmm." A low hum was building from the voices of the whole herd. Daisy had exhorted them to pray for the return of the Old Days, the Days of One.

"We ask that this one remain wild, that this one will know the life of those who came before. And we ask . . ." Calvin felt his mother begin to shudder convulsively, her whole being trembling.

". . . that this child be the one to bring humans back to the One."—

*So that's it,* Calvin thought. He hated to disappoint them, but he couldn't help thinking that Daisy had complained of feeling sick from being overmilked, and his own mother probably had at least a touch of milk fever, so both of them were likely to be hallucinating.

The ceremony was breaking up, in a tone of quiet reverence. Forty did not appear to believe in the possibility of hope, but this realism only pained her more deeply. She searched their faces for a glimmer of understanding that nothing would come of this prayer, while at the same time Calvin was flattered by the attention.

He was still thinking about how he would impress the humans the next morning as his mother was searching in a panic for a new place to hide him before she went to the barn for morning milking.

Gerry drove the tractor and short trailer down into the meadow. He almost missed the calf because it was standing up, unhidden, and raised its head to look straight at him as he drove the tractor toward the woods. Gerry had never before encountered a newborn calf in the field that wasn't completely hidden in some out-of-the-way place. But this calf seemed to know no fear.

Calvin stared transfixed at this strange animal that rode on another larger beast. Actually, he was more interested in the larger beast, because it had no legs or feet, even though it seemed to be the source of travel for the two-legged. It walked right up to him and slipped a loop of vine around his neck, then turned his behind in the direction of the large creature and began to push him toward it. Calvin could not believe that he was being treated in this way, and began to beller to let the human know that he would not resist going along for the ride.

Gerry was surprised that the calf was so cooperative. Normally he had to turn calves around and push them backward, because otherwise they would lock their legs and be impossible to move. He lifted the calf onto the back of the trailer, then led it up to the front, where he tied it. He didn't want the calf to be bounced around, but this bull seemed so curious he was unable to get it to lie down.

"C'mon, lie down, fella," Gerry coaxed, gathering Calvin's legs into his arms to set him on the floor of the trailer. Calvin resisted for a moment, then sensed Gerry's well-meaning intent and settled down on the rough plank floor.

Gerry fired up the Ford tractor and headed back toward the barn. Calvin was content to examine the bed of the trailer for a few minutes, then climbed to his hooves to look around when Gerry slowed to cross the ravine.

He could see everything, smell everything, hear everything. It was all so wonderful! The power of the tractor, which by now he had figured out was completely under the control of this human, he felt all the way through him, climbing up from the vibrations of the trailer bed into his legs and body. Calvin could not believe that his mother had wanted him to miss all this and stay hidden in the woods to become some wild animal!

After crossing two fields, Calvin's chauffeur idled the tractor again, opened the gate into the barnyard, and expertly backed the trailer up to the barn door. At least, this was what Calvin took to be the barn, since his mother had spoken of it as the place where all the cows went because of the farmers' mastery of them. It was confusing, though, because this human untied him, carried him into the barn, and put him in front of his mother, where he was tied to a square, dead tree trunk. Calvin looked up at his mother happily, then with concern at the look of anguish that leaped at him from her eyes.

"How did he find you so soon?" she demanded.

"I decided to follow your tracks out of the woods, Mother."

"Why? You were safe there."

"Yes. And bored. Oh, it was so amazing riding here on that creature."

"That creature? You mean the tractor. And it's not good. You're in grave danger."

"And you're too worried. How am I to be the child to bring humans to their senses if they don't even know I exist? Really, sometimes, Mother, I just don't understand what you want." Calvin sounded sincere, but his mother could barely control her anger at his impetuousness, his arrogant belief that he could know more about the danger he was in than she did. Gerry kept looking over at this odd calf, which seemed to enjoy being in the barn.

Calvin spent the milking time showing off for the cows, nibbling at stray husks of oats in the manger in front of Forty. Her anger had subsided quickly, replaced by a frightened, focused effort to think of an escape for her son. Calvin would hear nothing of it.

"You just wait and see, Mother. Everything will be all right," he said, nuzzling her cheek for emphasis.

"Maybe you can get free from that rope. Test it, Calvin," she urged.

"No, I won't do it. I won't indulge these paranoid ideas of yours, Mother."

"Calvin, you've got to get away. You've got to go back to the woods and hide from the humans."

"I don't understand you," Calvin sneered. "Don't they feed you? Isn't this grain better than just eating grass all the time? Don't the humans give you this barn to stay in during the winter, when you'd probably die from the cold? Yes, they take your milk, but I hardly think that is an awful lot to ask for what they give to you."

"Calvin, you don't know. They'll take you, they'll . . ." Forty was cut off by the glare she received from Dutchess. *You cannot tell,* the look said. *You know it. You cannot tell.*

". . . send you off to another farm to live," Forty compromised. She couldn't even explain to him that she had gained her human name from the tag in her ear, her sale number at the auction.

Dutchess continued to glare, to ensure that Forty would not continue. Her resolve to tell Calvin everything vanished with the realization that the only chance to save him was if he could believe, if they all could believe, that the prophecy was true.

"Is that it? I do want to stay with you, Mother, but if they decide to send me to another farm it could only be because it was the right thing to do."

"I suppose you're right," Forty said huskily. Dutchess nodded sadly.

"Of course. You can see that, can't you? Remember how afraid you were about whether I would be fed? That same human that gave me the ride fed me your milk," Calvin insisted, infatuated with the strength of his logic.

"Yes, of course." Forty was wooden, without even the faith to hope.

Gerry was still puzzled by this calf. When he had filled the metal pail with Forty's milk and gone up around in front of the stanchions to feed her calf, he was amazed at how calm and obedient it was. He began the same way he always did for a calf of that age, backing it up against the wall and straddling its front shoulders, holding it in place with his thighs as he plunged its snout into the warm yellowish milk with his left hand. He was prying open the corners of Calvin's mouth with his index and pinkie fingers, maintaining his grasp with the thumb and heel of his hand across the bridge of the calf's nose.

Calvin suckled greedily on Gerry's milk-soaked middle and ring fingers, and instinctively bucked the pail once, as all calves do to their mother's udders. But then he relaxed, fixed a knowing—almost bemused—eye on Gerry, and drank deeply and evenly without suckling. After half a minute Gerry was able to set the pail on the floor between his feet and straighten his stiff back, all the while marveling at the calf.

The only thing Gerry had to do after that was lift the pail to tilt it toward the calf so that it could lick and suck out the last drops in the bottom. Gerry pulled the pail away with his right hand and rubbed the calf's head, just behind where its horns would be growing in, with his sticky left hand. The calf responded warmly, yet with a puzzling reserve.

Gerry took the pail back to the barn floor and dumped the rest of the milk from Forty into it. It was too yellow and filled with colostrum to put into the bulk tank, so he took it outside and tossed it in the weeds where Daisy's infected milk had been dumped.

The machines on Peanut and Dutchess were almost done and ready to be rinsed out, so he took all of the machines to the alleyway where he already had drawn the bucket of cold water for rinsing. The cows were nervous and bellering to be let out, but Gerry didn't care. His father would have let the cows out first, but he had his own rhythm of finishing the milking.

Part of the bellering was coming from Forty, but she wasn't calling to be let out. She was desperate for Calvin to escape, something he could not have been less interested in.

Gerry finally was finished with the milking machines, having brought them up into the milkhouse to be stripped down and scoured out later by his sister—or, if she had her way, by her mother.

"C'mon now, Daisy, you gotta stay in," he said as she strained at her stanchion. Once Peanut and Dutchess had gotten around her, he picked up the pace, pulling the bolts free and sliding the stanchion boards clear in groups of five, chasing each group into the barnyard before they could shit on the floor.

When he got to Forty, she was flinging her head back and forth, bellering even louder.

"Get out of here! Git!" Gerry shouted, after pushing Forty's snout and finally resorting to letting the other cows out so they could push her out of her stanchion. She fought Gerry, she fought Thunder and Wings, she refused to let Dutchess coax her out of the barn. But Gerry's father finally chased her out of the barn with a solid oak stick that he normally reserved for ornery bulls. Gerry wanted to leave the barn door open because of the heat and humidity, but closed it so that Forty would forget her calf and go off to graze.

The door made no difference to her. She bellered and paced in front of the gate to the river pasture all through breakfast, which got King barking at her. After twenty minutes she was joined by Queenie, who was not considered to be awfully bright but was usually pretty sensitive, and superstitious.

Perhaps it was the prophecy that had moved Queenie. When she joined the chorus, King started barking louder, and it seemed that even the birds began to sing louder and more insistently.

They were eating oatmeal—Bob with milk and lots of sugar, Edna with lots of milk and little sugar, Renee sparingly. Gerry's, to Renee's disgust, was piled onto buttered, toasted homemade bread.

"Jesus, that dog is driving me crazy!" Bob finally snapped. This made Gerry wince, because the dog was only doing what he thought he was supposed to do. Besides, his father was always picking on King, and wasn't Forty really the problem?

"Hey, Dad, any chance that we'll keep Forty's calf?"

His father fixed a stern look on him, without replying.

"You know the answer to that question. Too expensive. I even wonder a lot of the time whether it's worth it with the heifers. Why?"

"Well, nothing really. I was just wonderin'. Besides, that calf is kinda funny. Different."

"Is it sick or something?" Bob demanded.

"No. It eats real good and everything. It's just different. Acts like it's trying to talk or something."

"Gerry, don't think you can get out of haying by acting crazy."

"I'm not trying to get out of anything. That calf's just funny."

By this time Dutchess and Pet had joined the chorus, which sent King into fever pitch.

"Jesus, get that dog in here and shut him up," Bob demanded.

Before Gerry could begin to get up from the table, a thought struck him hard.

"Hey, Dad. Have you noticed that all this time that calf hasn't been makin' a sound? That's unusual."

Gerry's father jumped out of his chair. "Jesus, that's right. Something's gotta be wrong." He was out of the door and running across the driveways while Gerry was still holding up an oatmeal-covered piece of toast, stunned. Gerry saw his father run in that old-man way—elbows pumping faster than the rest of him—and was transfixed until he saw his mother's questioning look. *Aren't you going to follow him?* her eyes said. Gerry jumped up and ran to the barn after his father.

Once he had cleared the milkhouse door, Gerry saw his dad a step and a half in front of the strange calf, his right hand outstretched, palm up and open. The calf was sitting on its back haunches, but its front legs were straight in under it. It looked like an eager Irish setter waiting to be petted. Bob reached his hand out, and the calf licked it, but not in a subservient way.

*Slightly salty, but otherwise nothing remarkable,* Calvin mused. *I wonder if he's going to offer me some grain?*

"Dad, see what I mean about him? That calf is special."

Gerry's father turned his gaze toward him, without seeing him, looking straight through him.

Gerry suddenly became aware that the din outside the barn was growing even louder, as Thunder had joined in.

"Dad, are you okay? The calf's not sick, right?" Gerry waited. He watched his father's eyes glaze over.

“Aren’t you supposed to be greasing the haybine?” Bob asked sternly.

“Yeah, I’m on my way,” Gerry replied over his shoulder, knowing enough not to look back. He left the barn, got the grease gun out of the toolshed, and went directly to where the haybine was parked at the base of the circle drive. From this vantage point he couldn’t see much, but he knew that he didn’t have to.

Even before he was finished greasing the power takeoff shaft, his father strode out of the barn, looking straight ahead. Gerry wanted him to turn in his direction, or go to hook up the rake, but his father went directly to the house. Gerry knew that his mother would be on the phone in another minute, calling to have the calf picked up, along with Daisy, for the beef auction.

## CHAPTER FOUR

# Peanut

(1968)

Peanut decided to leave right before it was her turn to be milked. Although it had nothing to do with Farmer Bob, Peanut felt that she should say goodbye.

Once he had adjusted the milking machine, she craned her head around to nudge his left arm, then gently mooed to him. Farmer Bob chuckled and replied, "Morning to you, too."

She was somewhat hurt that he had misunderstood her goodbye as a hello, but what could be done about it? Besides, she was sure that she was doing the right thing by leaving, and that Farmer Bob and Gerry and everyone else would understand once she was gone.

She was sure because she had seen the look on all of their faces the day the strangers had come.

*Which route should I use to run away?* She thought about probing along the barbed-wire fence and walking until she could get on the back road. But she gave up that idea, because of the stories she had heard about the Long March, and her fear of being discovered and forced to return to the farm. Also, since she was short-legged and hefty, she loathed the idea of trying to climb over a two-strand barbed-wire fence.

The river was the answer. Just walk herself in part of the way and swim the fifteen yards or so of the deepest part of the river until she could get to the opposite shore. Then there was a stand of pines to find her way through, and after that an open meadow to cross before she could begin to look for the highway.

Peanut was positive that these were her choices, because the pattern over the last several milkings had been to alternate grazing days between the mill piece and the river meadow. Any day now they would be herded across the road to graze in the alfalfa fields left from the fresh cutting of hay. But since she could see the wagons and baler still across the road, she was sure they would be let out into the river piece.

And she was right.

Her confidence grew with each step away from the barn. The sun was shining, the dew-covered meadow glistening. Peanut's life was all ahead of her, and just beginning.

The air was cool, as cool as it would be until early the next morning, so the rest of the herd fanned out to graze in the sunshine a short distance from the barnyard.

Everyone failed to recognize the meaning of Peanut's resolute tone and stride as she said goodbye and headed straight for the river. No one looked up, or replied, or noticed that she was gone. It wasn't that she was histrionic, just the opposite—she was unremarkably pleasant.

She hesitated for a moment as her hooves sank into the mud of the east bank of the river. If she stopped now, no one would ever know the plan, the dream, she had abandoned. There was no need to fear being teased. But she was just so tired of her ordinary life—of the sameness of it all—of being taken for granted by all of her so-called friends.

*This is classic running-away thinking,* she thought. *I remember hearing Renee, and I think Gerry, too, muttering these same things on their runaway attempts.* She waded farther into the river, arching her head and neck up out of the dark water.

*But they didn't have a plan. They weren't running to something, but away from some temporary problem.* She was swimming now, rather gracefully she believed, head held high out of the water weeds. *Besides, my life will be so wonderful, just like theirs.*

The far bank of the river was steeper, but she scrambled up and didn't stop moving until she was in a clearing in the pine grove where she could dry off on a soft bed of needles with a warm August sun for comfort.

Peanut allowed herself to slip totally into the daydream of her new life.

The circus.

It left her breathless with excitement. So many things she could do. Circle one ring and carry poodles on her back. Perhaps charge and fight with the wild animal trainer. But she just knew, she knew, that she might end up working with the clowns, chasing them around and performing her two-hooved mule kick. That would be okay, though. Everyone starts out paying her dues. Peanut was confident that she could work up to the glamour.

Two months prior to Peanut's running away, a teenage prank had brought a small circus troupe, lost, to the farm. A couple of bored kids driving home from school on Route 932 had decided to turn all of the road signs ninety degrees counterclockwise. The first driver in the circus caravan then took his first right-hand turn past the highway department onto Sand Road—in order to stay on Route 932, he thought.

Seeing that the highway was turning to gravel just past this farmhouse, the driver elected to turn around in the convenient circular driveway.

It was early in the afternoon, unusually warm for this time in June. Bob was working on the haybine when a truck pulling a long horse trailer swung into the upper driveway, moving faster than it should.

The truck slowed before it reached the base of the turn where he was working, then picked up speed again to climb the small hill in front of the barn. Two trucks with shorter trailers and another panel truck were following close behind the first, and were already in the driveway before Bob angrily flagged them down.

"What the hell you doin'?" he demanded of the first driver.

"Look, I'm just tryin' to find the shortcut to the interstate." The driver was in no mood to argue with Bob.

"Well, it don't run down my driveway!"

"I was just followin' the signs."

"Oh, that's right. Somebody screwed that sign around on the end of the road," Bob said grudgingly.

"So if we go back the way we came and turn right we'll get to Route 81."

"Yeah."

A lanky, slope-shouldered man trotted up to the lead truck, ignoring Bob.

"The Ford's overheatin' agin," he drawled. "Won't make it to the 'spressway."

"Jesus, Drew, what am I supposed to do 'bout it?"

"Well, there ain't nothin' ah kin do, neither."

"You could let the motor cool down and put some more water in it, couldn't you?" Bob said to Drew.

The lanky man shrugged and looked at the lead driver, who scowled and shook his head.

"All right. Where can we park these things?"

"Well, you've gotta keep out of the upper driveway. Do your animals need watering, too?"

"Shit, yeah. Prob'ly. 'Zere a way we can do that?"

"The barnyard's fenced in, and there's a water tank out back. Just back the trailers up to that gate, and once they've unloaded, park your vehicles in the grove across the road." Then Bob frowned for a moment. "Say, you ain't goin' to be lettin' any tigers out, are ya?"

The lead driver, who was also the owner/manager of the circus, started to reply, then thought better of it. His typical sarcastic response to such a question would get his whole outfit kicked out of this oasis.

"Naw, we won't let the dangerous ones out." He thought for a moment. "Much obliged" surfaced as the thing to say at that point.

The circus's lone elephant, a morose eight-month-old named Toby, was let out to drink first. Before he was finished, Farmer Bob's herd, earlier scattered all across the river meadow, was pressed up along the barnyard fence gawking at the newcomer.

Toby was followed by two worn zebras, whose circus task was to provide an exotic flavor to the horse routines. But they were so arthritic that one couldn't even traverse the barnyard to the water tank and had to have buckets of water brought back to her.

Still, the cows were fascinated by the special treatment, mistaking the zebras for some kind of royalty.

Farmer Bob's bull, John, was jealous of the attention the zebras were getting, especially the male, but was also curiously excited.

Peanut and Young Smitty kept their eyes on Farmer Bob's face, which was lit up in a way they had never seen. The deference he was showing these strangers was unprecedented. It left them feeling envious and, at the same time, awed.

"Look at the way he fawns over them," Young Smitty said, disgusted.

"He's not fawning, he's just . . . impressed," Peanut said.

"Well . . . that striped thing is a hussy," Bossy chimed in. "And the way they're falling all over her, it's disgusting."

"She's just special, can't you see? And Farmer Bob is treating her the way you're supposed to." Peanut was starry-eyed, enchanted.

Drew lazily shooed the zebras back onto the trailer, fired up the truck, and drove it across the road into the shade. His boss then swung his truck and trailer around the driveway once more, backed it up to the barnyard gate, and let out six gorgeous palomino horses. Stately, graceful, they paraded to the water tank and drank long and deeply, always proud and regal in their bearing.

John was enraged by this invasion of his territory, but he was powerless to stop it. The first two horses, having drunk their fill, wandered over near the fence to nibble at the already closely grazed barnyard grass. Peanut pushed her way through the pack to get as close to them as possible.

"I'll bet your life is exciting, isn't it?" she asked.

The horses cast quick sidelong glances at each other. "Oh, yeah, you wouldn't believe it," one casually replied.

"You see, Smitty? I told you . . . Smitty!" Peanut was embarrassed that her friend hadn't chosen to follow her. Charlotte snickered.

"And what do you eat most of the time? Oats, I'll bet."

The second horse fielded this one. "Oh, yeah, oats most of the time, corn, basically whatever we want."

"Oh, my. I knew it."

"What did you think of that alfalfa juice we had this morning?" the first horse asked.

"Alfalfa . . . oh, yeah, I know what you mean. I didn't like it as much as the clover salad we had yesterday."

"Clover salad! You mean with different kinds of clover mixed together?" Peanut interrupted.

"Well, isn't that what you get in your clover salad?" the second horse asked innocently. Suddenly it seemed that the first horse was choking on some coarse piece of grazing, before it spread to her partner. They staggered back toward the trailer, snorting and leaning on each other as they moved away from the fence.

"Clover salad. Oats whenever you want. Shows in front of thousands of people." Peanut couldn't get over it all.

It was the same daydream since the last full moon. Run away to live the same life the circus animals lived. But for now she was suddenly keenly aware of how hungry she was.

Peanut threaded her way through the pines, padding quietly on the carpet of needles. The quiet of the grove made her feel elegant, graceful. On the far side she found plenty to eat, even if the grass was tall and coarse.

She grazed her fill as she moved toward the setting sun, in search of the highway she believed would lead her to the circus.

"Gerry! Where's Peanut? Back o' the barn?"

"Naw, I didn't see her out there, Dad. Is she missin'?"

"Why do you think I wanted to know? Jesus Christ! Where the hell is she?"

"You want me to go look for her?" Gerry was anxious for a chance to get out of the evening milking. Haying had gone well that day, they were done before milking, but it was really hot and sticky.

"Merle was comin' over right after he finished movin' the elevator, wasn't he?"

"Yeah."

"Check *all* of the woods along the river, Ger."

"Okay." Gerry was out of the barn door before his father could change his mind. Once across the barnyard he selected a stem of timothy, unsheathed it, and began working on a piece of walnut, from one of his mother's cupcakes, that was stuck in his teeth.

*Now where would she be? The river's too deep to cross, and that cliff is too steep to climb up or down. She must be by that old logging road past the foundation.*

Gerry walked along the barbed-wire fence that bisected the pasture lands west of the back road until it went into the woods. When he was midway between the edge of the pasture and the ravine that cut across toward the river, he turned west.

It was possible that he could miss her in the ravine or if she was hidden in some thicket, but it was unlikely. A cow would have to be either very sick, dead, or planning on hiding to accomplish that. Peanut had no calf to hide, so she'd have no reason herself to want to avoid being found. Once he reached the river he'd take a right-angle turn and sweep the woods heading north until he got to the next fenceline.

Nothing left to do but keep moving and looking around. Gerry soon fell to daydreaming.

*He's behind one and two, Cuellar is really crafty on the mound. He waits on the pitch, sees it as if in slow motion—looks like a screwball coming in before it breaks away. Waits . . . waits . . . swings inside out . . . connects on the sweet part of the bat just before it takes off outside. . . . Ball rockets off to the opposite field, left-fielder frozen in place, clears the fence still parallel to the ground . . . frozen-rope-line-drive home run. . . . He runs the bases with hustle and humility, the best rookie hitter since Ted Williams. . . . A complete ballplayer, covers ground like the young Willie Mays . . . tucks and does a quick somersault after making a diving catch, comes up throwing, one bounce and the ball is waist-high on a line inside the plate, runner thrown out at home. . . . Leading the league in average and RBIs, shot at the triple crown . . . Now in the World Series, takes a vicious early cut to back up the third baseman, then lays down a perfect bunt on the next pitch to score the guy from third . . . but so good it rolls to a stop, and the pitcher, pulled toward first by his follow-through, can't come over to pick up the ball. . . . With his speed, no play at first. . . .*

Gerry had made the turn before the river and was halfway to the fishing hole by now, not having seen any unusual signs that would indicate where Peanut was.

He slipped back into his reverie.

*Leaps and robs Maris of a home run, almost two feet above the wall. . . .* A partridge was flushed from a thicket as Gerry passed by. Adrenaline jumped through him momentarily, then he slips back again.

*Twenty-gauge shotgun cradled across his left arm, treading carefully through the dead dry leaves, ready to turn, brace the gun, and fire in a quick reflex moment*—phut-tut-tut-tut-tut . . . a partridge taking flight—*that crisp clean fall aroma fills his nostrils. . . . The day is cloudless, warm enough for just a flannel shirt, sleeves rolled up to the elbows.*

Without warning, the edges of Gerry's daydream began to darken, slowing down and twisting into circus-mirror images of a scene bubbling up through walls of walls.

Just before Gerry could see his face, the whole picture went black.

When he returned to the barn, his father was rinsing out the milking machines. Gerry let the cows out, closed the gate, and scraped the floor.

"Didn't you find any sign of her?" Bob asked.

"No."

"Did you look *all* over?"

"Yes."

There was a dull look of hoarded pain behind Gerry's eyes that told Bob why he was so quiet. He had seen that look before, had lived at its source.

Bob stopped asking questions, stood looking off toward the woods along the river. The cows moved away from the gate, as if they were oblivious.

Peanut was out in the open when the thunderstorm struck, but the day had been so oppressively hot that she didn't even bother to seek cover. It was part of her new sense of freedom, letting the warm raindrops bounce off her.

She soaked in the downpour, glad for the respite from the heat. Lightning crackled all around, so blazing white that it seemed to heat the wind. Peanut smiled at it, knowing that no harm could come to her from the storm. Better things were in her future, about that there was no question. Her head was filled with the dreams, she was transfixed by them, she fell asleep with them.

Summer storms in the north country, born of deception, are made of cold, almost frigid air. Peanut should have known that, would have remembered if she had been back with the herd, which had gone into the woods with the storm and huddled together against the sharp drop in temperature. But she could not draw from the collective wisdom any longer; she was not even a cow in the ways that mattered.

That was why she panicked when she awoke, in the darkest part of the night, unable to draw in easily the tiny barbs of air. The sky swept clean by storm was star-filled, but they only served to remind her of how far away she was from them.

*Dark moon,* she screamed to herself. It was true. On this crystal-clear night, there was no guiding orb to pull her to safety, to point a path to where she belonged.

Peanut coughed as she climbed to her hooves, unable to stop. She wrinkled her muscles down each flank, not generating any warmth but testing how badly her body ached.

*Where do I go?* It was an old question, haunting her since she had arrived at the mud farm. Farmer Bob's son had appeared out of nowhere, shortly after she had been let out into the pasture, saying, "You should have seen her, Dad. From up there she looks just like a peanut." So they had given her a name she would never understand. Was peanut good or bad? No one else could tell her, either.

The storm had twisted and lodged all of the standing hay around her, and washed away her smell trail, even if she had been able to follow it now. So there was no path to follow, not even a clue to begin with. She struck out uphill in search of a vantage point to get her bearings.

Cresting the knob only revealed more hill to climb, a long steady rise away from the river. As she plodded, the darkness deepened, stars receding to a safer, mocking distance. Peanut's breathing was ever more labored, her eyes rheumy, legs aching. She longed for the comfort of her friends, the well-worn cow paths leading to familiar places of shelter, the taste of the morning grain, John's gentle firmness. She had been so silly, bewitched by those circus people, forgetting about everyone she really cared about. She had to find her way back.

Peanut toiled over the rim and immediately out of the standing hay so quickly she almost stumbled.

A garden with ripened sweet corn stared her in the face.

She trotted to the closest stalk and went to work. Although she had not been needy during her adventure, the corn was her first real taste of the life she had left the farm for. She cleared the first three stalks greedily, then slowed down, picking and choosing, as she traveled the rest of the row.

Satiated, she felt much less miserable, almost ready to continue on her quest. But as she moved away from the garden, the night cold returned, reminding her of winter, outside, when the barn was being cleaned.

*What if I never find the highway? What if the circus doesn't want me?* she fretted.

Peanut plodded away from the garden, preoccupied with thoughts of never again finding a home, living outside year-round, friendless and alone. She had no idea where she was as she crossed the Jonesen lawn, then clomped almost completely across the county road before she noticed the changing sound of her hooves on pavement.

*The highway! This must be the highway!* Peanut gamboled around in a circle, clattering gaily on the worn asphalt.

*Now which way to the circus?* she wondered. *The circus is probably in town, and town is a left-hand turn, so I'll go left,* she reasoned happily. So she turned left and trotted away from town, head up and eyes wide open.

The residential houses along the county road grew more scattered as Peanut skipped along through the darkness.

*What was it that Renee and Gerry used to say when they were kids? Lions and something and bears?* She was giddy, intoxicated with the prospect of success.

At three-thirty in the morning, traffic on Route 45 was rare. It was too early for the early shift, not late enough for the homebound graveyard shift. Traffic at that hour was comprised of hard-core drunks and teenage townies between after-parties. But mostly at that hour the stretch of road between the Jonesens' and the old cheese factory was desolate.

She had almost reached the thirty-mile-an-hour S-turn near Little Bend when she saw lights beyond the next hill. Whatever was heading toward her still was far away, because she could hear no sound. *Maybe those are the circus lights.*

At that prospect, still feverish, Peanut lost all self-control. She began to gallop straight up the middle of the road. The lights shot up over the top of the hill, four large blinding white beams with two pale yellow warning lights beneath. In her frenzy, Peanut ran faster toward them, head down and neck outstretched like a thoroughbred reaching the finish line.

She was halfway through the turn before she realized that the lights were not slowing down. In fact, they were on a collision course with her. She bounded once toward the roadside, to the center of the oncoming lane, before the lights caught her standing stock-still, looking every inch a cow stuck in headlights. She fainted.

"Uhnn . . ." Peanut's head throbbed. Her eyelids began to flutter open. The lights were now directly overhead, at treetop level. From somewhere just beyond the intense green light that enveloped her, she thought she could make out two standing figures. Whoever they were, she knew they weren't humans.

As the throbbing eased, she climbed shakily to her feet. Blinking anxiously into the hovering light that was lifting her from the ground, she tried again to focus, then remembered her mission.

"Hey, are you guys from the circus?"

CHAPTER FIVE

# John

(1969)

*Wires were falling from the sky, in gargantuan coils, blacker than night. Blacker than a blacksmith's anvil, than the coal for the forge. Each one settled down over him, then began to shrink, gathering in around him.*

*John would start to climb the side of the coil, kicking and scrambling to get out before it closed, almost making it out before the coil tightened viselike around his loins, shooting fire into his body, making him black coil.*

*It passed through him, bloodless, shrinking and collapsing into a tiny barb lodging in his gut.*

*Then a new black coil would fall.*

*He began to run, trying to get to the barn. The coils fell on their sides and rolled alongside him, stretching lines of deadly wire behind them as they went. Each time he turned, another coil would fall to cut him off, laying down a new line of barbed wire. He was pushed right up to the barnyard, the coils cutting off every avenue of escape.*

*Just before John attempted to run into the barn, it was crushed by a gleaming silver coil, its barbs glistening, blinding him. The black coils raced back and forth behind him, laying down new strands of barbed wire, pressing him forward into the silver coil, smooth and terrifying, as it shrank toward him.*

*John bellowed and kicked and turned, alternately jumping and falling to his knees, trying to battle his way out of this cage. The ground pushed him up and the sky forced him down, everything pressing his nose to the silver coil, which suddenly grew a barb that sliced into his nostrils and lodged.*

Everything stopped.

His dream changed form.

*John turned around, unobstructed, toward the river meadow. The sky was clear, pale blue, and warm. The entire herd was grazing lazily near the stone wall, some cows crunching on early green apples. John walked toward them, at first unsteadily, then feeling a loving sense of peace. He bent his head to munch on sweet clover, the nose ring now painless and forgotten.*

*Charlotte approached, followed closely by Thunder and Wings, who were nudging her and playfully nipping at her sides, then pretending to mount her. She smelled wonderful. Warm and musky, an irresistible aroma of desire.*

*Charlotte looked willowy, sleek, her eyes a yielding fire. She circled John slowly, seductively, a dance just beyond his memory.*

*John kept grazing, casually snapping up tender shoots of clover with his teeth as she circled into his peripheral vision. Wings and Thunder had gone off, humbled, leaving Charlotte to succumb to the inevitable. She pulled back her lips, baring her teeth slightly, nibbling his shoulder, engulfing him with her scent.*

*John raised his head, turned to look into her eyes, clear and unwavering, when he saw dark circles, the rounded lid of her eyes, closing . . .*

"Bruu-huurh!" John roared, jumping out of the dream, cold sweat stinging his eyes.

Bob had not asked the man who he was supposed to shoot, although he wanted to.

"What do you mean, you're going to tear down my woods? You can't do that," he said, with such certainty as to belie his fear.

The man didn't even bother to answer.

"Well, you've gotta give a man fair value," Bob insisted.

*Fair value for a property that's going to be condemned,* the man thought, snickering to himself. "The state gives us the authority to take the land if you won't sell." The man smiled slightly again; he could not help it. It still amazed him when people tried to resist.

Bob was trying to figure out how to stop this. Who did he know, what lawyer could help him? Couldn't his town supervisor stop this? That was his job, after all, wasn't it?

The man could tell this farmer was a fighter. It was part of his job to notify his bosses when he met some hardheaded landowner likely to slow them down. He hadn't by accident played cat-and-mouse with these people for three weeks, just trying to serve the papers.

He wanted to climb back into his Ford Fairlane and dry off his sweat, driving fast with the windows rolled down. He wanted a beer, in a nice shaded bar with a ceiling fan. He wanted this guy to realize how stupid it would be to fight, especially with a lawyer, when his 15 percent of market value might get bumped up to 25 percent after a year in court, with the lawyer getting most of the bump. And they would get the land anyway, clear-cut the woods, including the riverbank, spray it with herbicide so only weeds and brush would grow, cause him to question the grazing in the nearby pasture because of the poison, make him pay taxes on it because it was only a right-of-way, and break his will to fight the next time they expanded it to build another power line.

*Boy, I could really use a cold beer,* the man thought.

The man knew these things, almost wished he could tell these people why they shouldn't bother to fight, but also knew that they wouldn't believe him. They lived in another America, he could tell, one where a man's land was his own. In their America, a local politician not on the take might actually be able to stop some big project. It would matter that you were a World War II veteran and had been a good neighbor. You could fight city hall.

It was an America that was fighting in Vietnam to bring freedom to the people.

*Why am I even hanging around? The deed is done, the papers are served, they'll learn soon enough about what'll happen next.*

The husband wanted to punch him, he knew. The poor guy probably was angry with his wife, too, for accepting the papers, as if she could have stopped the power line if she had been out getting groceries this morning. The frustration, the helplessness, the powerlessness was evident in his face, clearer than the sky that day.

He was sure the farmer had known disappointment before, but this was worse than fighting the weather, which he knew couldn't be controlled, because the taking of land was made possible by his government, nominally on his behalf, for the furtherance of progress that he was born and raised to believe in. It was what his country was all about.

The farmer sagged into a chair at the dining-room table, his head in his hands. His wife looked shocked and frightened, as if she wanted to put her hand on his shoulder or somehow comfort and support him, but had forgotten how.

After a panicky moment she sat down rigidly in a chair next to her husband, protecting him by fixing a glare into the eyes of the man. Her look could not be mistaken. It said, *See what you have done!*

There was nothing left to do here. The man turned away from the couple and fumbled at the doorknob. "They'll start clearing the right-of-way in a few days," he said flatly, then pulled the door closed behind him. A tormented Border collie came slinking up at him from around the corner of the house, barking and scaring him into the car. Inside, Bob cursed, "Jesus, where the hell is that dog when you *need* him."

The Fairlane spun gravel as it careened out the driveway, the man already tasting the beer at Groh's Hotel in town.

The French Canadian crews had come through the woods three days after John's dream, clear-cutting a dozen acres from the riverbank to the back road. In the southeast corner of the river piece, the right-of-way passed within five yards of the barbed wire, affording the herd a viewers' gallery of the activity. Everyone had a different idea of what was being built there, from Thunder's guess that it was another farm to Dutchess's feed mill. Most of the cows sided hopefully with Dutchess.

John was quietly anxious about it, and when pressed, bellowed, "They're only cutting down some trees." The cows knew that wasn't true, but left him alone to brood.

After a few days the cows had become bored with the work on the power line, turning their attention to finding the best grazing when they were let across the back road, now that haying was done there.

Just as soon as they were across the road, the herd fanned out quickly to gobble up the ladino clover that was sprinkled throughout the near end of the lot. Dutchess, however, kept moving straight ahead for the Alfalfa Hill, where she knew she'd be able to graze the whole day in a small area.

Charlotte followed her, and White Brat, and Young Smitty, who was still grieving the disappearance of Peanut.

The alfalfa was magnificent, and they soon were full, lazily picking over the nicest stuff while working up their cuds.

"Dutchess, why do you suppose John's been so mean lately?" Charlotte asked.

"I suppose he's just doing his job."

"Whaddaya mean, doin' his job? He's s'posed to be nice to us," White Brat shot back.

"Well, honey, he's got more to do than just pay attention to us. Haven't you ever noticed that he protects us, like when those crazy horses were chasing us?"

"Yeah, but he's always s'posed to be nice."

"Just like you, right?" Young Smitty said distractedly.

"Hey, I just act up for Gerry and Merle's benefit. They don't care how they treat me, so I don't worry about how I treat them," White Brat snapped.

"Yeah, but you kick them, and then get a nose lead and sometimes worse," Charlotte said.

"Just my way of showin' them how I feel."

Young Smitty interrupted the argument. "If you think she's mean, you should have seen the first White John."

"Oh, I remember hearing about him," said Dutchess. "He *was* mean. He almost killed Gerry."

"Deserved it. The little creep." White Brat's bitterness was deep.

"What happened to him?" Charlotte was growing more curious for perspective. It was near her time.

"To whom? Gerry, or White John?"

"White John, the one that was mean." Charlotte chewed on her lip a little, nervous and excited.

"Oh, well, you don't have to worry about him, honey, he's long gone," Young Smitty soothed. "Besides, he was only mean to humans, not to us." Then more quietly she added, "But they said he was kind of rough sometimes."

They all lounged on the shady side of a small maple grove as the rest of the herd approached them. Young Smitty started staring off into space, absentmindedly switching flies off White Brat's face, who was doing the same for her.

Charlotte nudged Dutchess. "What did he do?"

"Charlotte, don't worry. Our John is different. He's gentle, he enjoys the dance, he's almost . . . romantic. Now, that White John, he was too full of himself, a bully, had to have his way all the time. But you don't have to worry about bulls like that, you see, because the humans don't like them around either. That's why they sent him away."

They all looked down for a moment, in a collective shudder. It was the custom to be silent after the telling of one's being sent away. It was done regardless of the feeling toward the one sent.

"He had his ring before the Long March, didn't he?" Young Smitty unexpectedly rejoined the conversation. "When I was just a heifer, I seem to remember hearing about his being mean over at A—Farmer Asa's farm." Her near-blasphemy raised some eyebrows, but no one spoke of it.

"Yes, I think you're right. Farmer Bob didn't know what to do about it, because the ring didn't seem to calm him at all. Then he attached a length of chain to the ring, so that when John lowered his head to charge he would trip over it. But John learned to charge head-up."

White Brat was grinning. "Sounds like my kinda guy."

Dutchess ignored her. "After he pinned Farmer Bob's son up against the barn door, they got rid of him. The next White John was okay, but he started eating too many green apples and was sent away." After the silence she finished, "And then we got the John we have now."

"Shhh," Charlotte whispered. "He's right over there. I don't want him to hear us talking about him."

John was approaching them, with a purpose. He circled the four of them, sensing the air, not so blatantly as to be crude, nor too discretely to make his purpose clear. Charlotte could not help but sit up a little straighter, to want to be noticed.

But it was not yet her time. All of her anxiety, and John's attention, was anticipatory of the fact. Dutchess and Young Smitty barely suppressed their smiles at Charlotte's posturing, while White Brat batted her eyelashes unsubtly at John. He wrinkled up his nose and coughed at her. Shreds of alfalfa flew out his snout. She was enraptured by his roughness.

John was confused. Why had he come over here? He smelled the air again, deeply, filling his huge chest. Nothing. He shrugged his shoulders, surveyed the whole herd, and puffed out his chest. From this vantage point on the hillside he felt completely in control again. The dream was just that, a dream, forgotten.

John even looked over to Charlotte, drank in her eyes. He jerked some fresh alfalfa from the hillside, letting its aroma fill his head.

The power line workers were unhappy with the weather, which was clear and hot. Of course, that made the work go faster, but there were no rainy-day breaks, to get paid just for showing up. Besides, at this rate they might finish too soon, before there were enough weeks in to sit back and collect unemployment through the winter.

They were racing across the western part of the county, getting the lines up before those crazy people fighting the line could get some leverage to stop them. It was so stupid to have to use bolt cutters to get people loose from trees to which they had chained themselves. On the other hand, it did slow down their pace and stretch out the job.

On the whole they preferred breaks caused by the weather or poor management to those caused by angry people. Rain, wind, ice, and foremen didn't yell at them about their values, look at them with those eyes, try to get them to question themselves and the work they did.

These farmers were worse, though, because they didn't say anything or yell anything, didn't even look at them. Whatever anger they had already had been swallowed, turned into meanness, mostly at themselves.

From their vantage points up on the towers they caught sight of Renee briefly, dressed in a sleeveless blouse and shorts. A cry of "Poon!" sang back and forth between the towers before she disappeared into the house.

That was the only time they saw her. The power line workers thought it was because her parents wouldn't let her out of the house.

They finished stringing the wires two days later, and continued their race to cut through people's land, their hearts.

John had been back to himself since that first day in the alfalfa, servicing the herd and defending the pastures from intruders. He was such a good-natured bull that he was even let out at night to graze, since Bob and Gerry were not afraid of his charging them in the dew-sodden fields before dawn.

Wings had gone into heat, danced with a grace unknown for her, and was bred back by John, happily.

It happened just after morning milking was done, when the cows were let across the back road by Gerry and Farmer Bob. Thunder and

White Brat were caught up in the fever, mounting Wings and bellowing.

"Looks like Wings is bullin', Dad," Gerry observed.

"Yeah. Betcha ol' John will take care of her pretty quick."

"Yeah, I guess so." Gerry was embarrassed at the crudeness of it all, especially since at the moment he was struggling so hard to make himself attractive to the girls in the sophomore class.

John moved toward Wings, his head up and neck outstretched. He nipped her shoulder, just below the white "V" on the ridge of her spine that had given her her name. She half-lifted her tail in response, circling to fill the air with the scent of her need.

Almost without pause, John strode to her, mounted her, and spent his seed inside her, renewing the cycle. Farmer Bob watched admiringly, a smug smile on his face.

"All those people that say you need sex education are crazy. Look at that. You just do what comes natural."

He looked to Gerry for approval. Gerry's brow was furrowed in confusion. Bob had no way of knowing how long his son would be damaged by this lesson. He tried again.

"Loves his job, don'tcha think?"

Gerry was still silent, trying to reconcile the image of John on Wings's back—pumping, groaning, tongue hanging out slobbering, eyes rolled back—with that of the sophomore girls, protesting for the right to wear halter tops, perfumed, coy, elusive, wonderful, some beginning embarrassedly to say, "Girls say yes to guys who say no," all so far out of his realm of possibility.

But what his father said was true. Wings looked somewhat weak in the knees, John's eyes half closed in exhausted rapture. Gerry knew that John and Wings would couple several more times before the day was done.

"Yeah, I guess he's enjoying himself," he replied sadly, wistfully. "I'll close the gate."

"Okay. Let's go get some breakfast, Ger." Bob was bursting with pride and relief. *Wow, that wasn't so bad,* he thought to himself. *People make it out so hard to talk with their kids. Well, glad that's over.*

As they walked up the road to the driveway, Gerry was thinking of John on Wings' back.

* * *

"Where do you want the cows to go out t'night?" Gerry asked.

"Aw, in the river piece, I guess. There's less trees for them to get hit by lightning under." Bob hated the muggy heat of July on his farm, when the thunder and lightning storms always seemed to hit at evening milking time, after a sweaty day of field work, so he could fret about whether the power would go off before milking was done.

*Geez,* Gerry thought. *Everything's gotta be negative.* Gerry knew he shouldn't think this, but he had been wanting it to rain so he could have a day off from haying.

His wish was granted only ten minutes after they were finished with supper. The sky was emptying so quickly that Gerry's Babe Ruth League baseball game was canceled, so he was as miserable about the rain as his father was about getting a field of mowed hay soaked.

Charlotte was disappointed, too.

It was so hot and humid that Gerry was letting the cows out a few at a time, as soon as they were milked. Charlotte and Wings and Thunder set out for the far corner of the river piece, to see if there was anything new where the woods were cleared. By the time the last of the cows had been unstanchioned, she and her companions were near the fence, trying to figure out where the thick humming sound was coming from.

"Don't look no different ta me," Thunder complained. "And there ain't nothin' looks like a feed mill."

"Have you ever seen a feed mill?" Wings demanded.

"Don't need to. Ain't no feed around. Whaddaya think I am, stupid?" She grinned at her witticism. Wings and Charlotte both winced.

"Where *is* that humming sound coming from?" Charlotte was nervous, but didn't know why.

The rest of the herd were working their way along the fenceline next to the road. The air was growing heavier and the humming louder. When the rain started, the humming was joined by a crackling sound.

It did not deter John. He came quickly across the meadow, almost at a trot, sensing that he was needed. And Charlotte was ready.

She had been completely absorbed in the mystery of the humming, when Thunder nipped her flank. She turned angrily toward her, eyes flashing, then saw Wings' look. It was her time. A pulse of fire flashed through her. And at that moment Charlotte saw John, head up, about to ford the small ravine that cut through the river meadow. Just as he dropped out of sight, she felt pincers of desire and longing grip her insides, in a part of herself she had been unaware of before that moment.

Instinctively she arched her back, raising her tail, and began to turn in a slow, dizzying circle. The longing crept up her insides, making her legs heavy and weak. It soared over her shoulders, the back of her neck, and settled into her brain.

Eyes half closed and mouth open, panting, she danced the dance. John knew long before he reached her how much she was in need.

Without fear, without pause, John ran to her, to replace her need with his strength, to match her desire with his.

The rain poured down, steam rose from them both, water droplets hung in Charlotte's eyelashes, seductively. There were no other cows around; they had vanished behind sheets of rain. But John could see Charlotte, look through her, into her, she was all that he could see.

Almost upon her, John began to rock back onto his rear hooves, then couldn't. His knees gave way. It was her dance. He had never understood it before, never needed it. Now it dissolved him.

Charlotte only knew that she must do the dance, to find the one meant for her. It did not matter that she had no choice, that John had none, that for time beyond memory there had been no choices. It had to mean something. And it did.

John danced, matching Charlotte step for step, gesture for gesture, passion for passion. Their circles closed into one.

Charlotte stopped, waiting for John to finish the dance. He rose to couple with her; she waited.

He set himself and reared upward, his front hooves lifted from the ground, pawing toward Charlotte. His eyes rolled back in anticipation of ecstasy. The humming noise gathered itself, swelled and thrust.

"Bru-huurh!"

A powerful shock had burst through him, knocking him backward. He tried again, rearing up once more, as the energy from the electromagnetic field of the power line searched for some source of grounding. It found John again, forcing him to earth.

"Bru-huurh!"

Charlotte was terribly confused. He had not come to her. She was filled with need. His scream was not from passion, but pain. What had she done wrong?

She turned to look at him just as he reared up the third time, saw the spasms in his hindquarters, his eyes shooting open, his fall to his knees, a scream unable to climb from his throat.

"Stop! Don't hurt yourself! Oh, please, just stop!" Charlotte was sobbing. John wanted to try again, desperately, but could not. His front legs were cement anchors, heavier and sunken more deeply than the bases of the towers. He hung his head, afraid to look at Charlotte, afraid to say anything.

The rain came harder. They stood apart, both looking at the ground, the herd all around them.

Thunder and Wings moved to Charlotte. She stared at the mud splattering up from the ground, unblinking.

"Come on, honey. It's okay," Wings whispered. Thunder nudged her gently. The whole herd moved off, except for John.

It took hours for the rain to stop, still more for the sky to clear, longer yet for John to move from that corner of the pasture, near the power line.

## Chapter Six

# Aretha

(1969)

"Who's that comin' down the driveway, Grenny Teller?" Bob yelled.

"No," Edna said. "It looks like they're delivering that cow you just bought."

"Oh, Jesus. They would come when I just lit up a cigarette. Renee, you're not doin' anything, are ya?" he asked innocently.

Renee looked shocked and then annoyed that he might even be asking her to do something in the barn. But Bob could not see her from his customary seat on the other side of the woodstove; only Gerry could. Gerry knew the look was mostly for his benefit.

"No, I'm not really busy. Do you need something, Daddy?"

Gerry's eyes rolled white.

"Could you run down and open up the gate, and tell 'em to put her in the third stanchion up on the right?"

"Okay. I just have to put my barn boots on," Renee said casually. She went into the kitchen, picked up her calf-height work shoes from behind the door, and returned to put them on. She pulled on her right shoe, lacing it slowly and deliberately.

Gerry couldn't take it any longer. He knew she was taking her time so he would have to go, or his father would have to go after all.

"I'll go, Dad," he said as he jumped up to get his boots.

"Oh, great. And I'm almost ready now," Renee complained. "I *was* going to do it."

"Yeah, sure." Gerry couldn't help himself.

"Don't start arguing with her," Bob said.

Gerry pulled his barn boots on and was out the door before Renee had finished crisscrossing the rawhide laces through the hooks on her right shoe.

"And don't let that bastardly dog out!"

Gerry forced the dog's nose back before he slammed the kitchen door.

Renee sighed meaningfully toward her father and began unlacing her shoes.

The driver had found the barnyard gate but had not figured out how to negotiate the truck up to the barn door. Gerry picked his way across the barnyard to open the gate to the river piece, giving the driver a better angle from which to back up.

"Huhloo, Gerry," the driver sang out.

"Hi, Stormy. How ya doin'?"

"Good, good. Say, izzat close enough to the barn?"

*Not if she decides to bolt, it isn't,* thought Gerry. "Let's let the tailgate down and back 'er up some more."

"Okeydoke. You know how to do that, don'tcha? Let out enough chain to hold the gate halfway up, then rehook it."

Gerry smirked. Stormy's reputation for laziness was well deserved. "Sure, Stormy, you just hold down your seat." He reveled in the chance to get a dig in on somebody.

"That's right. Lemme know if you can't handle it and I'll give you a hand." Stormy was much more practiced in jabbing egos.

Gerry braced his shoulder into the tailgate and, gaining some slack in the chain, unhooked a length of it, then rehooked it. Stormy backed the cattle truck so it was just inside the doorway, then joined Gerry inside.

"I don't know what your father was thinkin' this time, Jeremy, my boy."

"It's *not* Jeremy, it's Gerald," Gerry said. "What do you mean?"

"This cow isn't anything like the kind your dad usually gets. She's kinda spooky, too."

"Sure, Stormy, sure. What does she do, fly around?"

"Go ahead, make fun of it. You'll see."

They dropped the tailgate to find a haggard blue-gray cow staring directly at them. That was a little strange, but certainly not spooky.

"I see what you mean, Stormy. I'm scared," Gerry said.

"Okay, wise guy, you'll find out."

The cow swung sideways now, and swung her long neck back and forth, appearing to be frightened of something. But she was the only animal in the truck. She cocked her head, listening, shook her head in disagreement, then turned again to face the front of the truck. It seemed her invisible guidance told her she was not supposed to stay at this farm.

"C'mon, you bastard, get outta there." Stormy wanted to get rid of this cow and go home.

Gerry grabbed a hard maple club and climbed up in the truck. The cow let him pass by her flank. He rapped her on the side of her skull with the stick, without effect.

Five seconds passed. She blinked. Another five seconds passed. She looked directly into his eyes, but Gerry felt that she had no clue he was even in the truck.

He grabbed her head in both hands, trying to pull her around to face the back of the truck. She relaxed into his hands only when he pulled her, until she was standing on the barn floor.

They heard the milkhouse door slam shut. Bob, done with his cigarette.

"So where is she s'posed ta go, Ger?"

"This stanchion over here. The third one."

"Well, put some grain in front of it then. Show her the grain," Bob said.

Gerry sprinted to get a scoop of grain, ran back, and held it in front of the cow's nose. She reached out her tongue tentatively, tasted the fine bits of meal, and followed the scoop across the gutter. But as soon as Gerry reached through the stanchion frame to dump the grain in the manger, she dodged to the right, shoved her head past the stanchion, and began gobbling it up.

"Hey, you stupid thing. Cut it out! Boy, what a *stooopid* animal!" Gerry slid through the stanchion to get in front of the manger, stomping the cow's snout with the heel of his boot.

"Well, I guess I'm all set, Bob. Let me know when you need another cow brought over," Stormy said as he lifted the tailgate up into place. He wasn't about to fart around with this beast any longer.

"What's yer hurry, Stormy? All your experience here oughta come in handy," Bob yelled.

The cow jumped back, feinted farther right, got Gerry's stick against her ear, sidestepped left, and dived into the fourth stanchion. She grabbed one mouthful of grain before she jumped backward, too far to the right again, knocking Gerry down.

Bob found this to be exceptionally funny, especially since it made Gerry angry. He leaped to his feet, jabbing the maple stick into the cow's neck, screaming at her.

"Now stop that. There's no use in bein' mean to the animal," Bob found himself saying.

Gerry's jaw dropped open in disbelief. "I've seen you beat cows for less than that, for doin' almost nothin'."

Bob exploded. "*Jee*-zus. You don't know what you're talkin' about. If I ever hit a cow it's for a damn good reason."

"Oh yeah, well, this pissin' animal just knocked me down. I suppose that's not a good enough reason."

"You just calm down," Bob menaced. "This cow—" He was interrupted by the roar of the cattle truck as Stormy gunned it up the driveway. "Why, that lazy bastard."

The cow suddenly wheeled around and launched herself across the gutter, then trotted the length of the barn floor, Gerry and Bob in close pursuit. Without hesitation she negotiated the ramp over the reverse curve of the gutter cleaner, slipped and skidded into the door of the feed box, then gathered herself for a dash to the left around in front of the manger on the far side of the barn.

Gerry sprinted to the narrow alleyway between the old and new sections of the barn, unable to head her off. He was deceptively quick for his stocky build! "Jesus, you're slow," he heard his father say behind him. Coarse iron replaced Gerry's bones now, too heavy to move quickly. He slowed to a deliberate walk.

The cow braked abruptly two-thirds of the way down the stretch in front of the manger. In agonized, mincing steps she attempted to find some passage around an invisible barrier. *Ghosts,* she thought. *This barn has too many, too many.*

"Nice cow." Gerry's voice was sugar-glazed bile. "Why doesn't the nice cow just stroll over to Peanut's old stanchion?" He looked over his shoulder at his father. "Then why don't you just lock yourself up?" he added.

"Put her in Young Smitty's place. We'll move Young Smitty over to Peanut's stanchion."

*Well, I'll let her sleep up in my room,* Gerry thought, swallowing the words stillborn. "Whatever you say," he sighed.

He shooed, waved, and flailed his arms in a vain attempt to chase the cow past the invisible barrier. Feeling ever more foolish, he finally stepped across the manger and through a stanchion, clearing her path of retreat. As she began to move in the opposite direction, he paralleled her, walking more quickly when she picked up the pace.

"Slow down—don't get her running again," Bob warned.

Gerry was beside himself. *That's no problem. I'm too slow anyway, right?* Unable to speak the words aloud, he compressed their force into the muscles of his right arm, in which he held the club. He stood rooted in the thin straw of summer bedding.

"Just turn right at the alleyway," Gerry sneered. She did, angering him more.

"Now walk back down the floor. Second stanchion from the end on the left."

"Git down in that doorway so she don't run out into the barnyard," Bob ordered.

Gerry ran past his father, overtaking the cow just as she took a sharp left across the gutter and into Young Smitty's stanchion. Gerry's momentum carried him across the threshold into the barnyard. He reversed and ran to close the stanchion, arriving a moment after his father had slammed it closed.

"Sweep that grain over in front of her and give her a little more," Bob said.

Gerry fetched the broom and a quarter scoop of grain. The cow seemed placid, almost normal. He caught his father looking across the barn floor at the place that had spooked the cow. It seemed that his father had an idea of what it was, but if so he wasn't talking about it. Gerry concluded that the animal was just retarded, or crazy.

Bob turned on his heel and walked off, giving Gerry the chance to swat the cow's nose with the broom as he swept.

*Stop hurting! Stop hurting! It's not my fault! That ghost is yours!*

*It's not my fault!* she wanted to say, but could only beller.

Gerry finished sweeping and replaced the broom. Before he left the barn he looked over at the place where the cow had been spooked. "Wonder what's buggin' that crazy beast," he thought aloud.

Gerry had said nothing to his father about what was wrong with the cow, but he knew what Stormy had meant. His father usually bought healthy, well-fed Holsteins, and occasionally a Brown Swiss. This cow was freckled blue-gray, so thin the bones of her haunches jutted up painfully; her bag was smallish and uneven.

The color of her eyes was an unremarkable brown, made unusual by a thin violet tint around them fading into the white. It also seemed that she had an extra set of eyelids, or an extra depth to her eyes, because she could appear to be studying someone intently and at the same time not seeing the person at all. Despite all this, Gerry could have been okay with this cow if it had not been for her tail.

It was not there.

Just below the downward curve of her tail was a squared-off, blunt stump. The exposed meat was dark as dried jerky, purplish, like the edge of her irises. Every so often, when flies lit on her sides or there was some other annoyance, the stump would twitch. Either her body had never forgotten how to use the tail, or her mind had not accepted its loss.

Gerry was afraid to ask his father if this blue cow had belonged to Helmut Molshoc, a hard farmer whose pastures bordered on Bob's gravel bed and woods on the east side of the farm. Despite the proximity of the farms and the interest Gerry and Renee had in the Molshoc kids, Bob rarely spoke of Helmut. Once he'd heard his father speak of Helmut as being "odd," in a tone tinged with disgust.

It was not because of Helmut's rumored abuse of his wife and children, but because he had strange ideas about the treatment of his cows.

Helmut interpreted dominion in a very serious way, so serious that nervous, restless cows, tormented by flies, were not allowed to swish their urine-soaked tails during milking. Helmut believed, and his children when required would echo, that God had given man dominion because the beasts of Eden had not saved Adam. Their sin was original also, Helmut believed, and could be redeemed only by absolute subservience to men, so long as men were struggling to return to grace.

Helmut believed that it was unnatural for man to use unnatural methods in the breeding of animals in his domain, and when hormonal meanness ensued—or as Helmut would say, "the beast became rhiny"—there was no good reason to rid the bull of the offending appendages, so there was a high rate of turnover of bulls at the Molshoc farm.

Not so with cows. Cows that kicked might be sold eventually, but not before they had felt iron squeezing their nostrils, stretching their necks into stubborn, aching lines; not before a rope had been circled so tightly around their flanks, just before the haunches, that they could only feel their hind legs as numbness; not before Helmut had pulled their tails up and bent them back over their spines, stretching the cords of the anus to such a tautness that attempting to kick might tear tender flesh and muscle.

The fact was that Helmut kept his cows for a long time because not many other farmers wanted to buy them for milkers.

Especially since offending tails could be taken care of so easily, by binding the tail with rubber bands, ever more tightly as the circulation was cut off and the rotting progressed, until the tail fell right off.

It did not take many swishes of the tail to bring on this rectification, sometimes only one.

Bob never was able to understand how Helmut could act that way, especially to go so far as to hurt the price of his cows. His own belief was that his animals had feelings and that it was wrong to cause unnecessary pain. But his treatment of his cows was driven more by economic concerns than morality. He couldn't afford to think in ethical terms.

In fact, his economic views were the basis of his morality. "Ya know what the worst thing is that ever happened to this country?" Bob had once asked Gerry.

Gerry sighed and said, "Yup. Them letting the Beatles in here with their long hair."

Bob thought on that for a moment, having forgotten that was what he had lectured Gerry about the last time he had asked him a question.

"Well, yeah, that was bad, but the worst thing," lowering his voice to a conspiratorial whisper, "is that damn Pill."

Gerry was inclined to see it as a godsend.

"Why?"

"Well, there's not enough people, ya know."

Gerry was perplexed. He'd just been hearing something about a population bomb in social studies class.

"But I heard—"

"What? About overpopulation? That's a crock. Ya don't see too many people around here, do ya?"

"No, but—"

"There's not enough people in the world. Women haven't been having enough babies, so without enough babies people haven't been buying all the milk. Here we got all this milk and the women aren't having enough babies to drink it."

Gerry was stunned for a moment. "You mean to tell me that people should have all the babies they can just so there will be enough to buy all the milk we can produce?"

"Yessir. Then the whole economy will be healthy."

"Who's gonna buy the milk for them?"

"They can buy it for themselves, can't they?"

"Well, not in a lotta places. Like, what about Biafra?"

"That's just two tribes fighting over the same piece of land that's not worth anything when you're done with it. Soon as they stop fighting they can go back to getting fed by us."

Gerry's mouth was hanging open. His father looked at him, disgusted, and shook his head.

"What grade are you in now?"

"I'm gonna be a junior next year."

"Just goes ta show, school don't teach ya nothing."

Gerry shifted in his seat. He knew what was coming next.

"Whatcha takin' up in school, anyway, the teacher's time?"

"Renee, that's Grenny Teller. Can you go down to the barn to make sure he does the right cow?" Edna asked. "There's two in the barn now, with that new one from Molshoc's."

"Mother, are you serious? Why do I have to go to the barn? Can't Gerry go?"

"Gerry's raking and your father and Merle are baling, and I'm canning these berries." Edna paused, hoping Renee would not fight her.

"But I'll watch the pressure cooker," Renee whined.

"It's White Brat, in the new section of the barn on the right. I guess the new cow is speckled. Tell Grenny to just do White Brat."

Renee sighed, took a step toward the dining room and the stairs to her room.

"Better get going." Edna's voice was unwavering. "Now."

Renee quickly pulled on her barn shoes, laced them, and went out the door. Grenny had just gotten his equipment inside the milkhouse door. Renee held the door into the barn open for him and pointed him toward White Brat.

Renee had expected to return to the house as soon as she had shown the artificial-insemination man which cow to fertilize, but something caused her to stay. She watched as Teller cheerfully bared his right arm up to the shoulder, pulled a long plastic glove over it, and poured some semen into the palm.

Renee reflexively averted her eyes as Granny lifted the cow's tail with his left hand and began to shove his right hand up inside her. She focused on the cow's eyes, which had been agitated and red but now collapsed into a hollow, bloodless stare. She seemed to not want to be there.

Renee felt queer, as if she were assisting in the violation of this animal. She moved away just as Grenny's plasticized biceps disappeared into White Brat. Renee walked to the other end of the barn, where the new cow was stanchioned, hoping to get some fresh air and to calm herself.

The cow was at once nervous and calm, repulsive and beautiful, innocent and worldly. She was twitching while White Brat was being bred, feeling the plastic fist plunge into her. Renee stepped across the gutter and climbed between the stanchions to look at the cow's face. They stared into each other's eyes. *I know your name,* each was saying without words.

"Well, honey, she's done," Grenny bellowed. "I'll bet she'll be feelin' better real soon."

Renee and the blue cow turned to look at Grenny. The blank expressions on their faces rattled him a little.

"Y'know, Renee, these cows suffer when they're in heat. Bu-ut, this one won't have to worry about that again for a while." He laughed. "Well, got another call."

Renee snapped out of her trance, following him out the door and up to the house. She was still bothered by Grenny Teller's visit when Bob and Gerry came in at noon to eat.

* * *

Dinner was fried hamburger with cooked onions, yesterday's boiled supper potatoes browned in butter, fresh cucumbers from the garden, and blackberries served with sugar and milk. Gerry ate ravenously while his sister picked at her food.

"Did Grenny come over to breed that cow back?" Bob asked, after finishing the last of his coffee-soaked crust of homemade bread.

"Yes, he did. About an hour ago," Edna replied.

"Hope this one sticks," Gerry mumbled around a mouthful of berries. His father became instantly angry at the thought that he might have to pay twice for artificial insemination. Sometimes the cows weren't even breeding back, so it would have to be done again.

Renee was looking sternly at their brother, shaking her head. "You are so disgusting."

"What?" Gerry asked, genuinely confused.

"Don't talk with your mouth full," Bob said.

*My family is so sensitive,* Renee thought. *Talking about breeding animals when they're eating.*

"You gonna let her out after we eat?" Gerry asked.

"Who?"

"White Brat."

"What about that new cow?" Renee asked.

"So, you saw that new cow?" Bob asked, surprised.

"Yes."

"Whadja think?"

"I don't know. She's kind of interesting," she replied, disinterestedly.

"Don'tcha think she's kind of gross?" Gerry said, grinning at her.

She scowled and curled her lip at him.

"You are so disgusting," Gerry said to Renee.

She turned in her seat, facing her father, ignoring Gerry. "She looks different from the other cows. I like the speckled blue and the blue in her eyes."

Bob smiled. "Is that what we should call her?"

"Old Blue—that's a good name for her," Gerry said, attempting to get back into the conversation.

"That's not very imaginative," Renee offered.

"Yeah, Ol' Blue," Gerry insisted.

"Blue sounds okay to me," Bob said.

"It's too obvious, too ordinary," Renee complained. "Maybe Blues would be better, or someone who sings the blues."

"Connie Francis sings that blues song," Edna cut in. "What is it, 'Hawaii Blue,' something like that."

"Connie Francis! But Mother, that's not a blues song. Connie Francis!" Renee was incredulous.

"Old Blue. Good Ol' Blue."

"I know, Aretha Franklin. R-E-S-P-E-C-T. Let's call her Aretha," Renee concluded.

"R-E-S-P— What? What is all that?" Bob said.

"Just somebody who sings, Daddy. Let's name her Aretha."

Edna nodded approval to her husband, he nodded back, and Gerry scowled.

"Aretha. What a stupid name."

"Can I let her out, Daddy? Are you going to let her out?" Renee continued.

"Well, so long as we can get her back into a stanchion for milking. Would you give us a hand?"

"Sure. I know she'll go in without a problem anyway."

"Well, then, go ahead. Uh, and let White Brat out, too."

"Okay," Renee chirped. She got up from the table to get her work shoes.

"Uh-hem . . . are you gonna help your mother with the dishes?" Bob inquired suspiciously.

"Don't I always?" Renee replied sweetly.

"Gerry can help me get started, while Renee's down in the barn," Edna said.

Gerry was confused now, looking to his father for support. As Renee left, Bob sucked the last drop of coffee from his cup, set it down on the saucer, and slid it over in front of Gerry, ignoring his look of silent protest.

"Gosh, it's great that Renee is getting interested in the barn again, isn't it?" Bob said.

"Yes, it is," Edna agreed, with an ironic smile.

Renee unstanchioned Aretha and White Brat, then shooed them out of the barn. Aretha moved slowly, looking back over her shoulder at White Brat, who walked woodenly. Once in the barnyard on their way to the stone-pile pasture, a field rented from a neighbor no longer in farming, Aretha slowed down so White Brat could catch up to her.

"It'll be all right, believe me," Aretha said. "It's nothing to feel ashamed about."

White Brat could not answer. She was still in shock. She could only keep moving forward, heading in the direction of the rest of the herd.

"Your ghosts will come back, don't worry." Aretha was desperate to help White Brat feel better.

Finally, White Brat turned to her, glaring. "I don't fucking care if they come back. Leave me alone."

Aretha froze in place, ashamed of herself for badgering. She fell back, shuffling slowly toward the herd.

"Ooh. So this is the new cow," Bossy said, then gasped as she saw the stub of her tail. Aretha looked through her, the same way she had looked through Gerry.

Silence rippled outward from White Brat and Aretha as they walked grimly through the center of the herd. Young Smitty moved from the edge of the woods on a beeline toward them, communicating silently to the others to let her be alone with White Brat. But Aretha was blind to Smitty's intent, and continued to shadow White Brat even after Smitty fell in step with her. Perhaps it was because her only connection at this farm was to her, and her ghosts.

"Go away," Smitty hissed.

"She'll be all right. Her ghosts are still right here, waiting to come back." Aretha seemed matter-of-fact to Smitty, but was nearly overcome with fear.

"Her what?" Smitty stopped to look Aretha directly in the face. White Brat paused in her tracks, then also turned around to face Aretha, her eyes hollowed out by denial.

"Ghosts. Two left her, when that man was inside her. But they are hovering there." She nodded over White Brat's head. Smitty looked to the place where she had indicated and saw nothing.

"Why don't you just leave her alone," Smitty insisted.

"What happened to her will happen to all of us. I've heard about it, from others who came to my old farm. It's the human way of giving us calves without a bull."

"But ghosts! What do you mean by ghosts?"

"Hers are lost parts of herself. Her pride and dignity left when she was violated." Aretha started to quiver, shaking in sympathy with White Brat, who was engulfed by the shakes. "She's coming through it now."

Smitty turned to watch her friend, as White Brat's knees buckled and shudders ran through her.

"She'll be like that for a while. Then she'll get mad and fight back. Eventually she'll get used to it, like everybody."

Smitty looked at Aretha in fear, worried that she might have some powers that could hurt her.

Just then Aretha cocked her head sideways, seeming to listen to a voice outside of Smitty's hearing, then focused her eyes into Smitty's.

"Her ghosts are not like yours. Hers belong to her. Yours are from someone else, someone close to you . . . your mother . . . and another . . . a friend."

"How do you know that?" Smitty gasped.

"My ghosts . . . talk to me. They tell me what they see."

Dutchess joined them now, to help comfort White Brat and to check out the new sister. Dutchess and Smitty together would determine where this cow would fit in the Order.

"Ghosts? That's ridiculous," Dutchess asserted. "There are no such things. You know that."

*You won't let yours in,* Aretha thought.

"You had better go away, *now,*" Dutchess commanded.

*They're swirling all around your head, like a bee swarm.* Aretha pondered the frenetic activity around Dutchess's head, thought better of pointing it out. She turned and walked off toward the woods, drifting into a meditation.

Dutchess waited for a moment until it was clear that Aretha was in retreat. Turning to Smitty, she hissed, "How could you? She's a new cow!"

"Yes, I know, but she seemed to know some things about . . ."

"Ridiculous! She's a new cow. There is nothing she could know."

"She was telling me about my mother . . . and, I think, Peanut."

"Nonsense. She'll have to become part of the Order. Just like everybody else. Or do you want to get rid of the Order?"

Smitty shuddered internally. The Order was one half-step above chaos, with brutal struggles over rank and privileges. She had always wondered, only to herself, if it was a practice among all of their kind, or just peculiar to this farm. Her mother never had endorsed it fully, in fact had fought against it.

*Mother. Oh, you were taken away moons ago. How could that new cow know about you? Maybe you're alive, at that other farm.*

Smitty turned to go after Aretha.

"Where are you going?" Dutchess snapped. "Have you forgotten your friend here?"

She had. White Brat was slipping back into sullenness, which could either be dangerous or a return to her normal mood. She had fought to her position in the Order, as low as it was, so her meanness had served her. Smitty had a flash of insight. *We are worse than the chickens,* she thought.

*"Smitty!"* Dutchess shouted her to attention. "What's the matter with White Brat, anyway?"

"I . . . I don't know, Dutchess. But the new cow said . . . well, she seems to be getting better."

"Good, good. You had me worried there for a moment, Smitty. We need the Order, even more now. Don't forget what it's done for you."

Young Smitty had indeed benefited from the Order. She had been recruited into it, was second from the peak, and just at that moment hated herself for it, for the betrayal of her mother, and her mother's spirit of independence.

*Mother,* she thought. She took a quick look at White Brat, grazing almost calmly, and set out to catch up with Aretha.

Aretha was almost in the woods, searching for a path through the thickets of blackberry bushes that barricaded the hemlock grove. She wanted to be alone. She was afraid that she had already jeopardized her chances for acceptance by any of the cows.

She was right.

It was not just that she'd had a run-in with Dutchess, but also because of her tail, and the entire herd was at loose ends because of John. To have a bull that was too mean was a problem, but mostly for the humans. Not having a bull was a problem only if the herd was unused to artificial insemination.

But John was still there, at least in the physical sense, and it had all of them confused and on edge. He was a constant reminder that something very real was wrong, and worse, there was no way to set it right. John had lost all sense of himself, moping around on the fringes of the herd when they were out in the pasture, and sitting quietly in his stanchion during milking.

After three cows were not bred back within two weeks of John's trauma, Farmer Bob had reluctantly contacted Grenny Teller to use artificial insemination. He kept John, hoping that somehow he would turn around, but as each day passed without change, both John and Farmer Bob became more depressed and withdrawn.

At first the cows were sympathetic to Charlotte, and distant toward John, but after his funk lasted a few days, much of the herd seemed to assume that it was Charlotte's fault and began to pay attention to John again. This lasted only a few days, until Wings and Forty and Bossy were rejected by John, who, despite their affections, grew more miserable every day.

Then the cows became openly hostile to John, turning their frustrations upon him with all the viciousness of the vengeful oppressed.

"John, are you going off on your own tonight? A little romance in the woods all by yourself?" Wings had baited him.

When White Brat and Aretha had come out into the pasture that day, news of Aretha's tail had spread like wildfire, adding to John's torment.

"Have you seen your new mate yet, John? She's really beautiful."

He shrank into himself, and tried to move away quietly from more torment.

"Hey, John, she has something missing too, John, just like you. It ought to be fun watching you two try to get together." Wings kept pressing him, and he kept going deeper within himself, until finally he retreated into the woods.

He had blasted through the blackberry brambles fringing the hemlock woods, heading straight for the river. His voice was pounding his head from within. Unable to do his work, he had lost his understanding of his identity, while constantly being reminded of the expectations others had of him. He had completely lost touch with his bullness.

"Whaddaya think you're doin'?" Thunder challenged.

"I'm going to talk to . . . I'm going to the woods," Smitty replied.

"In a big hurry, ain'tcha?"

"I just need to get into the shade before milking."

"Okay, sure. I'll go with ya."

"You don't have to do that. I'm just kind of worn out because of White Brat and all."

"Yeah, and that new cow."

"What about the new cow?"

"Ain't you worn out by the new cow, too?"

"Why would I be? She's just new, that's all." Her quavering voice was making even the dim-witted Thunder suspicious.

"So she's just new, huh? What about her tail?"

"What about it? Her tail has been cut off somehow. I don't see what that's got to do with me."

"She's gotta be put in the Order," Thunder insisted.

"Well, I'm sure she will be," Smitty replied evenly. "Don't you think so?"

"But, Dutchess said . . ." Thunder sputtered.

"Dutchess said what? Doesn't she want the new cow to be put in the Order?" Thunder was visibly confused, so Smitty kept pressing. "If you and Dutchess are trying to destroy the Order, you won't get away with it."

"Dest . . . whu-ut? Hey, whaddaya tryin' ta do?"

"I'm trying to protect the Order," Smitty lied. "And I'm tired right now. So I'm going to the woods to rest."

"But Dutchess told me—"

"Dutchess told you to keep an eye on me," Smitty interrupted. And then she gambled. "Come with me if you don't believe me."

Thunder's brow furrowed in concentration. She looked back over her shoulder at Dutchess, unsure of herself.

"Well?" Smitty pressed, anxious to get away.

Thunder's face suddenly relaxed, then brightened.

"Uh . . . sure. Let's go."

Smitty suppressed a shudder, resigning herself to sitting at the edge of the woods with Thunder until milking time.

"Ruh-unh . . . Unnh . . . Ruh-unh."

John did not know what the sound was, but he sensed that it was not threatening. Blackberry bushes, ferns, skunk cabbage, and orchard grass had grown so thick around the base of the overturned, decaying elm tree that he could not make out the source of the noise. He circled the upturned roots carefully, but without fear.

It was Billie, the most miserable and angry cow on the farm, neck outstretched and taut, eyes rolling back, tail lifted and back arched, panting and sweating.

She was freshening.

John had never been present at the birthing of a calf, mostly because he had never been interested. His mates always had gone off on their own, if they could, to have their babies in the wild, hoping to hide them so they could grow up.

John circled around behind Billie, unable to pull himself away from this sight. The calf's nose and mouth were visible, straining through a film of membrane to break through to the air. There was no sign of the front hooves emerging, so, while John had no idea of this, the calf and its mother were in trouble.

She strained and moaned, then rested. The flesh across her ribs swelled and contracted as she panted. Billie knew she was in trouble. She rolled from haunch to haunch, rose to her knees and dropped, then rolled again. Her meanness was her only strength against collapse.

John moved to her, knelt down, and nuzzled against her haunch, rubbing the side of his head and the underside of his neck against the mouth of her womb. He did not know why he did this, he knew only that he must somehow try to help.

Billie was first startled by John's intrusion, then weakness forced her to relax to his massage. If she had known it was John, she would have preferred to die.

He made no sound.

A blue-speckled cow crashed through the blackberry bushes, eyes frantic and red. John bolted, thrashing through the ferns and grass toward the river. Billie launched to her hooves, then collapsed.

John stood on the cliff edge, looking down past the hulks of ancient farm machinery dumped there, to the river. Early green apples from the trees on the cliff edge crunched under his hooves as he walked.

"I should go back there. I should help somehow," he repeated to himself, tormented by his helplessness. He began to tear apples down, chewing them nervously while he paced along the cliff edge, searching out a course of action.

"You saved her, you know."

John whirled around to face the blue cow, who he realized must be the new arrival at the farm.

"What do you mean?"

"She had her calf, a healthy heifer, just after you left," Aretha said. "She's already moving the calf to a better hiding place."

"Ye-ess," John exulted. "I mean . . . that's good." He settled back into his misery, feeling even more lost than before.

"Oh, no, now your ghost is back," Aretha observed. Immediately she regretted saying anything, turning away to cover up.

"My ghost? What are you talking about?" John asked.

"Oh, nothing. Don't listen to me. Sometimes I say things without thinking."

"No, you meant something. What is it?"

"Your ghost is . . . part of yourself you have lost," Aretha said, mustering a delicate tone. "It's why you feel useless."

*You're ugly,* he thought. *And that butchered tail makes me sick.*

"So, they couldn't wait to tell you about me. Who was it, that bitch Wings?"

"No, you don't understand. No one told me anything. I can see ghosts."

He looked up into her eyes, wanting to believe her, but afraid to think she might actually understand.

"What ghosts have you seen?"

"Are you sure . . . I can't say. I'm afraid."

"They did tell you."

"No. That's not true. . . . All right, there's a calf ghost in the barn, and another one, a cow, but I don't think she's dead . . ."

"Peanut," John breathed.

". . . and there's a human ghost, too. You can feel it around all the humans. They're all sad, and don't talk."

"Neither do we," John warned.

"Why not? Who is it?"

"Don't ask. It'll only cause trouble."

They both fell silent, awkward in realizing that their only connection was as outcasts. John munched more apples.

*I hate freckles, and she's so scrawny,* John thought.

*What is happening here? Everyone is so uptight. But he's really kinda sweet, helping that mean one freshen.* She nibbled absentmindedly at the sweetly rotting fallen apples.

"Hmmph. Bet they'll have you in their Order," John thought out loud.

"What? The Order? What's that?" she said, frightened at the ominous sound of it.

"Aw, don't worry. It won't be that bad." He chuckled. "You probably scare 'em."

She surprised herself by laughing. "I think you're right. Especially that Dutchess."

*"Dutchess,"* John roared. "If you've got her scared, you'll be running the place."

"Yes, she was really pressuring the friend of that one that's missing—"

"Must be Smitty," John interrupted.

"—and making that cow that was just bred by the man . . . oh, I'm so sorry."

"White Brat," John said, ashamedly. "It's okay. It's not your fault."

"No, I mean I made her feel worse. She really felt violated."

John couldn't speak, or even look up at her. He chewed the apples thoughtfully.

"You *will* help her, don't worry."

"Don't say that. You don't know."

"Yes, I do. I saw it. I saw you helping that mother have her baby. Whatever is bothering you doesn't have power everywhere."

John finished crunching some apples, letting the fermented juice fill his head. He swallowed and listened. A breeze through leaves, birds calling, no humming.

"What did you say? Did you say I'm all right?" he said excitedly. Until this moment he had not noticed the intriguing violet of her eyes.

She looked into his eyes. "You're fine. There's no need to worry."

*That blue is so . . . exotic. And that tail. It's so different, so . . . inviting,* John dreamed, his eyes a little unfocused from the apples.

He turned a slow circle, never losing contact with her eyes. She turned with him, disbelieving.

"You won't be lonely anymore," he said to her. As they coupled she began to cry.

Before he lay next to her, exhausted and sleepy, John cried.

When they were missing at milking time and Gerry was sent to look for them, the sight of them lying together asleep made him confused all over again about the sophomore girls.

## Chapter Seven

# King

(1969)

The dog shoved his nose between the mattress and springs of Edna's bed, and kept nudging the mattress until she rolled out of bed. It was five past five. She was late. A thunderstorm had cut off the power, screwed up the clock.

*Good thing for the dog,* Edna thought, as she padded out to the kitchen to put the milk on the boil for cocoa.

King could only think about "out," beginning his day. He waited in front of the bathroom door while Edna was changing into her housedress, blocking her passage back to the dining room. She emerged from the bathroom and turned right to check on the milk, while King hugged her right ankle, slinking along a half step behind her. When she paused in front of the gas stove, he stood between her feet and the cake-pan drawer.

A ring of tiny bubbles had formed around the rim of the saucepan. She waited for the froth to begin rising before she turned the gas off, knowing for years now that it would not spill over. All this while King leaned against her legs, waiting for the click of the dial to signal him to herd her toward the door.

He stayed just behind her and to the right, watching the flexing of her calf muscles to be sure she was going to the door. She turned the knob and pulled, the door teasing him a moment before it unstuck and burst open. He lunged for the opening as if it were prey, running free into the chill dark before morning.

The birds could not yet be stirred, so King struck out to locate Scout, the Molshoc dog, to go on a woodchuck hunt. Scout was an ancient mongrel with rat-brown fur often matted with cow manure he had rolled in, or burdocks or other sticky nettles. He was slow-moving and pensive, but a wonderful companion.

King loped leisurely to the east of his farm and up the hill to the Molshoc chicken coop, where he found Scout huddled in the chill.

"Hey, Scouter, wanna go huntin'?"

"Too early, King. My bones hurt before the sun comes up."

"You sure? I think Grampa's up and eatin' on the hill."

"I'd like to, Kinger, just can't."

"Okay. See ya later."

King raced directly back across the frost-sodden pastures between Scout's farm and his own, hoping that Gerry was up. At this point in the fall there was not even enough grazing left for the cows to be out all the time, so they were in the barn now at night. Nothing for King to do but wait for after morning milking for a chance to herd.

*No lights in the barn—they must still be drinking cocoa,* King thought as he headed up the side-porch steps to the kitchen door. Once there he pushed his nose against the door, first gently, then hard enough to rattle the windowpane slightly.

*The dog,* Edna thought.

"That son-of-a-bitchin' dog," Bob said as he sucked on his cigarette.

"Must be King. I'll get him," Gerry said. He leaned forward to lower the front chair legs to the floor, then slid back from the table to get to the door.

*He's going to break that chair someday,* Edna worried to herself.

"It's good to see that he can move around this early, isn't it, Mother?" Bob jabbed.

"Yes." She put on her agreeing smile for him.

As soon as he was let inside, King could sense that they were picking on Gerry again. Sometimes his mother would have to call him three times in the morning before he came downstairs, especially now that he was sixteen and had older friends who could drive at night. It was a constant struggle now to keep Gerry sufficiently rested to help out on the farm, Edna felt. Often the good-natured ribbing that his father had always engaged in when Gerry was getting up was turning more serious, and bitter, from both of them. King would have helped, if there had been any way for him to help, but he had problems enough of his own. Bob thought that the dog was even lazier and more no-account than his son was getting to be, which was no mean accomplishment.

"Boy, he must have been out really, really late last night," Bob said with glee.

"It was after one before the light was turned off," Edna replied. Her voice walked a tightrope between a guilt trip to Gerry for keeping her up, and sadness that she was compelled to participate in this sacrificial rite.

The maddening part of the morning routine for Gerry was the sameness of it all. When he was in the bathroom he'd mouth the words of their script. The weather, the hired man, Gerry, Renee, the dog—all were sources of complaint for Bob.

King had settled underneath Gerry's chair, which was tipped backward again. Edna watched nervously as King wagged his tail back and forth beneath the chair legs. King was keeping his eye on the angle of the rear chair legs so that when they began to tilt to the vertical he could scoot out from under.

"Jesus," Bob exclaimed, looking out the window. "Merle's down to the barn already. Let's go."

Gerry jumped up and got to the door a second behind King.

"That dog doesn't need to go out. He'll just wanna come in the barn and get the cows goin'. Leave him in!" Bob commanded.

Gerry held the side of his foot up against King's nose as he eased the door open, then stepped through quickly and slammed it shut. King looked disappointedly up through the door window at Gerry's disappearing back, then turned his head to make sure that Bob was going out next.

Knowing that Bob and Edna would not let him out, and that Renee—home from college—would not be up until late morning, he dropped his head and retreated around the corner of the refrigerator toward the dining room. Bob tugged and tugged to unstick the door, and when it finally burst open King sprinted out ahead of him.

"Goddammit. Worthless animal," Bob complained. He looked at

Edna to emphasize how it was her fault. "He's a sneaky bastard." Edna was silent, busying herself by tearing yesterday's bread crusts into King's dish, which she knew would bring him back inside in about two minutes.

King had always been treated well by Edna, who had compensated for her children's entry into teenage nastiness by babying their new puppy, a Border collie, bred to herd cows. She lavished food on him such as his predecessor, a mutt also named King, had never seen nor tasted except as table scraps.

In fact, as a puppy this collie had been loved and fussed over by the entire family. Renee saw in him a second chance to prove herself in pet care, having neglected a horse to auction when she was twelve. She never managed to persuade her mother to let any of the barn kittens sleep in her room. Renee had grown terrified of chasing the cows, too, and this dog offered the prospect of release from that fear.

Bob's interest in the dog was practical, too, but he once had been so fond of King as a pup that he allowed him to ride shotgun on the seat of the truck as he plowed the driveway in his first winter. After failing as a cow dog, King was never again accorded that favor.

But Gerry loved him despite his failure, and even championed him, believed in him. As time passed, this loyalty only served to estrange Gerry further from his father, which somehow seemed to strengthen the bond between boy and dog.

The annoying part of this situation, Bob thought, was that Gerry had as much reason to want a real cow dog on the farm as did Bob, or Renee.

Her fear had begun on the Long March, when Bob had bought out Asa North's herd and decided to move them by a cattle drive on the back roads for the three miles between their farms.

One cloudy, threatening summer day right after morning milking, Bob had brought his hired man and children to the stone farm to round up his new herd and begin the drive to the mud farm. Gerry and Renee were excited and scared at the prospect of herding the cows all that way on the back roads. For Gerry it was pure cowboy stuff, right out of the movies, except he didn't have his own horse to ride. In fact, Renee had to beg her father to let her ride the old work horse, Dewey, on the roundup. She finally convinced him that she would feel safer on the horse if they ran into any problems with the new bull, and then her father relented.

Most of the time Renee was on the horse while Gerry had to walk, even when they got onto the back road and some cows wandered off into the brush. It wasn't much like how Gerry had thought it would work, from Westerns he had seen.

They had started from the barbed-wire gate to the pasture on the top of the hill at North's farm. The pasture had short-cropped grass, "from too many cows on too little meadow," Gerry's father had snorted, and it was so studded with stones that neither Renee on the horse nor her father in his pickup could start the roundup. It fell to Gerry to circle out behind the herd and get them started toward the gate.

Old Smitty, Daisy, and Miss Jerome stared at him dumbly while he chucked pebbles at their haunches. They had become so accustomed to Asa and his wife shooing them away from the gate that this new human wanting to chase them the other way was very suspicious. So they moved slowly at Gerry's urging, a few at a time, while others moved off in different directions, until their bull could investigate.

*Where do you think you're pushing my cows to, little man?* the bull thought toward Gerry.

There was no reply.

*This is my farm, and my herd.*

The little man said nothing, only started throwing pebbles frantically. Then he looked all around him even more frantically, until he discovered a thick stick, which he brandished toward the bull.

*You're not scared, are you, little man?* The look on the boy's face belied any thought-message he might have been trying to send to White John. The boy was almost scared out of his wits.

Asa circled around to the boy's side from the opposite direction, so that John did not see him until it was almost too late. He had begun pawing the ground and snorting, angry at the arrogance and lack of response of this small human, when the old man rapped him firmly on the side of his nose and pronounced, "Git."

Confused, John began to turn in the direction of the old man, then sensed his sadness. Whatever was happening was not something that the old man really wanted, but it was also something that could not be fought. White John started to move toward the gate, and the reluctant cows fell in line.

Once they reached the gate, Bob asked what the holdup was, but before Gerry could answer Asa interrupted, "Cows were just curious at somebody new in this old pasture, Bob. But your boy did a good job of getting them started. Wish my boys had as much interest in the farm."

Gerry still was frightened from his brush with the bull, but at the same time pleased with how the old man had described him.

*This cattle drive could be fun after all,* he thought.

The feeling lasted for the first mile of the trip, until the cows had to be turned off Colson Road onto the back road, near the decaying shell of a country schoolhouse that still stood on the Salter farm. Bob had left Renee on Dewey in the middle of Colson Road as a barricade. A firm believer in leadership, Bob was steering a half-dozen cows up the back road with his pickup truck to point the way.

Gerry was on foot about a dozen cows back from his father, while Merle, also on foot, was to keep the stragglers on track from the rear. The mutt King was hunting woodchucks with a younger, more ambitious Scout in the county road piece on the Molshoc farm.

Bob's fervor in keeping the lead cows moving had allowed the bull to slip back in the pack. He grazed on the inside of the turn of the road while a dozen cows passed him by, lifting his head and turning full around to startle Gerry and block his path again.

*So there you are,* he thought to the small human. Gerry quickly looked around for help and saw none. His father's pickup truck was out of sight, Merle at least a quarter-mile behind him, and he was mortified at the thought of looking weak to Renee.

Gerry yelped in fright and jumped backward. The bull closed the gap. Gerry brought the stick down across the bull's forehead. White John shook his head menacingly. Gerry sidestepped to his left, toward Colson Road and Merle, but the bull was faster, lowering his head into Gerry's stomach, lifting him off the ground and between two strands of Salters' barbed-wire fence.

Only the hood of the heavy raincoat that Gerry was wearing prevented his neck from being torn up. And although he was now on the other side of the fence, Gerry wasn't safe from this bull.

Renee knew it, too.

She began kicking her heels into Dewey's ribs even before the bull had charged, but the horse only plodded ahead slowly across the gravel of the intersection. And once he reached the other side, Dewey bent down to gobble up some roadside clover and stood rooted, ignoring Renee's prompting.

Gerry was still lying flat on his back, motionless. The bull ripped up the tender shoots of grass around the base of the cedar fence post near Gerry, which had been snapped and was now dangling in the air, suspended only by the strands of wire attached to it.

Renee looked back down the road toward Merle, who was rousting two first-calf heifers from out of the ditch, too preoccupied to see her frantic waving. She wanted to yell but couldn't, afraid that the bull would turn on her.

White John snatched a mouthful of timothy from the edge of a bull thistle, then swung his head back for more. The most sensitive part of his snout was stung sharply by the nettles of one flower.

"Ee-errnnnh." He swung his head from side to side, smashing the fence post again, separating one strand of wire from it.

White John went crazy, backing and turning around and around, snorting to get the barbs free from his nostrils.

The noise brought Gerry back to consciousness. He sat up, pulling the hood of his raincoat back to get his bearings, and stared straight into the enraged eyes of the bull.

White John had a renewed focus for his anger, in the terrified face of the little human sitting on the ground before him. He lunged toward Gerry, oblivious to the remaining strand of barbed wire that stretched across his path, until it caught him square in the forehead and rubber-banded him backward.

Renee had been frozen on the still-grazing Dewey, until the sight of Gerry's terror reversed the polarity of her emotions, sent her storming after the bull. She somehow found Gerry's stick in her hands and cracked the bull across the bridge of his snout.

"Git away from here! Git! Git!" she screamed. He looked at her menacingly, disdainfully, taking a half-step toward her to increase her fear, a low guttural growl in his throat.

She didn't buy it. Renee stepped toward him and cracked the stick down hard on the top of his head.

"Now git!" she said.

White John was stunned for a moment, having forgotten why he was getting ready to charge.

*You don't want to hit me, girl,* he thought to her.

Renee felt that she would fall into his eyes if he didn't turn away soon.

John wasn't sure if she would give. They stood riveted in place for a long moment, staring each other into paralysis. Gerry was sitting absolutely still, holding his breath.

*You don't want to hit me,* John thought, the message oozing from him toward Renee. He took a tentative step toward her, then pawed the ground with his left front hoof. Renee felt an overwhelming weakness wash over her, making it an effort to stand.

Suddenly John dropped his head and lunged toward her. She reflexively smashed him behind the eye with her stick, feeling that she would cave in beneath him.

*"Git outta here! Now!"* Merle yelled, waving, all arms and legs. John turned away up the back road as Renee collapsed in relief. Merle was such a welcome sight, he looked so strong, that Renee never knew she was the one who had made White John turn away and run.

It was Saturday, a crisp, glorious fall morning on the edge of Indian summer. The milking was done, the gutters had been cleaned and the manure spread, and the hay and oats had been done for weeks. The World Series was to be on TV that afternoon: it couldn't be a more perfect day.

"Gerry, do you want any more eggs?" his mother asked.

"Naw, four's enough, Ma. Could use a couple more pieces o' toast."

"Homemade or boughten?" She had the suggestion of a smile.

"Homemade, of course . . . un-less . . ." He looked at her impishly. "Naw, homemade is good."

"Two slices or four?" Her expression was grave, but she secretly loved his teasing.

" 'Zere any more coffee?"

"Yes. Probably another whole cup."

"Okay, then." He stroked his chin thoughtfully, tugging on an imaginary goatee. "Give me three slices. As many crusts as you can find, my good woman."

Bob shot a stern look across the table at his son. "This ain't no restaurant, buddy." When Edna passed by him with the coffeepot he held up his cup, wordlessly. She filled it just above half, so Bob could cool it with cream, still leaving some for Gerry.

Gerry did his best to smile and joke away his chagrin, complimenting his mother profusely on her bread. Bob's quiet signaled that Gerry was not to be forgiven. Edna had been unbothered by Gerry's teasing, but suffered through an act of feigned hurt.

Gerry couldn't wait to finish breakfast, but three thick slices of bread were too much to handle with less than half a cup of coffee to dunk them in, and he couldn't leave until he had finished eating everything. King was back in under his chair again, anticipating some scraps from Gerry's plate, but Bob's gaze was fixed on the unfinished toast.

Gerry carefully palmed one half piece of toast in his right hand, on the far side of his plate. Bob pretended to be preoccupied with something out the window. As Gerry brought the toast to his lap, King could smell that food was on its way. He slid out, spun around, and dived under again, now facing Gerry's right hand.

"What's the matter with that dog, Edna? Hasn't he been out today?" Bob asked.

Gerry suppressed a sigh, still clutching the toast. King heard his name and "out," and bounded for the door, looking hopefully at Gerry.

"Only for a little while," Edna replied.

"Guess he oughta go out then, shouldn't he?" Bob rose and turned to open the door for the dog, giving Gerry the chance to put the toast back on his plate. King bounded out the door and raced across the yard to bark at the swallows nested under the eaves of the barn.

"Jesus, that damn dog. Always causing a racket," Bob said as he settled back into his chair to sip the last of his coffee. He smirked, satisfied, when he saw the half piece of toast back on Gerry's plate.

The three sat in silence, virtually motionless, for two and a half minutes.

"Well, I think I'll make some orange juice and have some toast with it," Edna announced. "Gerry, could I have one of your pieces of toast?"

"Sure, Ma. Have this one. Can I have some OJ, too?"

Bob was defeated, and looked it. He had never been a good loser.

"You two'd be havin' breakfast all day if they'd let ya," was the best complaint he could manage. "Edna, if you get done eatin' anytime t'day, how 'bout goin' to the Massey dealer with me?"

"All right. Just give me time to do the dishes."

Gerry looked at his mother hopefully, itching to get started on his day.

"Eat up that half piece of toast. Here, wash it down with this," she said, handing him a glass of orange juice.

Gerry gobbled down the toast and drained the juice glass in one gulp. Mournfully, he began to clear dishes from the kitchen table, grumbling about his lazy sister still sound asleep upstairs.

"Gerry, do me a favor, take this out to the dog," Edna said, handing him the last piece of toast. "I'm not sure if we'll be back by noon, so Renee might have to get you lunch," she continued.

"No problem." Gerry was already out the door. He ran after King, who was still circling the barn barking, rousting the cliff and barn swallows. These were birds that terrorized cats, swooping down on them in waves. But somehow King was able to flush them out from their nests at will, making them scatter in panic.

"Err-ruff . . . errr-ruff, ruff," Gerry barked, in unrestrained joy, wanting to be King's buddy. King was confused, though, and hung his head, ashamed.

Gerry did not know that the dog could not tolerate being mimicked by a self-conscious being, that no animal could, because it was a cruel reminder of how the creator had limited humans, caused them to question themselves and their identity.

*Being able to become so many things is the road to craziness,* Scout had told him once. After listening to a fight one time between Helmut and Gunnar, his oldest boy, Scout shook his head sadly and said, "And they call us mad."

King stopped barking as soon as Gerry mocked him, then Gerry, flustered, ran back around the corner of the barn in an attempt to get King to chase him. King was still hurt and confused, but so much in love with Gerry that he couldn't resist.

"C'mere, boy. C'mere. Look what I got for ya," Gerry coaxed as he waved the toast at him. King jumped at it, tore the piece out of Gerry's hand, and gobbled it up. They chased each other around the yard, breathless, scattering neatly raked piles of leaves.

"Boy, I'd like to go huntin'," Gerry said aloud, then a gray wall slid down his mind. He stopped short. "Better go see what time the game is on," he said, before he turned to run into the house, the storm door slamming behind him.

King waited, and waited, for his pal to return. He was still waiting when Bob and Edna emerged, Bob growling, "Lazy goddam mutt," as he passed by.

Gerry was sitting in Bob's recliner chair, engrossed in TV cartoons.

King waited about two more minutes for Gerry, standing still in the yard, before he began investigating smell-trails. The crisscrossing paths of a red squirrel and two moles carried him across the southeastern corner of the lawn, where a crow's cawing invited him to a chase across the Old Woods pasture. Remains of a small woodchuck that King and Scout had killed the day before were their carrion. He made three obligatory passes at them, letting them know who was boss, before he tore off for Scout's farm.

"Scout, Scout, ready ta go?"

"Sure, Kinger, nothin' to do here."

"Let's go then, quick."

King hated Scout's human, Helmut, for good reason. Scout was fed irregularly, and abused regularly, by Helmut, who refused to allow his wife and children to feed the dog. They did so only when they were absolutely certain that Helmut was not around, because they all had heard that "what the dog gets is what he deserves" for displeasing his master.

They started to leave too late. As they turned the corner of the barn, King almost ran into Helmut.

"Git outta here, you sonuvabitch, you hell-dog," Helmut screamed as he kicked at King.

King dodged him easily, scampering away to a safe distance.

"And you bastard, where d'ya think yer goin'?" he yelled at Scout.

King watched Scout freeze in his tracks, losing his character.

"Yer a no-good waste of my time, ya vile creature," Helmut spat in Scout's direction. Scout stood still, expressionless, only the mistiness of his eyes revealing his hurt. But he felt all the words, like bullets impacting flesh.

Helmut smelled like old meat to King, like waste. Not the pungent richness of fresh kill nor even the subdued heartiness of jerky. He smelled like rot; fetid, putrescent, maggot-ridden excrement, almost too rank for flies to tolerate.

"Err-ruff . . . errr-ruff, ruff," King snarled. Helmut turned toward him, his face contorted with rage.

"I'll send ya ta hell, ya demon beast. No creature of God threatens me."

King began to growl again, squaring his head into his shoulders. Helmut abruptly turned on his heel and disappeared into the barn, where Scout knew he kept one of his shotguns. King's eyes narrowed into angry slits, sensing an attack.

Scout looked at his pal pleadingly. *Get out of here,* his eyes said.

*No. That human is evil,* King's eyes answered back.

*He is not your human.* Scout looked toward him, his eyes becoming clear, sharp and stern. *Go away.*

Helmut burst out of the barn door, with a twelve-gauge shotgun split in his hands. "Now you're going back to hell, you sonuvabitch," he declared as he racked the gun and raised it to his shoulder.

King was transfixed by the sight of it. He had not seen one for many hunts, but had loved being around guns when the old man was still alive. He would go hunting for pheasants or partridge this time in the fall, when the woods were bright from the leaves and the sun. Although King was not born to hunt, he could follow the smell-trail of the birds, and loved to be in the woods when the scent of the final blossoming of much of the earth filled the crisp air.

The old man was very methodical in his hunting, only tolerant of Gerry once he had learned to be quiet while hunting, but he enjoyed having King along. King thought for that instant of how much he would like to go hunting again, but Gerry never went anymore, and the old man was gone—

"Grrrr. Errrrowww. Err—*roww,*" Scout snarled, lunging at the back of Helmut's legs. Helmut jumped half around, misfiring up into the air.

"Why you . . ." he roared at Scout. But Scout kept moving, growling and snarling at King as he stalked in his direction. King was stunned.

"What are you doing?" he growled back.

"Get out of here . . . *now.*" Scout's snarling became even more angry and frantic. He lunged at King, biting at his right shoulder, just below the throat. King reacted instinctively, tucking and rolling away from Scout, then spinning around into a crouch. His teeth bared and gleaming, King let go a guttural growl so fierce that Helmut raised the shotgun to his shoulder again.

*"Grrr-rowww,"* Scout screamed, lunging suicidally at King. He fell short of King again, letting King lunge into him before catching him and rolling together down the side hill away from the manure chute at the end of the barn.

"Get outta here, he'll kill you," Scout growled as they rolled.

"What?" King was incredulous.

"Just get outta here. I'll catch up later if I can."

"He would kill me?"

"Probably . . . but he won't kill me. Just get outta here."

"Gotcha. Come find me in the Old Woods if you can."

"Go right to the swamp now. Be quick," Scout urged.

*"Grrr-roww,"* Scout insisted, for Helmut's benefit. King sprang off on a dead run, disappearing into the swamp before Helmut could gather himself to fire again.

"Look at that, Edna. That dog's a worker." Bob pointed out a Border collie threading his way between rows of haybines, tractors, balers, rakes, disks, drags, and combines.

"Yessir, Bernie's always circulatin' through here, all day long, keepin' this machinery in line," said George, the ancient tending the counter at Zelzac's Farm Implements.

"Isn't that somethin'. Ya know, we got a dog just like that, papers and everythin', but he ain't worth a damn," Bob complained. Edna was silent.

"Blacksmith hound, huh?" George asked.

"What?"

"Said you got a blacksmith hound."

"Whaddaya talkin' about? My dog's just like that one, a Border collie."

"But you said he didn' work?"

"Yeah."

"Well, then, he's a blacksmith hound, I tell ya."

"What the hell's a blacksmith hound?"

"When ya kick him in the ass he makes a bolt for the door," George finished. Bob chuckled appreciatively; Edna smiled in a noncommittal way.

"That's a good one, George. Ain't it the truth? Wish I knew what was wrong with the bastard."

"Well, howja train him? Out in the field?"

"Oh, yeah, just like you're supposed to, on a short leash."

"On a leash! Who told ya to put him on a leash?"

"Well, that's the way you're supposed to. An old-timer told me, an' he had three cow dogs."

"Trained 'em on a leash, ya say? Man, that don't make sense to me." George shook his head. "Say, did that fella have a lotta cows?"

Bob was suspicious, and defensive. "Wahl, Jesus, George, he wasn't farmin' for a livin'."

"That explains it then. A dog's gotta be able to move if there's a lotta animals ta herd, especially if there's a bull around." George winked at Bob to calm him down. "But don't worry about it. Ya prob'ly ain't ruined him."

"Not any more than he's ruined the rest of his farm," came a voice from behind Bob.

"What the hell?" Bob snapped. He turned around to see his neighbor from across the river, Pete Jonesen.

"Jesus, I shoulda known. Well, how ya doin', horseball?"

Pete grinned at him, then began poking at his ribs.

"Hey, cut it out. Yer messin' with more'n you can handle," Bob said as he poked back. "Tell ya what, George. This guy thinks he's an expert on ruined farms 'cause of what he's done to his place."

George chuckled, shaking his head.

"Aw, yeah, George, if it weren't for Edna he'da gone under years ago, the way he spends his time sittin' under shade trees," Pete needled.

"Shee-it. You'da starved ta death without Peg. Don't she still cut your meat for ya?"

"I'll hafta send both o' ya off to 'bedience school with Bob's blacksmith hound if ya keep it up. Bob, whyn'tcha pay for yer parts," he winked at Pete, "for a change." Bob glared at him. "An' get outta the way for my big-money customers."

"Yeah, Bob, let me buy George's next Cadillac, willya?"

"Don't let me stand in your way, Pete. I can see he's waitin' for you so he can retire," Bob smiled. He reached for the brown paper bag with the tractor wheel bearings and turned for the door.

"Hey, Bob," George called. "Just a minute." He spat tobacco juice generously on the cement floor next to the counter. As Bob walked back to talk with George, Pete touched Edna's elbow, signaling her to move off to talk.

"Edna, you're all done with your oats, aren'tcha?"

"Oh, yes, Pete, a long time now."

"How about the corn?"

"You know Bob doesn't put in corn anymore. Doesn't believe it's worth it. Why?"

"There's no reason why you can't come over to visit, then. Peg is bakin' a couple of her special pumpkin pies."

"Probably made fresh, from scratch, right?"

Pete nodded.

"She still won't let her secret recipe out, I'll bet."

Pete nodded again, and laughed.

"It's the nutmeg, isn't it?"

Pete turned his head away for a telling moment.

"Then you can come over, soon?" he said, changing the subject.

"We haven't been out since . . . it's been years, Pete. Bob doesn't seem to want to see our old friends," she whispered, taking a glance around the edge of the display to see if Bob was still speaking with George. "I can't push him. I can't get myself to," she finished.

"I understand what you're sayin', Edna," Pete said sadly. "Do your best. He really needs to get out."

"Yes, I know," she whispered, as Bob strode away from the counter.

"Give 'im another chance, Bob, I would," George yelled as Bob and Edna left the store.

*George knows more about sellin' you stuff you don't need for a price you can't afford to pay than he does about trainin' cow dogs,* Bob thought. *Even if I did give it another try, that lazy bastard wouldn't chase cows. Knows he doesn't need to,* he thought as he looked over at Edna, who was staring blankly out the windshield.

Tom Seaver had given up four runs by the fourth, but Donn Clendenon had come in on Al Weis's sac fly in the seventh, so the Mets still had a chance against the hated Orioles. Gerry was glued to the TV screen, not even leaving the living room for commercials.

Renee had made him four toasted peanut-butter sandwiches, delivered them with a tall glass of milk into the living room, and left him alone.

Art Shamsky was just grounding out in the ninth when Merle drove into the yard, a half hour after Gerry was supposed to have grained the cows, put the milking machines together, and shot down some hay.

*Oh, no, I'm in trouble,* Gerry thought. *Dad could be home any minute, too. He'll skin me.* He laced up his work shoes furiously and burst out the kitchen door.

Gerry found Merle in front of the manger on the far side of the barn, shaking his head that there was no grain there.

"Sorry, Merle, got caught up watching the Series. Can you grain 'em for me?" Gerry pleaded.

"Don't know how much they get. What else ya gotta do?"

"Shoot down the hay, put the milking machines together, and get the cows."

"Well, I'll shoot the hay down, then, I s'pose."

"Thanks, Merle. You're a lifesaver."

Gerry loaded the wheelbarrow with grain and fairly flew down in front of the mangers, tossing scoops of grain in front of the cows. "Lessee, now, Bossy gets six and a half," he muttered as he thought, *Something's wrong.*

*Wait a minute, I'm late, that's what's wrong. No. Something else. Merle's gone up to the mow. He'll know which side to get the hay from. What is it?*

He stopped, poised just past the chute doors on the far side of the barn, listening to the muffled sounds of Merle grunting and complaining about having to shoot down the hay.

*Merle,* Gerry grinned. *That's not new.* He tossed three scoops of meal in front of Forty's stanchion. "Ohmigod, the chutes!"

*"Merle, Merle, wait!"* he yelled, grabbing the wooden handle to pull the chute open. The chute door caught on one side. Gerry pushed it back, straightened it, and pushed it open again, all the while yelling, *"Merle, wait!"*

Finally the chute door relented, just as the unmistakable sound of a bale hurtling down hit Gerry's ears. He jumped out of the way as the bale hit and bounced toward the stanchions.

"Jesus, *Merle!*" Gerry yelled.

Silence.

"What?" Merle finally replied.

"I've gotta open the chutes. You almost killed me."

"Sor-ry," Merle complained.

"Lemme get the other one, *okay?*"

"Go ahead."

Gerry ducked between the stanchions, cut across the barn floor and through to the manger on the near side of the barn. He reached up, dug his fingernails behind the handle, and slid the chute half open, then stretched up onto his toes and heaved it again. Only a two-inch span was blocking the opening now. He reached up once more, standing on his tiptoes, and shoved the chute door all the way open. As he turned to finish graining the cows, a bale whistled down the chute, almost knocking him over.

"Mer-erle!" He waited for a reply. "Aw, forget it," he muttered to himself, running to finish his chores.

After he had grained the cows and put the milking machines together, Gerry ran up the driveway and down the road to the gate for the alfalfa pasture.

"Ca-boss. Ca-bo-oss. Come, bossy," he pleaded. Almost a third of the herd was on its way to the gate, the grain hogs and leakers. The rest of the herd seemed oblivious to him.

*Oh, man, I've gotta get them up here somehow. King. Where is he?*

"King! Ki-ing! C'mere, boy!" he yelled. Then he whistled, a thin, barely audible teapot sound.

"Nuts, he could be anywhere," he grumbled, just as King shot out of the woods on the far end of the lot, heading straight for the herd.

King had been hunting woodchucks with Scout once he had gotten away from the Molshoc farm. They wanted to get Grampa, whose burrow was on the uphill corner of the Alfalfa Hill lot.

Scout ambled along the hilltop in full view, showing no interest whatever in Grampa. Grampa took the bait, standing up on his hind legs several yards from the entrance to his burrow, his curiosity piqued. Scout moved away into the woods while Grampa nibbled on his lunch.

All was quiet, no threats anywhere.

Then Grampa caught a whiff of dog, stretched up farther, searching the air for the direction of the smell. The old dog was nowhere in sight. Grampa relaxed, and bent down to eat some more. The wind shifted, delivering a blast of dog. Grampa turned to flee back to his burrow door, only to see the black-and-white dog closing in on him, too quickly for Grampa to get back.

Grampa feinted to the right, then bolted to the left toward the gnarled black cherry tree by the stone wall at the pasture's edge. King was on his right flank now, and Scout in front to the left, just beyond the stone wall.

"We got him," King barked to Scout.

"Turn him toward me," Scout barked back.

King angled toward the cherry tree, closing in on Grampa, who was hurtling toward the stone wall, and Scout, poised atop the stone wall to see in which direction the woodchuck was going to break.

"We got him, we got him!" Scout barked. King snapped at Grampa's hind leg, just missing, when Grampa suddenly dived into his new entrance, between the base of the tree and the stone wall.

"Aw, shit, Scout. He's too smart for us," King gasped, pawing distractedly at the gravel around the woodchuck hole.

"He's a smart one, all right. That's why he's been around so long. But ya ain't gonna give up, are ya?"

"Can't give up, Scout," King replied, despondent. "Wish I knew why, but I can't."

"Sure, ya can't let them put a label on ya, just because they think they know everything."

"Whaddaya talkin' about?"

"Haven't ya ever noticed, Kinger? Humans think they know the name of everything."

"Ain't that the truth."

"Yer born ta chase, Kinger. It's in yer blood. Don't make no sense ta fight it."

"Guess you're right. It's like an ache, ya know? Like an itch ya can't keep from scratchin', but don't want ta go away either."

"Yup. Hey, didn't your humans go to town today?"

"Ye-ess! I can chase the cows in!"

King exulted, and took off on a dead run to find Gerry.

"Go get 'em, King! Get the cows! Get 'em!" Gerry was shouting. King veered sharply to his right and into the center of the herd. He nipped at Billie's heels, turning her around and toward the gate.

"Don't get too close, you bastard, or I'll kill ya," Billie said.

"You can't even get close enough to try," King boasted, bobbing and weaving away as John lowered his head to take a run at him. King turned hard on his right hip to circle behind John and snap at his heels.

"These are my cows! Get out of here!" John threatened.

"They're still yours, don't worry. I'm just gonna get them up to the barn."

"Yeah! Go, King! Bring 'em, buddy!" Gerry cheered. Most of the herd were moving briskly toward the gate now, and Gerry could hear Merle slamming the stanchions closed on the lead cows. He had gotten off the hook for being late, and King was the major cause.

By the time the last of the cows had crossed the road and Gerry had closed the gate behind them, Bob and Edna were pulling into the driveway in their blue Chevy Biscayne. King was gnawing at a late-season flea on his left rear haunch, resting near the side porch.

"Lazy sonuvabitch," Bob complained to Edna as they passed by.

King and Scout rendezvoused in the gravel-bed lot, where they took turns rolling in freshly spread manure, rewarding themselves for chasing in their cows. King smelled so ripe that Renee refused to let him in the house at suppertime.

Gerry tried to sneak him through the door when he came up from the barn.

"Oh, no. Don't let him in. That dog is disgusting," Renee sniffed.

"Aw, c'mon, Renee. He smells like a dog. He can't help it." *He is kinda rank,* Gerry thought. If anyone other than Renee had been complaining, he would have gone along with it.

King was confused. When he was a pup, Renee had coddled and babied him, and fed him exotic treats. But now she seemed to hate him. Not just him, but all dogs. And even the cows, too. Renee was lost.

"I don't care why he smells. He's not coming in here." She held her toe in front of King's nose, barring the door.

*What's she complaining about?* King thought. *She smells like tortured flowers.*

"He's got to eat his supper, Renee," Edna said quietly. Before Renee had even finished sighing, Bob was climbing the porch steps.

"What the hell's the holdup?"

"I don't want to let the dog in. He stinks," Renee said.

"But . . ." Gerry interrupted.

"Then leave him out."

"But . . ."

"Now dammit, we're gonna eat supper, an' I don't need to be smellin' that dog while I'm eating." His father's expression convinced Gerry it would be futile to argue. He shooed King off the porch.

"Well, Sweet Pea, how's college?" Bob asked.

"It's okay. I'm doing pretty well in some of my classes," Renee replied disinterestedly.

"Some? Why not all of 'em?" Gerry piped up.

Renee ignored him. She was picking out the pieces of carrot and potato from her mother's stew, leaving the beef and gravy behind.

"Yeah, why not all of them?" Bob demanded.

"Because I'm not interested in them, Daddy," she replied evenly.

"Not interested? In what?"

"In all of my classes. Some of them are boring."

"Boring? I'm paying for those classes. They better not be boring."

"Well, maybe not for everyone, Daddy. Some people like them, I guess. Just not me."

"Which classes are you talkin' about, Renee?"

Renee glanced over at her mother for support. Edna would not look at her directly.

"The a . . . the accounting classes. I can't stand accounting," she blurted out.

"*What? Accounting?* That's what you're supposed to become, Renee. An accountant!"

"I know, I know. That's what I said I would do, but I've changed my mind." She could see that he was still angry.

"I really tried, Dad. I *did.* But I just couldn't do it, so then I started not liking it, because no matter how hard I tried, I was getting bad grades, and it made me so upset I wanted to quit college."

She gauged his look of alarm. "I thought, I'm not smart enough for college. I just can't do it, and I wanted to drop out. That's when Hugh convinced me I could stay in college."

"Who the hell is Hugh?" Bob demanded. He looked at Edna angrily, while Renee looked at Edna, alarmed. *Why didn't you tell him about Hugh?*

"Uhn . . ." Edna cleared her throat. "You know Hugh Dyson, Bob."

"Dyson. Jake Dyson's boy?" Bob accused.

"Yes."

"Well, Jesus, Edna. He's gonna be takin' over the bank once he's done with college. Then he'll be takin' over this farm."

"Daddy!" Renee cried.

"Dyson. Hugh Dyson. I don't believe it, Edna. Our daughter goes off to college to become an accountant, but that's boring. So instead, she wants to run off with the son of that bastard."

"*Daddy!* He's not a—" Renee screamed, before Edna froze her with a glare. *Don't you say it,* the look warned.

"He is my friend." Renee bit off the end of each word precisely. "He has kept me in college. He is not a bastard."

Edna's throat, cheeks, and forehead were blotched red, but her expression was stoic, her eyes granite.

Gerry had grown to despise his sister, for her snottiness, her aloofness from the farm, the family, their school. Her coolness toward her old friends was an embarrassment to him. But now he could not join his father in the attack, could not point out how she had become arrogant, superior in her attitude toward him, because he realized that he would be sitting in that same seat before long. He welded his eyes to the pieces of cube-steak gristle left on his plate.

"Well, he may not be a ba—" Bob began. Edna turned her glare on him. *You don't want to do this,* she warned.

"Uh, he may not be a bad kid, but I don't like his family, or what they stand for. All they ever cared about was robbin' this town blind. They've been doin' it since their old man was runnin' rum across the lake, durin' the Depression. They made their money by stealin' then, and they haven't forgotten how. And if you don't watch yourself"—he paused to glare back at Edna—"you'll end up just like 'em."

Before anyone could respond, Bob shoved his chair back from the table, picked up his cup of coffee, and walked away.

"News is on," he grumbled over his shoulder.

Edna looked at her daughter helplessly. Gerry quietly sneaked out the kitchen door.

"Well, Mother, I guess we're supposed to do the dishes now," Renee said.

Waves of shame washed over Edna as she silently cleared the table, unable to meet her daughter's eyes.

* * *

Bob was still planted in his recliner chair in the living room, the local news giving way to Huntley and Brinkley, then a *Honeymooners* rerun, then *Jeopardy,* and now *The Sonny and Cher Show.* Bob didn't really like Sonny and Cher, but he was in his TV trance. As long as Gerry was willing to get up to change the channel, there was nothing to break the spell.

He was reading the auctions section of the *Journal.* Edna rocked in her armchair, lost in *Reader's Digest.*

Gerry sat on the far side of the woodstove, where he could have some privacy. He hated it when he discovered his parents studying him while he was paying too much attention to Cher.

Renee breezed into the living room. "Hugh is coming over, and we're going out," she announced. Bob looked at her angrily. She was dressed in a short skirt, not a miniskirt, but far shorter than what she had been allowed to wear in high school.

"I don't think so, not dressed like that."

"Dad, I'm not arguing with you about this," she replied. "This is the way I usually dress."

"It is not," Bob insisted. Renee sighed and turned to walk out of the living room.

"Don't you turn your back on me," her father shouted from his recliner.

Lights shone into the living room. A car was sitting in the driveway, motor still running. It was Hugh, in his new Mustang.

"He's here. I gotta go," Renee said.

"Just a minute."

"Daddy," she replied shrilly. "Please don't make a scene."

"Listen, Renee. He should at least come in here to meet us." Bob's voice grew quiet. "He can have that much respect."

Renee switched on the light and stepped out onto the front porch, waving to Hugh to come into the house. Gerry was gritting his teeth, his TV show interrupted. Edna and Bob stood just behind Renee in the doorway to the dining room.

The car door opened, and Hugh started climbing out. But before he could get himself completely out, King crept from the shadows of the garage and lunged at him. Hugh jumped back in the car.

"Ooh, that dog. Make him stop, Daddy," Renee pleaded.

King was barking fiercely at this strange car. *Hmm, this smells funny, nothing at all like a farm,* King thought. *But like something I know. What is it? Oh, yeah, like the Teller truck, the one the cows hated so much.* He barked even more ferociously.

"Daddy, make him stop."

And for that moment, despite his failure to chase cows, his disobedience, and all the other ways in which he fell short of Bob's expectations, Bob could clearly see the value of King, his dog.

## Chapter Eight

# Renee

(1969)

Daddy, do something!" Renee was frantic.

Her father was unmoved. Renee turned to Edna. "Mom, can't you stop that dog?"

"King," Edna called, her voice weak from tension. "Ki-ing."

King paused from growling for a moment, turning toward the porch as if looking for direction. His feeder human seemed to want his attention, but she looked unsure. King looked to his master. His expression was grim, unshakable, and it signaled approval. King jumped up, snarling at the cowering figure in the car. He clawed at the window of the driver's door, growling all the while.

Hugh jerked away from the window, falling into the space between the bucket seats of his Mustang. Embarrassed and angry at his predicament, he thought for a moment, a long moment, about restarting the car and driving away. "I don't need this shit," he muttered to himself. "Certainly not from the Scotts."

Gerry crowded his way onto the porch, grinning at the sight of a Dyson trapped by his dog. "Want me to get him to stop, Renee?" he offered.

"Yes! Get that animal away from him!" Renee screamed.

Gerry stepped down from the porch to call King, noticing for the first time the expression on his father's face. Gerry, too, turned weak.

The best he could muster was a feeble "C'mere, boy." King heard, but was reveling in the approval from Bob.

"I'm leaving," Renee announced. She disappeared inside the house for an instant to grab her jeans jacket, then strode by her family to the car. "Thanks for all your help," she said over her shoulder.

*"King!"* Bob's voice was sharp, and hard. King stopped barking, dropped down on all fours, and looked toward the porch for further directions. He was very pleased with himself.

"Get away from that car," Bob commanded. King willingly complied, retreating to lie next to the bottom porch step.

"Are you going to come back in?" Bob asked his daughter.

Renee opened the passenger door of the Mustang. "I don't think so," she replied tiredly.

"Hugh, would you want to come in to see my parents?" she asked.

Hugh studied her face, then looked to the grim pair on the porch under the bare lightbulb. He had no desire to go into the house, but he did not want to appear weak.

"Do *you* want to go back in?" he asked firmly.

"Uh, no. No, that's okay," Renee replied.

"We'll just leave, then?"

*He's letting me find my own strength,* Renee thought. "Yes, let's just go."

"Sure, Renee." Hugh shifted into reverse and turned his head to navigate back out of the driveway. Renee could not see the expression on her parents' faces, only her mother half-raising her hand to wave goodbye. She could not stop herself from waving back, although the dark inside the car kept her mother from seeing the gesture.

*Whew, that was a pain in my ass,* Hugh thought. He looked over at Renee, smiling at her beauty, her honey-brown hair. She had so much strength that he was amazed at her lack of confidence in herself.

They were going to visit Hugh's parents, for Renee to meet them, before going out dancing. Renee was anxious about this meeting, since most of what she had heard from Hugh about his parents had been bad, really bad, and scary. Racist remarks that her father made unselfconsciously were stated more quietly and subtly, but not with less belief, by Mr. Dyson, according to Hugh. *Why does he even want me to go over there?* Renee wondered.

She tucked her right foot under her, half turning so that she could study Hugh more closely, under the thin instrument light from the dash.

He looked possessed. Maybe it was the green fluorescent light's unworldly quality, or the glint of green returned from his iris, but he seemed to want something badly, beyond hunger. It could have been his aquiline nose that was too fleshy, or his longish short hair (not quite to his paisley collar), or the mustache that almost cornered his lips but shrank from extending to the sides of his chin. He seemed half formed, in transition, slip still wet in the mold.

Hugh caught her studying him and smiled his disarming smile, his you're-so-much-more-interesting-than-I-am, why-don't-we-talk-about-you smile. She did not want to talk right now, but she knew he was uncomfortable in silence. Perhaps the slip might harden.

"So . . . what was that all about, anyway? Your old man looked mad. I thought he hated that dog," Hugh said.

"He does. He's always mad at the dog. He's always mad at everything. I don't want to talk about it."

"But you can't do that, babe, can't ya see?" The light in Hugh's eyes softened. "You have to deal with that stuff, or it'll take you over. It'll own you."

"I know, but I just don't want to talk about it. There's no point. It's not like I can do anything for him. He's wrapped up in his own bad vibes. It doesn't even have anything to do with me."

"And how do you feel about that?" Hugh prompted.

"I feel . . ." She paused for a moment, annoyed. "Why are you asking me all this? It's not like you don't have problems with your father."

"Wha . . ." Hugh was embarrassed, caught. "Sorry, babe, I'll drop it." He was relieved when she responded with silence. But once he arrived at the corner of 932 and the Old State Road, by the planked water tower on the southeast corner of town, he noticed her studying him.

"Wanna hear something?" he offered.

"Okay, sure."

Hugh slid a Creedence eight-track into the tape player. They cruised down Main Street, eased left onto Gary. Hugh sneaked a look out of the corner of his eye. Renee seemed quiet, pensive. He took a right onto Hamilton to glide up the hill to his house as John Fogerty wailed about a "Bad Moon Rising."

The Dyson house was not ostentatious, not conspicuous in its display of the wealth within it, not either much of a home. The asphalt driveway, freshly sealed in preparation for winter, composed most of a reversed S, providing shelter of white pines and an eight-foot-high sculptured hedge from the unwanted gaze of fifty-cent-a-week Christmas Club depositors and overzealous tax assessors. It was chilly, but Hugh decided against the garage.

Renee kept well behind him as he approached the porch veranda, lit up by night security lights.

"C'mon, Renee. What're you doing? They won't bite, you know."

"Hugh, do we have to do this?" Her nerves were fire. "Can't we just go out?"

"No."

"No." The first voice was Hugh's, the second a more jocular echo. "You must come in and meet us properly," it insisted.

"Ma, I wish you wouldn't listen at the door like that," Hugh complained. Renee was stunned. She wanted to retreat to the car, but could only manage a feeble "I'm so sorry."

"It's all right, dear. You're not the first to feel that way." Mrs. Dyson's tone begged the continuation *and you won't be the last.*

"We know that Hughie has told you some horrid tales about us, none of it true," she continued good-naturedly. "It's part of his college rebellion"—this last delivered as she guided Renee through the heavy oak outer door into the front-room hallway.

"Here, dear, let me take that, uh, jacket," she persisted. "My, isn't that a sweet little dress." She turned and smiled pleasantly at her son, who was reddening visibly from embarrassment at his entrapment. When he shifted his gaze from Renee's legs to meet his mother's eyes they said, *Haven't you looked at her legs long enough, dear?*

"Where's Pa?" was Hugh's best effort at diversion.

*Pa?* Renee thought. She had never before heard from Hugh any other reference to his father than "my old man." She wanted to feel more comfortable about it, but wondered at the shift. Also, this Pa was wholly unlike her grandfather, known to her by the same name. Her Pa had been a shambling, sourball-candy-distributing if sometimes cantankerous old farmer. The Pa of Hugh's inquiry was more dignified, aloof, the gentry. The tone was more in keeping with "Judge."

"He is in the parlor, setting up the pool table." Renee could swear she heard Mrs. Dyson say "billiards." Hugh looked back past Renee toward the entrance, and to the right, where two sliding French doors were pulled closed. As he took a step toward them, Mrs. Dyson grasped Renee's hand and led her in the opposite direction, through a paneled door and left into a sparkling modern kitchen, then left again through a windowed, hardwood-floored dining room to another set of sliding French doors that matched the ones in the front-room hallway.

"Go on ahead, dear. Jake . . . er, Mr. Dyson is anxious to meet you."

Mrs. Dyson's glance at her son as she passed by, on her return to the kitchen, confirmed his suspicions that they were being drawn, inescapably, into an elaborate trap.

"Well, come on in, Hugh," said a baritone voice from the other side of the door. "Come and show me your friend."

Hugh rolled his eyes at Renee before he opened the door, ushering her into the pool room. Hugh's father beamed at them, as if his switch had just been turned on.

"So good to see you . . . Renee, isn't it?" he soothed.

"Yes," she replied, feeling uncomfortable that he was still holding her hand and now cupping her elbow with his left hand, turning her in an arc away from Hugh, to his right side.

"Let's see, the Scotts," Mr. Dyson boomed. "Your grandfather bought that farm, at first, didn't he?"

"Yes," Renee blushed.

"Then your old man went in with him after the war, right?"

"Ye-es," Renee answered. She had stiffened at the "old man," knowing that Hugh's father was several years younger than her own, and not a veteran.

"Sit down. Sit down right here next to me. Edna, Edna. You know, your mother was really bright, smart and . . . and good-looking when we were in school," Hugh's father continued. "Everybody thought she would go on to college, or go to work someplace where she would end up running the place. We were very surprised when she got herself tied down on the farm."

Renee's mouth dropped open slightly. *Is this for real? What is he trying to do here?* she thought.

"I'll bet you're just like her, though, a real sharp, take-charge kinda gal." Mr. Dyson was struggling to maintain eye contact. Hugh's jaw was turning to granite.

"Uh, I don't know, Mr. Dyson," Renee said. "In fact, I'm not even sure about what I'm doing in college."

"Mr. Dyson? No, no, it's Jake. You don't have to call me Mr. Dyson." He touched her forearm, which was resting in her lap. "But I'll tell you what," he added in a confidential tone. "Since you're polite and show respect, you shouldn't worry about whether you'll do all right. You will."

He turned to glance meaningfully at Hugh, while his hand continued to rest on Renee's arm, fingertips grazing her thigh.

Renee saw the blood drain from Hugh's face.

Mr. Dyson didn't.

"That's one way, one good way, you're different from the other girls he brings home," he said into his son's face.

Renee crossed her legs, lifting her left hand to pull a few loose strands of hair back past her shoulder. She teased the hair near her temple until she was sure Mr. Dyson's hand was firmly back on his own lap, supporting one side of a heavy tumbler of gin.

"Pa," Hugh asked sharply, "do you want me to get you a fresh drink?"

Mr. Dyson frowned and shook his head, uncomprehending. Then he remembered Renee. "Oh, no, not for me, thanks. But I'll bet your young lady would like something, wouldn't she?" He turned toward Renee, who was already out of her armchair.

"I'll get something if you like. Hugh?"

"No, I don't want anything." Hugh had jumped up as well. "Maybe we should go."

"No, no. Not at all," Mr. Dyson insisted. "Now, Hugh, don't even suggest that you should be going. Your mother wanted us to have some coffee and cake together, at least."

"Oh, is that what she's doing? Let me help her," Renee volunteered.

"Hugh will do that," Mr. Dyson announced, looking at neither of them. "Won't you?"

"I . . . I guess so," Hugh replied.

"No, please, let me go." Renee was close to pleading.

"Not a word of it. You're a guest, Renee. Besides, it will give me a chance to get to know you better," Mr. Dyson insisted.

"But if Renee wants to help Mom . . ." Hugh said.

"She can do that later," his father finished. "Son," he said to Hugh, in a stage whisper, "your mother wants to speak with you."

Hugh was completely disarmed, and speechless. Renee had no idea why that amused her, but that relief was broken by the knowing wink Mr. Dyson gave her.

"Have your talk with your mother, Hugh, I'll be all right," she found herself saying. *How bad can this be?* she thought, as Hugh reluctantly disappeared through the French doors into the dining room.

The wood paneling in the billiard room was dark, the light from the chandelier was muted, and the hardwood floor was stained a deep walnut. Renee was studying all of the furnishings, asking about each one in great detail, chatting about how beautiful it all was, anything to avoid being cornered by Hugh's father.

*What is Hugh doing? Where is Mrs. Dyson?*

"You don't really believe that she's good for you, do you, Hughie?"

"Yes, Mother, I do. She's a wonderful person."

"Yes, yes, Hughie. She's a fine girl. No one is saying she isn't sweet, and bright, but how far do you think she expects to go in life?"

"Am I supposed to care? I'm not sure how far *I* want to go in life," Hugh shot back.

His mother paused, sighed briefly, and patiently returned to the attack. "Her parents are farmers, struggling farmers, and do not appear to be going anywhere."

"Yes, but Renee is not like her parents. They don't really get along. She's not interested in that farm. There is no telling what she'll do."

"And that's the point, son." Another sigh. "Why did you insist on going to that state college when your father had you admitted to Brown?" she asked the ceiling.

"I like it there. And I love Renee. . . ." It was the first time he had used the word to describe his feelings for Renee, and it surprised him.

"Of course you do, she's a lovely girl. But you're young, you're both young." She sensed a vulnerability. "And you said yourself that she's not sure what she wants to do, whether she even wants to stay in college."

"But I'm helping her with that. It's the one thing that's made me feel good about myself."

"Of course, dear, you're very sweet. You're a savior, I've told you that. But the wrong kind of person, someone not like us, not like our family, might not understand. The wrong person could take advantage of your sweetness, dear, and hurt you beyond repair."

"Yes, yes, this is a wonderful room, Renee." Mr. Dyson was irritated. "But let's talk about you, dear."

"Well, I'm not very interesting, Mr. Dy—Mr. . . . J-Jake."

"There you go. It's Jake. We can be friends, Renee, you know that. And," he added, "I find you interesting. All young people are interesting."

Renee was caught off-guard. Her father never found anything she liked to be interesting. He hated young people. Everything about young people. The way they dressed, the way they walked, the way they cut their hair, their music, their . . . youth.

Renee stopped retreating. "Do you really think so?"

"Yes, of course I do," Mr. Dyson pledged. "Don't you agree? Young people are so refreshing, so . . . stimulating. The trouble with old people is that they act old, and think old."

*Wow. That's the truth,* Renee thought.

"Your grandfather went to Brown, just like his father. Of course, I met your father after he had already decided to go to Dartmouth, so that couldn't be helped," Mrs. Dyson continued. Hugh was distracted, staring off in the direction of the French doors.

"Hugh, are you listening to me?"

"Yes."

"Do you understand what I'm saying?"

"Yes," Hugh sighed. "I should be just like your father."

"Now why do you have to say it like that? Your grandfather was a wonderful man," she sniffed.

"I know, Mother, I know."

Renee did not know what to do. She couldn't believe what was happening. Her body was numb, motionless. The rest of her fled.

She remembered shaking, from anger. But there was nothing she could do but bury it, and tremble rather than explode.

*"C'mon, Renee, we need some help. The cows are out!" Gerry had shouted at her.*

*It was a quarter past seven in the morning, fifteen minutes before the bus would come, and a stretch of barbed-wire fence that ran along the edge of the garden was down. Renee's grandfather was supposed to have fixed it, but had somehow forgotten.*

*"I can't go—the bus will be here any minute!" Renee was mortified at the thought that she would be seen chasing cows by the snotty kids on the bus.*

*"So I'm s'posed to do it all by myself?" Gerry screamed back at her.*

*"I don't know. The bus is coming. I just can't." She could feel the tension rising up inside her, because there would be trouble no matter what she did. But between her mother's disapproval and the social castigation from the bus kids, she chose to bend to the bus kids.*

*"RENEE! GET OVER HERE AND HELP!" her father bellowed.*

*"I CAN'T, DAD! THE BUS!"*

*"I SAID GET OVER HERE! NOW!" Renee jumped reflexively, the spikes of her father's anger lodging in her backbone. She moved stiffly in the direction of the garden, fighting back hot tears.*

*Billie had discovered the sagging strand of barbed wire first. "Hey, looks like it's time fer a little fun, girls." She was followed by Thunder and White Brat. Gerry had circled around behind them to keep them from taking off down the back road, but when her father had chased them from the garden next to the maple grove, they had bolted up the road toward the top of the driveway.*

*"Get back there! Git!" she warned, sneaking looks over her shoulder for the arrival of the bus. She had managed to get Billie and Thunder turned back from the driveway toward the gate, when the new White John surprised her coming out from behind the sweet corn.*

*"G-git!" Her voice was suddenly hoarse, frozen. "Dad," she whispered, "I can't get . . ."*

*"JEE-ZUS CHRIST," Bob raged. White Brat had turned away from the road and trampled a row of green beans.* I'm not goin' back in there till I get some more corn, *she thought.*

*"Dad," Renee pleaded, too softly for him to hear. White John turned toward her for an infinite moment.* You know you can't stop me, *he thought toward her.* You don't want to try. *He moved slowly toward her, from an angle, almost like a dance. She felt weak and trapped. White John snorted and spun back to the corn.*

*"GIT BACK THERE, YOU BASTARD," her father yelled.*

*Renee got away from the garden, chasing Thunder and Billie the rest of the way to the gate. Merle had straggled up the driveway from the barn to the road, and Grandpa Scott had pulled his International pickup truck partway across the road at the edge of the garden. Bob, Merle, and their father alternated between chasing White Brat and White John back and forth down the rows of vegetables and glaring at Gerry and Renee standing together on the other side of the gate.*

*"C'mon, can't they get this over with before the bus comes?" Renee whined quietly to her brother.*

*"Are you kiddin'? If we miss the bus maybe we can go in late, or even get the whole day off," Gerry grinned.*

*"No way—you just end up working all day. I'd rather be in school with my friends."*

*"You would."*

*White John was approaching, with Merle on his right flank and Grandpa behind, driven along the line of the fence. He took the gate on a trot, like a show horse building to jump a rail. White Brat was entirely spooked from being shouted at, having lost all self-control when she gained her freedom. She was panting now, and so tired that Bob was able to drive her up to the gate.*

*"C'mon, c'mon," Renee was saying under her breath, as Gerry was trying to close the gate with his grandfather's help. He had almost fitted the loop of wire over the top of the cedar post when Grandpa interrupted him to restart the process. Gerry stepped back while his grandfather lifted the bottom end of the gate post out of its wire loop with his shaking, liver-spotted hands, squinted through his thick glasses at the shaved end of the post, then replaced it carefully to make sure the loop was higher up on the post.*

*Merle was already walking off to go home for breakfast, but Renee knew better than to try to leave yet. Her father was still winded from chasing White Brat and was now dividing his attention between glaring at his father and son trying to close the gate, Merle walking away, and his insubordinate teenage daughter.*

*"I got it, Grandpa," Gerry said.*

*" 'Twasn't closed right," his grandfather retorted.*

*"It was good enough," Gerry insisted.*

*"They why'd the cows git out?" the old man said, looking confidently into Gerry's eyes.*

*Gerry looked from his grandfather to his father, then down at his sneakers. Nothing could get him to betray his grandfather.*

*"What? You wanna know how they got out? Look at that goddam top wire. That's how they got out," Bob spat. When the old man walked over to the fence, Bob closed in for the kill. "Wasn't that the part you were supposed to fix?" he asked triumphantly.*

*Renee could hear the school bus gearing down as it climbed the hill by Westals'. It would be there in half a minute. "Can't we just go get on the bus?"*

*"WHAT?" Bob spun around.*

*"Can't we go now?" she snarled at him.*

*"Well, who ever said ya couldn't go?" Bob snarled back.*

*"Fine," she shouted, hungry for the last word.*

*Bob was so angry he could not think of a retort, though he wanted to punish her for her disinterest in helping and in his discrediting of her grandfather. He was so wrapped up in his anger that nothing could console him, not even when Renee stepped in a fresh splatter of cow manure in her haste to retrieve her books and get on the bus.*

*Renee's sudden entreaty to get a ride to school so she could change her shoes was met with a smug "I thought you were in a hurry to get to school?" So she got on the bus, humiliated, and Ronnie Belson announced to the bus that Renee had her shitkickers on today. It produced a rage that never left her, a feeling of not being in control, of having someone who didn't understand her ruining her life, of helplessness in fighting against her father's authority.*

So she cried, and shook with anger, but did not fight back.

"Now, now, you'll have to stop that. Renee, you'll have to stop," Mr. Dyson said, as he moved away from her.

Renee was trembling uncontrollably, her eyes red and filled to overflowing.

"Renee, stop it. You could give people the wrong impression," Mr. Dyson continued. He rose stiffly and moved off to freshen his drink. Renee slumped in her seat and began to sob.

"Just remember that you let me do everything that I did, Renee, so it's your responsibility," Mr. Dyson stated. Then in an ever more clinical tone, "Why don't you just stop that and pull yourself together. You won't fool anyone."

Renee was trying to find a place inside herself to go to, where she could be safe, where she would know what to do. What would Hugh think if she was crying? She had cried before in his room at college, and he had become distant, coldly analyzing the source of her hurt without sharing her pain.

*I've got to pull myself together, and only tell Hugh about this,* she thought, rising from the leather sofa and smoothing her skirt conscientiously.

"There. That's better." Mr. Dyson soothed, giving Renee his handkerchief. "No sense making a fuss of a little misunderstanding. I was only trying to get to know you."

"Everything's ready," Mrs. Dyson warned from the dining room as she approached. Hugh's father leaned on the bar, unmoved. Before Renee could open the doors, Mrs. Dyson burst in with a coffee serving tray, Hugh in tow carrying another tray loaded with fancy cookies.

Mrs. Dyson searched Renee's face, noted the red eyes, the uneasiness, the involuntary glance toward Mr. Dyson, and knew what he had done. She set down the tray on the mahogany coffee table, then braced herself for the rest of the story. She turned to face her husband with a hope for trust in Renee, but Mr. Dyson's frown and the slow shaking of his head meant "tramp," "slut."

"Hugh, I know we were going to have coffee, but I'm not feeling well," Renee said shakily.

"What's wrong, Renee? You look like you've been crying." Hugh shot a fierce look at his father, who was studying Renee as if to see what was bothering her.

"I don't . . . know. Maybe it's my sinuses," Renee lied.

"If you want to go now, that's okay, dear," Mrs. Dyson said flatly.

Mr. Dyson held Renee's elbow and looked into her eyes. "Is there anything we can do to make you feel better?" His voice was pure concern, but his eyes were empty. Renee's head was spinning.

"I . . . I guess the air would make me feel better."

"Fine. We can get better acquainted some other time," Mrs. Dyson said coolly.

"I hope you feel better, dear," Mr. Dyson said. "And come back to see us again."

Hugh was flustered, but escorted Renee directly into the hall and outside. He glanced back to see his father shaking his head again, while his mother was dutifully rearranging the cookies on their silver platter.

Outside, Renee gasped in the chill October air.

"Are you all right?" Hugh asked.

"Yeah," she said. But she wasn't.

She was desperately trying to think of where she could go, but deep inside she knew that she would be going back to her parents' house.

It was where she lived, even though it wasn't her home.

## Chapter Nine

# Gerry

(1970)

Gerry was in the barn, scraping the mud and manure off the floor and getting ready to lime it. Although it helped to dry the moisture from the floor, he hated to spread the lime because it made his hands seem so old and cracked. So when his father returned with the tractor and manure spreader, Gerry startled even himself with how angry he was about it.

"You know that I could have driven the tractor, so you could spread the lime," he screamed. "You always do the things I want to do."

"Aw, hell, yes," his father snorted. "You're supposed to do the things I want you to do."

"Well, not anymore. I'm not going to be pushed around."

Bob turned his back on his son and broke open three bales of hay to feed the cows. Gerry watched him stride away, apparently ignoring him. But every few steps he stopped, turned around in Gerry's direction, and waved derisively at him. His father's face was contorted with bitterness.

Suddenly Gerry found a rifle in his hands.

His father was at the other end of the barn now, sifting the lime back and forth from hand to hand, growing ever more angry. Gerry pulled the rifle butt to his right shoulder, eyed down the sight, and pulled the trigger.

The one shot caught his dad full in the chest and knocked him back against the feed box, where he slumped to the floor. Gerry was sobbing.

The length of the floor seemed about two miles. Everything looked distorted, as if seen through the bottom of a shot glass. But when Gerry finally reached him, his father was sprawled on the sidewalk in front of the newspaper office in town and the editor and his brother, the feed-store owner, and the school principal were all looking down at him nonchalantly.

"Ohmigod, where did that come from?" Gerry was sweating, the sheets stuck to his chest and legs, even though it was only mid-June. He lay in bed attempting to sort out his feelings about his father from the events of the previous day, looking for the trigger of this dream.

*Let's see, chores, school, the ball game . . . shit, the ball game.*

It was horrible, being pulled in the sixth for Slack, just because he'd lined out to the left fielder in the fourth. It was so unfair to be expected to deliver every time in the clutch, every time, or be pulled just because he wasn't a townie. Sometimes Gerry thought that was the point, that they could wear him down and get him out of the lineup entirely by humiliating him.

The part that pissed him off was that Coach waited until he was in the on-deck circle and Jonesey was on with one out before he yanked him—like he was going to hit into a double play! That out in the fourth had been a shot, a line drive. And what was Coach looking at, anyway, staring off into the stands, when he made the move to pull him? If it weren't for his friends on the team, Jonesey and Herm Cullen, Gerry would be tempted to quit playing, at least that's what he told himself when he was on the bench.

But it wasn't true. He lived for playing ball.

Once the shame of his benching had washed over him again, he was still clueless about the dream. His father hadn't even been there. Besides, if he thought for too long about his humiliation, it might interfere with his play that night, so he let it pass.

*Let's see now, run it back to morning chores. Got up at Mom's second call, went down to the bathroom, got picked on while we were having cocoa, was late chasing the cows in, got yelled at . . . nothing unusual there.*

School wasn't anything special, just like always. Gerry lacked an inclination toward academic subjects, the Regents track, so he was enrolled in shop and Ag classes. But the truth was that he didn't like those either, mainly because his father insisted that he take them as preparation for taking over the farm.

Ag left him uninspired, and in metal shop he was downright dangerous, having once almost blown up the shop trying to light a gas oven with a worn flint. And what was worse, Mr. Nelson (Sergeant Joe) Friday, the Ag teacher, was a by-the-book land-grant man, so enraptured with scientific agribusiness that he announced on the first day of Ag 3 how good it was that two-thirds of the class would not make it in farming.

There was absolutely no way that Gerry could attempt to please both his father and Sergeant Joe at the same time, so he just drifted through Ag, despite Sergeant Joe's complaints about his not living up to his IQ and his father's insistence that he follow in his own footsteps.

"The Bulk Tank—Storage System of the Future," Sergeant Joe had boomed out as the title of his lecture yesterday. "This technology will be the dairy farmer's *choice* for inexpensive, hygienic"—he built to a crescendo—"*ee*-ficient milk storage." The only thing Sergeant Joe liked more than new technology was ee-ficiency.

But something seemed out of whack to Gerry about this bulk-tank deal. He'd say something about it if his friends in class wouldn't think he was a jerk. He looked up from the cracks in the tile floor to gauge the boredom of the other kids and guessed it was sufficient to take the risk of speaking up.

"Uh, Mr. Friday?"

Sergeant Friday paused to see where the annoying sound was coming from, while the back row turned their attention from the cool sunlight outside the window to their panicking classmate. Gerry would have backed out, but Sergeant Joe was glaring now. If he didn't ask something, they'd all get a lecture and a reprimand for interrupting him.

"What is it?" Friday demanded, focusing on Gale Richards, in the seat next to Gerry. Gale was about to pass out.

"Suh-suh-suh," Gale stammered, everyone biting lower lip in anguish. The only one in the room who didn't know about the Sergeant Joe nickname was Sergeant Joe.

"Yes. Go ahead," Friday snapped.

"Suh . . . ss . . . suh . . . ss . . . ss . . . ss," Gale leaked.

"Spit it out, Richards." Sergeant Joe's eyes were live coals burning Gale's courage.

"Suh, suh, suh, suh, suh." Gale was kicking over, like a Chrysler on a twenty-below morning. Gerry felt his heart smash through his breastbone.

"Mr. Friday, it was me," Gerry interrupted.

"Suh, suh, suh . . ." There were flecks of foam in the corners of Gale's mouth.

"Don't interrupt him," Sergeant Joe commanded.

"But . . ."

"Suh, suh, suh, sar, ser, sir, sir?" Gale's eyes were almost completely white.

"What is it?"

"It wuh, wuh, wuh, it wasn't me," Gale said.

The class eased back into their seats.

"You were saying, Mr. Scott?" Sergeant Joe was still glaring contemptuously at Gale, whose mouth hung open, fishlike.

"I was the one asking the question, Mr. Friday," Gerry confessed, the last bit of moisture abandoning his own mouth.

"Well," Friday said, continuing to hold Gale on his line. "What is it?"

"We already got a bulk tank, an' everybody here's either got one or's gettin' one, 'cause we have to."

"Your point, Scott?" Sergeant Joe turned his full attention to Gerry, allowing Gale to slump and gasp for air.

"Well, didn't you say somethin' about the storage of choice, or something? We didn't have any choice, 's far as I know."

Red, then gray clouds passed over Friday's face in a single moment. "In order to improve hygiene, lower bacteria count, and raise the consistency and taste quality of the product, the state has determined that bulk-tank storage is necessary." Friday was well versed in the latest farm-regulation press releases.

There was only one week left of school, their new, expensive, more ee-ficient product storage system had already been put in, and most of the back row were lost outside the window again. Gerry debated letting it pass.

"But won't it take more electricity?" Gerry asked.

"Probably."

"And make it easier for local milk plants to be bought out by larger companies and closed?"

"Yes."

"Then couldn't we get stuck with higher trucking costs? And more of a problem to cool the milk if you lost power?"

"I'd like to know where you get those ideas from. They sound un-American to me," Sergeant Joe warned.

Gerry recognized this as his cue to shut up and let Sergeant Joe go back to his lecture. His eyes were glazing over already.

It wasn't Ag class, he was pretty sure, yet the answer was still escaping him.

"Gerry! Time for milking!" Edna called. He had lost track of the passage of time, missing the sunlight streaming in his window. Gerry got up, dressed, and went downstairs to renew the morning routine.

"What's wrong with you?" Bob greeted him.

"Whaddaya mean?"

"Edna, didn't you only have to call him once? Something must be wrong," Bob teased.

"No, I'm okay," Gerry said. "I was already awake before Mom called." Then he quietly went off to the bathroom, afraid that if he lingered his father might somehow discover the patricide dream. For extra measure he washed his face before he reemerged from the bathroom.

"Well, how'd your game go last night?" Bob asked.

"Okay," Gerry replied, not looking up from the Formica design on the table.

"Just okay? What happened, did you lose?" Edna asked.

"Naw, we won." He clammed up again, then thought that might be suspicious. "Uh, I got a hit."

"Only one?" Bob looked surprised.

"Yeah, but I got a couple of walks," Gerry lied.

"You mean you let 'em pitch around ya," Bob snorted.

"No, they were bad pitches."

"Can't hit like ol' Duke Snider, huh. He could hit anything, not like those Yankees who needed ice-cream cones served up."

For some reason which Gerry could never fathom, Bob had been a Brooklyn Dodgers fan. Maybe it was because of the arrogance of the Yankees, or because the Dodgers were always the underdogs, but Gerry found it surprising that the team that had broken the color line had his dad as one of its fans.

Bob smiled and changed the subject. Gerry lapsed back into quiet worry about the dream. It made him nervous all through milking, especially whenever he was in front of the manger.

"Hey, Jonesey, it's your favorite. Jell-O with carrot peelings," Gerry announced.

"Yuh, love it. Gimme some more." Jonesey made a sucking sound through his teeth, making Gerry laugh. Besides being Gerry's best friend on the team, Jonesey was the lunchtime comedian. He had discovered the adhesive qualities of the lime Jell-O with carrots when they were sophomores, by sticking it under the chairs and tossing it up onto the ceiling.

"How d'ya like that Coach last night?" Gerry asked. "I can't catch a break with that guy."

"Y'know, it's only because Slack wants to play center."

"Yeah, I know, but he stinks in center."

"Naw, he's okay."

"Whaddaya mean, he's okay?"

"He is okay. He's not bad."

Gerry was visibly upset. "So you like him playing center?"

"Yeah, sometimes."

"What the . . ."

"He makes me look better." Jonesey looked at his friend out of the corner of his eye. "He makes more errors."

Gerry laughed. "You asshole." Then he laughed again. "He'd have to make a lot to make you look good."

Haying season would begin in a few days. It was a time Gerry dreaded, because haying brought out the worst in his father. He was trying to find some way to help, to stay out of his father's way, and to figure out the dream.

There were two greasers on the plunger arm, fifteen on the knotter, three inset on the wadder, one on each side of the threader arm, and more yet on the tension and wheels. Something was comforting about greasing the baler, although he never knew what it was. And for that matter, something was good about taking care of the rake and the tractors. Gerry guessed it was the finality of it. There was no ambiguity involved in doing those things, no need for thought, and there were no decisions. There was no way you could screw up, decide wrong, be left open to getting called stupid. All you had to do was fit the grease gun nozzle over the greaser, pump in the grease until you could see it beginning to come out of the joint, and move on to the next one. Gerry had volunteered to grease the baler as soon as breakfast was over.

"No need. I already greased it yesterday, while you were in school," Bob said.

"Then how about the rake?"

"Rake's okay right now. I need a hand with the baler once chores are done."

"But the gutters aren't that full."

"It's been three days. They're full enough to clean."

"Oh, okay." Gerry stood up quickly from the kitchen table and deposited his plate, cup, and silverware in the sink behind him, a rare courtesy to the dishwasher.

"You don't hafta be in a hurry," Bob ordered. He still had the last gulp of his coffee, and two Lucky Strikes to smoke.

"That's okay, I'll bring the tractor around and start the gutter cleaner," Gerry said on his way out.

"Jesus, Edna, what's got into him?"

She nodded her head in reply. A new worry.

Gerry fired up the tractor, backed the spreader beneath the gutter cleaner, and started it. He had wanted to get everything done before his father could arrive, but Bob was suspicious of Gerry's enthusiasm. When he arrived in the barn to find Gerry conscientiously scraping bits of chaff and manure off the returning paddles of the gutter cleaner, he became even more suspicious.

Gerry did his best to avoid making eye contact, and when the gutters were cleaned he quietly began shaking a fresh layer of chaff into the gutters. Bob spread the manure as Gerry limed the barn floor, then washed and washed the dryness from his hands. It did not seem to want to come out.

The baler was waiting, a job Gerry dreaded. It was an intricate piece of machinery that would pick up hay, wad it into bales, thread twine around the bales, then tie a knot. The knotter was like sorcery to Gerry.

It made him thankful that he didn't have to figure out how to make a machine do that.

But now it wasn't working. The timing was off. Somehow the threader arm came through the bale too early, or too late, so that the twine wasn't tying.

"Drop the power takeoff in, easy, Ger," Bob said. The familiarity made Gerry blush a little, because of the dream.

Gerry slipped the p.t.o. lever into gear and eased out the clutch. Then he nudged the hand throttle until it was about halfway open and climbed off the tractor.

"Now feed that hay in, *easy*," Bob reminded. Gerry reddened again at the warning. Same old story. No middle ground. The things that Gerry didn't know how to do or had forgotten how to do he had to face without guidance. And the things he knew innately, could do in his sleep, he was lectured about.

Gerry stood in front of the baler, waiting for the signal from his father to start pushing hay into the front for some test bales. Bob was behind the twine holder, staring at the knotter, looking at the threading arm, as if by the sheer force of his concentration he could make it work right. It was almost as if there was a prayer being said so that when the threading arm went through, it would go through at precisely the right time, and nothing else would have to be done.

The low hum of the power takeoff and the movement back and forth of the baler sent Gerry back into his haying trance—the attitude he had to maintain to get himself through, what with equipment breakdowns, and problems with the weather and the need to make decisions in a hurry about whether you could mow a field down, have it cure, and get it baled before the next rain came. Haying always was the season of greatest stress.

And as Gerry had to face the prospect of what he was going to do with his life, and felt the pressure to become a farmer, he necessarily wanted to make more decisions, but that was fraught with peril. So although he saw things that he knew were obviously mistakes, he had learned to keep quiet, to let his father make the decisions, and simply to stand there being yelled at if things didn't work out.

"Start feeding her in," Bob yelled.

The prayer was over.

Gerry had a bale out, already broken open, and there was a pile of loose hay behind it. He grabbed the fork and started pulling the hay up, under the bar, so it could be swept into the baler by the tines. The baler started to settle into a familiar singsong hum, as the hay was jammed into the wadding chamber, heading down toward the threading needle. Gerry kept an eye on the p.t.o., whose cover was a little loose, and would sometimes rattle and fly back in an alarming way. Although his father knew about the cover, too, if it should rattle back at the wrong time, disturbing Bob's concentration, it would mean trouble. Gerry fell to daydreaming.

He'd had problems with power takeoffs before.

Once when Helmut Molshoc had come over to look at the old Ford tractor, to buy for his farm, Bob fell into his salesman pitch, which meant that Gerry had to be his assistant operator. There was a mowing machine hooked on the p.t.o. with the mower lifted off the ground by the hydraulic sway arms. Gerry climbed up on the tractor to start it up on his father's request. Helmut's son, Gunnar, was sitting up there with him. Gerry put the clutch in, jiggled the gearstick to neutral, turned the key almost ninety degrees to where the switch engaged the best, set the throttle one-quarter open, and pushed the starter. He was fortunate that it only cranked through four cuh-cuh-cuh-cuh's before it fired.

So far, so good. But once it was idling all right and Helmut and Bob were looking at the mower, Helmut with his foot resting on the connecting rod, Gerry turned around to see what his next order was and the heel of his boot nudged the p.t.o. into gear.

"Jesus," Bob shouted.

Helmut jumped back, the mower clattering to life for two seconds before Gerry could shut it off. "Why, if I had a son like that I'd kick his ass," Helmut said, glaring at Gerry.

Gerry didn't attempt to meet his eyes but instead looked at Gunnar, whose eyes seemed to answer, *Yes, you would.* Bob said nothing at first, but glared himself at Gerry and then said, "You know better than that."

Helmut was notoriously tight with his money, and Bob had been saying over morning breakfast that it was unlikely that Helmut would buy the tractor, but when he left shortly thereafter, Gunnar in tow with head hung down, Bob had his opportunity to focus his ill fortune on Gerry.

"Hold it! Hold it! Hold it!" Bob was yelling at Gerry, who was still feeding in the hay at a steady pace, although the threader arm had kicked up through the bale and the needles had been sheared in two by the wadder.

"Son of a bitch. Don't you pay attention to what's goin' on? Couldn't you hear that?"

Gerry thought he actually was supposed to answer. He was searching his daydream memory to see if he had heard the sound of the needles being sheared. He decided it was probably best to say nothing, and stood mute as his father cursed at the baler and his son.

"Help me crank this thing back to get the needles out." Bob had come around to the front of the baler, unhooked the p.t.o., and pulled the flywheel backward to get the needles to retract. "Why can't you pay more attention to what's going on? Jesus, you'd think by now that you could do something as simple as feed hay into the baler without breaking it."

Gerry felt the heat rise up in his neck and in his cheeks, but focused all of the anger into the counterclockwise turning of the flywheel. When the needles were finally retracted, and Bob went back and saw them broken, he fell into another fit.

"Goddammit. Now I've gotta go buy a brand-new set of needles. The timing is still off."

He stormed away up to the house to get Edna to call the New Holland dealer. Gerry stood rooted in the same place, hoping for some new order to come.

Just before he reached the top porch step, Bob turned around and yelled, "Go get the rake from up on the Alfalfa Hill, down in the corner by where the lane is. Ya know where I'm talking about?"

Gerry said, "Yeah," halfheartedly. He went to find the Ford tractor, fired it up, and headed down the back road to get at the Alfalfa Hill piece. He left the Ford in third gear, put the throttle about half open, because he wanted to take longer than he needed to, so he could cool down, and so that the chances would be good that his father would be gone before he got back with the rake.

The back road from the Scotts' house that led to the woods and the power line was bordered on the west by pasture and the east by a hayfield. This year the field was planted in a crop of oats, still green, that was just reaching a couple of feet high. Gerry was lost in his thoughts on the trip down the back road, but as he chugged along the lane he looked back toward the oats and saw some strange holes in them that you could not see on the level from the road.

It looked like two or three circles in the oats, perfectly round, as if some huge cookie cutter had descended and chopped down through the oats, and lifted them up out of the ground into the sky.

His first thought was, *Damn, Dad is gonna be mad at this,* and he even began readying himself for some kind of accusation that he had been involved in knocking them down. But once he'd hooked up the rake and headed back up the road, he decided to stop and look to see if he could figure out what had happened. Maybe if he could, or if it wasn't as bad as it looked, he could somehow redeem himself. So when he got past the swamp and almost a third of the way up to the turn, he pulled the tractor and the rake off to the side of the road as best he could, and picked his way over the fence and into the oats.

The cows were across the road, in the pasture nearest the power line, and they hadn't been paying any attention to the oats across the way until Gerry's presence attracted their interest. By the time he got close to the first circle, a whole bunch of them were pressed up against the fence.

"I wonder what he's doin'?" Charlotte whispered to John.

"Oh, just going over to look at something in the oats. Sure wish he would somehow loosen up that fence or get it knocked down so that we could get at it."

"Yeah, that sounds good. Think he will?" Thunder asked.

John, Charlotte, and Young Smitty just looked at her, incredulously.

"I don't believe how dumb you are," Charlotte finally said. "You're dumber than that bobtail over there." She swung her head in Aretha's direction.

John was silent, not wanting to incriminate himself by going to Aretha's defense, although it hurt him that she was still an outcast.

"No, Thunder, I don't think that he's going to take the fence down so that we can get into the oats," Charlotte said.

"But it doesn't make sense that he's over there right now, because they're not ready, and if Farmer Bob finds out that he's knocking them down, he'll be mad."

"Yes, he will," Bossy said as she joined them. "Have you noticed how funny Gerry's been acting lately?"

Gerry had reached the area where the holes were. They were perfectly round, and the spots were perfectly flat. There was an eerie scent that was faintly metallic, but not like anything that Gerry had ever smelled before.

Once he looked at the holes he had an overwhelming desire to look up into the sky, as if there were some connection between the sky and what had been left there. Because he saw that no other creature had made a path there, it looked like whatever had caused the circles had just dropped out of the air.

Gerry knelt in the bare space, felt the twisted, uprooted stubs of oats, saw in some places where they were just knocked down. Unable to fathom what could have made such a design, he tore some of the oat stalks from the ground to take back to his father for evidence. When he got back to the tractor, he sniffed a handful of oats, picking up again the strange metallic scent along with something very familiar that he couldn't identify either.

"G'wan, you stupid animals," he yelled at the cows pressed up against the fence. "G'wan, you're not gonna get any of these oats."

And then for a reason Gerry didn't even understand he climbed back off the tractor, walked across the road, pulled a handful from the bundle he'd collected, and tossed it just over the fence. Then he climbed on the tractor and headed back up to the house.

They swooped down on the oats as quickly as they could. Thunder was first to get there and nearly had gobbled up the entire gift from Gerry before Young Smitty could wrestle some away. As she chewed and their scent filled her nostrils she was struck by a lightning bolt of memory. She bent her nose down and sniffed at the stalks left by Thunder, smelled them all, smelled them three times, then whispered, "Peanut."

Gerry had timed his trip perfectly, because when he returned, his father and mother were gone to get parts, leaving a note behind on the kitchen table that they probably wouldn't be back for dinner.

King was off hunting woodchucks with Scout, so his only company was Renee, who was just getting up. They didn't argue nearly as much as they used to, mainly because Renee had become so withdrawn and pensive the last several months.

Gerry didn't know whether it was because of college or because she had broken up with Hugh Dyson. Renee was very quiet, brooding, or at least that was the way she acted around him. Though she was even more confrontational with her father over any issue, a particular vehemence was reserved for the war that was still going on.

And Gerry sensed that might even be part of the reason she had laid off him, because now that he was reaching draft age she seemed to have gained sympathy for him, at least much of the time.

"Gerry, you're such a pig, you know that, don't you?" Renee offered this matter-of-factly, without the shrill tone of their fights in the past.

"Whaddaya talkin' about?" Gerry was washing down his third toasted peanut butter sandwich, guzzling the last of the milk from a quart Mason jar.

"You're disgusting, drinking straight from the milk."

"I always have—what's the big deal?"

"Aren't you ever going to grow up? I had to make dinner, I'll have to clean up after you. I have to wait on you while you're watching TV. Don't you see anything wrong with that?"

Gerry sat in Bob's recliner chair, confused by Renee's question.

"I . . . I . . . It's what I always do. It's what Dad does. . . ."

"Sure it's what Dad does, and Mom lets him do it. They don't know any better."

"I'm just minding my own business, Renee. Leave me alone." Gerry tried to look past her at the TV. He had no idea where this conversation was going, but already he wanted no part of it. Better not to think about this stuff.

"Yeah, well, your own business includes me waiting on you when Mom's not around, so that makes it my business, too."

She hated being the apprentice Edna, with the expectation that she should have married some teenaged sweetheart and had kids right away, like other girls from high school. She felt guilty for a moment about not having called her friend Patty, who was already tied down with one baby, expecting another. She knew she wouldn't be calling her today, either. It would be too depressing.

"Okay, okay. I'll take my stuff out to the sink. Next commercial." Then Gerry closed off to her, fell into his TV trance. It was the same reaction he had to his father, to become indifferent.

Indifference counteracted ambition. It permeated his life. It wasn't that apathy had engulfed him—he cared deeply, but not about anything confusable with ambition. Occasionally he would get pangs of conscience, but once he would start to think about following his father, his head began to feel thick and heavy, like an oversized sponge saturated with aged lead paint. He would have to lie down.

TV was a godsend. It ordered his time into twelve-minute segments, and even provided commercials to relax through if the drama was too intense, allowing it to flow by him pacifically. For time was his enemy, the measure of how much he should have accomplished, how much closer he was coming toward figuring out what he was supposed to be doing with his life—and its presence was total, unwavering, suffocating.

Time was even more his father's enemy. What else could make a man drive himself so hard, to build and raise and construct and tear down and start all over again so unceasingly?

"There's always something to do," was Bob's dictum.

And his father was even more absorbed by TV. The TV trance was so total that often he would not bother to change stations, but instead learned to like what was on rather than risk breaking the spell. The volume was adjusted by one of his kids, or by Edna. If TV sedated Gerry, it made his father helpless, set adrift on waves of air.

Gerry never suspected that his father did not know who he was, either. Bob's fights with his father, and his wife and kids, showed how unhappy he was, how much in need of the feeling that he was doing something of value, the right thing.

These always seemed to Gerry to be expressions of his father's bad temper, of his desire to have more control over the people working with him than anybody could expect to have, of his own poor choices and lack of faith in his ability to change the circumstances of his life.

"You didn't have to stay working with your father," Gerry would say.

"You didn't have to hear him every day ask me to stay."

And that was the end of the argument. It was an act of God that had kept Bob stuck on the farm, unhappy to the core of his being.

* * *

"Why don'tcha take over the farm, Ger," his father asked during milking. "You know why the Old Homestead is abandoned. You know what happened to the Sand place."

*Oh, man, not this again. Why does he bother? He's got to know I'm not interested in it,* Gerry thought.

"Aw, Dad, you know what you always said about farming, that you'd have to be crazy to want to farm it."

"If a young man had any ambition today he could be set up right in farming. It's a gold mine. You'd be on King's Row." His own statements from the past bounced right off him.

Gerry sighed and turned his attention off. Focusing his eyes just to the right of his father's face, he let his mind drift.

*What I'd really like to do is . . .*

". . . 'forty-two they was dyin' for people."

. . . *But that would take too long, even if I got . . .*

". . . The second time I bought the farm, they was just startin' a milk strike. . . ."

. . . *And she's too beautiful to even look at me. . . .*

". . . But a man who had some am-bition . . ."

Gerry's head started to ache, a slow dull throbbing. He couldn't wait for milking to be over, so he could get away and go play ball.

He had completely forgotten about the dream.

His father was up when Gerry got home. He'd slipped in the kitchen door to be quiet, but Bob met him in the dining room and switched on the light.

"So, how did the game go?"

"Uh, okay. I got a couple of hits."

"Who won?"

"Uh . . ."

"Where you been?" Bob was looking directly at Gerry, but Gerry kept his eyes averted.

"Over at Jonesey's house."

"Some kinda party over there?"

"Yeah. I was mad at Coach. Got benched. I can't figure it out."

"Whadja do wrong?"

"Nothin'. That's just it."

"Did the Slack kid go in for you?"

"Yeah. . . . Why?"

"Can't you figure it out? What kinda game did you have?"

"Well, I had a great night at the plate, two for two, no errors, and I made a shoestring catch of a liner in the third. It was my best game ever." Gerry looked confused.

"Do you know what Ol' Man Slack looks like?"

"Not really."

"Well, he always wears a button-down golf cap, and yachting shoes, wire-rimmed glasses."

"Wait a minute," Gerry started. "He sits . . ."

"Just past the visitors' bench," Bob finished. "On a line with the first-base coach."

Gerry pulled out a chair from beneath the dining-room table and slumped into it. He whistled softly.

"So that's where Coach is looking when he pulls me. How did you know?"

"I was sitting behind your dugout tonight."

"Oh." Gerry's embarrassment deepened. It would figure that his father would be a witness to his humiliation.

Bob sighed and motioned Gerry back into the kitchen, where he closed the door and pointed to a large rectangular folder on the table.

"Wanna show you something," he began. Gerry sat and stared vacantly.

"I didn't want to be a farmer, y'know." Gerry had heard this opening line before. He was having a hard time concentrating.

Pause. "Uh-huh."

"This is what I really wanted to do." Bob undid the knot on the folder and pulled out some line drawings. Gerry's jaw dropped open.

One was a brooding portrait of his grandfather, another a scene of a tractor on its side, its driver trapped under a rear wheel. Bob was spreading them out on the tabletop, silently, gently, easing them into place.

The third drawing was of a cow freshening, striking in its detail and its power. Gerry couldn't take his eyes off it.

"My father hated this one." He tapped the bottom of *The Freshening*. "Had a chance at a scholarship to an art school. The recruiter even came out here during milking. Old man said no."

Gerry was shocked. He had had no way to prepare for this moment. A heartfelt talk with his father was out of the realm of his experience and expectation, like what he was feeling now, from smoking his first joint. His father's drawings had more depth of feeling and understanding than Gerry had believed he was capable of. He was dumbfounded.

"Whadja do, Dad?" he finally managed.

A long pause followed, in which Bob's expression turned in degrees from wistful to malevolent. "I stayed here."

Gerry was still staring at *The Freshening*, which was coming to life before him. The twelve-year-old boy standing on a milk stool to assist in the birth was now standing on tiptoe, and the cow engaged in the breech birth was rearing its head back sideways over its neck.

"Musta been some party at Jonesey's, eh?" Bob baited.

"Yeah." Gerry spoke to the painting.

"What were ya celebratin'? Yer team didn't even win."

"Weren't celebratin'. We were mad about what happened." The drawing was frozen in place again.

"What? That you got pulled from the game?"

"Yeah, and about Martin." Gerry's hands had been resting on the tabletop, but now he was conscious of how they were holding him upright, balanced in a pocket of air.

"Martin? Ya mean Grover Martin's boy?"

"Yeah." For the first time since the drawings were unveiled Gerry took his eyes off them and tried to look directly at his father. Sitting across the Formica tabletop, he couldn't figure out what was keeping him suspended in his pocket of air.

"Well, what about him?"

With great effort Gerry resisted the temptation to look under the table to see what was holding his father up. "Ringer got yanked from lunch yesterday." The tractor in the second drawing rolled sideways toward Gerry. He jumped a little in his seat.

"For what?" Bob's face was huge, as if Gerry were standing in front of a movie screen. Gerry stared back into it.

"He's a senior, just turned eighteen." The old man's nostrils were flaring so that Gerry was afraid he'd be swallowed up by them. He couldn't will his eyes to blink.

"So? So what?"

The drawings stopped moving. Bob's nostrils were calm.

Gerry's eyes met his. "He hadn't signed up for the draft."

Ringer Martin, one year ahead of Gerry in school and the team second baseman, had been dragged out of lunch two days after his eighteenth birthday by the local draft board chairman and a rotted English teacher aspiring to vice principal.

"Oh," said Gerry's now-normal-sized father. He stood up from the table, pulled the drawings together, and secured them in their folder. "G'night," he said, as he carried the drawings off to their hiding place.

"G'night," Gerry replied, now alone, wondering how he was going to get himself up to bed without arms, since he could no longer feel them.

## Chapter Ten

# Edna

(1971)

She had heard him go up the stairs, the telltale squeak of the third step at 1:48 A.M., allowing her finally to drift off to sleep. When King came in at two minutes of five to shove his nose between the mattress and the box spring, she had already been awake for twenty minutes.

The wind howling outside her window had snapped a branch off the crabapple tree out back, scraping it along the west wall of her bedroom before it was lost in late-February snow. It had sounded like a wild animal being buried alive.

*Are the pipes frozen?* Edna wondered. When the water pump wasn't running on bitter-cold mornings, this was always her first thought. She pulled on her housecoat, slid her toes into worn slippers, and padded to the kitchen. The toilet was okay, but the hot-water faucet in the bathroom would not produce even a drip. She decided not to say anything about it to Bob unless he asked.

He didn't ask. Besides grunting "G'mornin' " to her he didn't say anything until Gerry came downstairs, on Edna's third call. The dog's nose was pointed toward the door all that time, and Bob was sitting closest to the door, but she could tell by the set of his shoulders that he was not going to move, was not ready to brave the blast of arctic air to let the dog out. She got up to open it.

*Gotta go, gotta go, gotta go,* King thought as he circled in front of the door. A cold gust of air blasted him immediately. King paused, hesitated, wondering whether he really needed to go out.

"Jesus Christ! Get out! Close the door!" Bob yelled. Edna started to comply. King backed up a step, then forward, then looked up at Edna for guidance.

"Make up your mind," she warned, and King moved forward enough for her to close the door behind him. Bob shook his head at her.

"Guh-morn," Gerry breathed as he passed through the kitchen on his way to the bathroom.

"Pretty late night again, huh?" Bob asked. Gerry ignored the question, pretending that he couldn't hear through the bathroom door. Actually, he was gritting his teeth at every word.

"So when didja get in? Three o'clock?" Bob asked, this time louder.

"About quarter to two," Edna offered reluctantly.

"He probably won't be worth a damn at school."

Edna was silent.

"Ev'ry since he got his night license he don't pay any attention to gettin' home at a decent hour."

She nodded slightly in agreement.

"An' he needs a haircut, too."

Gerry's hair was down over his ears, barely past his collar in back. By 1970 standards he was a Marine. But he had learned how to keep it long in front by combing it back to keep his father happy, then letting it drift down over his eyes when he needed to be part of his generation. Despite his efforts to please his father, Bob hated the way Gerry's hair sometimes would flop down, and especially that he could not force him to get it cut the way Bob liked anymore. Gerry's hair had become an obsession for his father.

Edna silently nodded in assent. She never spoke aloud about it, not even to her husband, and she studiously avoided making any sign of disapproval when Gerry could see. Although no one was absolutely certain how she felt, Bob took it for granted that she agreed with him. For Bob it was enough that his son knew how he felt about the hair.

"Y'know, you're startin' to look like a woman," he leveled at Gerry as soon as he came out of the bathroom.

Gerry sat down and stared straight ahead, not yet awake enough to want to get into an argument. The only thing Bob disliked more than long hair was being ignored. He leaned over toward Gerry and challenged, "Ya know what the worst thing is that ever happened to this country?"

"That Martin Luther King?"

"No," his father scowled, as if he had never said that to Gerry before the assassination.

Gerry suppressed the urge to sigh.

He remembered a similar conversation from before, the same conspiratorial tone, the same sense of helplessness in the face of his father's peculiar logic. That time the worst thing that had ever happened to the country was when they got away from the way Indians lived.

Gerry had wanted to say something about all the Indian land being taken, but he had known it was hopeless.

"Yup, things started to go ta hell when women weren't doin' all the work at home."

Edna had worn her noncommittal look.

"The man used to go out and hunt and fish all day, and his squaw had to take care of everything else."

Gerry had been perplexed. He couldn't remember hearing his father say anything good about Indians before.

"But I heard . . ."

"Yeah, yeah, about women's liberation. That's bullshit. Ya don't see Indian squaws complainin' about women's rights."

Gerry couldn't remember ever seeing a real-life Indian.

"No, but."

"And there's not enough babies bein' born now, the economy's goin' bad."

"Yeah, but."

Bob's voice had dropped to a whisper. "Women aren't doin' their job. They're not havin' enough children to drink all the milk we can produce."

"What?" Renee had exclaimed as she came into the kitchen. "What are you saying is women's job?"

Bob looked over at Gerry, rolling his eyes.

"Nothin' you'd understand," Bob mumbled.

"Nothing I'd understand. About what women are supposed to do. What does that mean?"

"I'm talking' to your brother. It means you're stickin' your nose in where it isn't wanted."

"I can't believe you! You're trying to tell my *brother* about *women*, and you don't know . . ."

Gerry had been spared then from the full treatment by his father's argument with Renee, but Renee was not here to defend womanhood this time. He glanced nervously over at his mother, who was noncommittal, sphinxlike.

"It was those goddam Beatles . . ." Bob continued.

*It was those goddam nigger jazz musicians,* Edna swore she had heard. It was her father's voice. *They never shoulda let them niggers get their own bands, have their own bars. They got uppity,* he had tol[d] her. She worshiped him, he was the best father, taking care of her. Sh[e] had never crossed him, never argued, only listened and believed.

Edna's father had died when she was eleven, chewed up by a w[...] puller he was operating for the first time, trying to help break a st[...] He had not yet outlived his time as God in his daughter's eyes.

Edna's mother had moved her children to Lowmarket to be [...] her family, where they could pinch and scrape their way throu[gh the] Depression together.

"Talkin' to you is like talkin' to a wall," Bob concluded. [...] hair had almost descended over his eyes. "Well, let's get to t[...] See what troubles I got today."

Edna was tremendously relieved that they were leaving [...] having discovered the frozen pipe. Now if she could get it t[...] fore milking was done, it would keep Bob from getting in[...] Renee's break from college was coming up soon, and Edna [...] to come home, so she needed for Bob not to be in a mood [...]

She waited to hear the drone of the vacuum pump b[...] the dark morning wind, then went down into the cellar wi[...] Renee had left behind. Standing on an overturned co[...] reached the nozzle of the hair dryer up close to where [...] disappeared through the floorboards.

Her left hand clamped her right wrist, holding th[...] the soreness in her shoulder and elbow. Her legs ache[...] in any extreme weather. When the pain in her arm [...]

unbearable, Edna concentrated on memories of pumping a
water from the well at her grandfather's farm. By comparis
ing out this pipe was a blessing.

Just when the pain of the present was breaking through aga
water pipe shuddered and rattled. Edna held the hairdryer up fo
other agonizing count downward from ten, then shut it off and
down on the coal bucket. The cold surrounded her almost immediately
troubling her daydream of the bathroom at her father's house, with the cast-iron tub on lion-claw legs, a tub she could fill with as much hot water as she liked. She could hear the water running into it.

"Ooh, no." Edna jumped up in alarm. She had left the hot-water faucet open in the bathroom sink while she was thawing the pipes, and now the water was spilling out onto the worn rubber tiles of the floor. It had soaked into the throw rug before she got to the faucet, so she had to pull it out of the bathroom and sop up the water with towels so there would be no evidence when Bob returned from the barn.

Edna let the dog in the house, added coal and stoked the fires, and made all the beds before contemplating another rest. When she finally sat down in the kitchen she felt again how slowly the fire was coming up. It was almost seven, about twenty minutes before Bob and Gerry and Merle would come up from the barn, and still devil-dark outside.

Against her will, the sound of winter crept into her. The cold made the house pop, as if it were shrinking out of itself. It made Edna want to curl up, near the fire, not do anything. It took all her energy to sweep the kitchen floor and maintain her equilibrium, remain the model of honest effort. But on these days she was always close to spilling over, to wanting to get to the sun.

The men were late coming up from the barn. It used to make her worry about Gerry's being ready for school, but once he and Bob had started arguing about President Nixon and the war, she was grateful for the lack of time. Gerry had had to jump up from the table without finishing his fourth piece of toast because the snow had drifted around the '62 Chevy he drove to school. Just before he left to rock his car out of its snowdrift, he delivered a parting blast.

"I suppose you think Calley's a hero, too."

Bob ducked into his shoulders. Edna blushed. They both were horrified by what they were hearing about My Lai, and angered at the country-western songs holding Lieutenant Calley up as a hero. Bob had

seen terrible things during World War II, but was disgusted by this. Edna was inclined toward unbending patriotism, mostly because of how she and her family would look if they appeared otherwise, but she was no fool. She had known long before the My Lai story finally came out that there was something deeply wrong with this war. She was also afraid of losing her children, and she suspected Bob was afraid of the same thing.

If only she could talk to him about it.

Bob said nothing, sat drinking his coffee and smoking his cigarette, listening to the sound of Gerry's car as it rocked back and forth and finally heaved out of the driveway.

"There's more toast, Bob."

"Okay, I'll have another piece."

"Edna, stay away from the lettuce," Herm whispered as Edna unjammed a grocery cart. "They're marked way down, but frost got to 'em someplace."

"Okay, Herm. Any specials on meat besides the ones on the board?"

"Only on chuck steak, but between you'n me," his voice lowered again, "I'd only buy it for cutting into stew meat."

"That's fine. Have you got three pounds' worth? I like to make a big pot if I'm making it."

"Should have. It'll be all wrapped for ya when ya get to the back."

"O-kay." She hesitated. "Yeah, thanks, Herm." She remembered now that it was the assistant manager at the new supermarket in Onlius who had parceled off some gristly cube steak on her the first time she had tried that store. The prices were good, but Bob noticed the difference in the meat and complained.

Besides, her legs had hurt from walking back and forth down the aisles trying to find everything by herself. The only help she'd gotten was from that pimply, overeager kid, and that had turned out to be no help. So she went back to Zerrillo's, where it cost more but you could trust whatever came wrapped in butcher paper, and it was closer to home.

"You stop that, this minute," a large woman was threatening. Her two children were whining for some store cookies, Fig Newtons or Oreos or something. The older one looked like she should be in school, but Edna guessed that she was home sick by the way both of their noses were running. *Hmmph, no boots or hats on either of them,* she snorted to herself.

The older one was skinny and knobby, the bottom of her stretch pants missing the top of her socks by a couple of inches. She dropped a bag of cookies into the cart while her mother was yelling "I'll break your arm" into her little brother's face. He began to bawl tearlessly, his stout arms stretched out straight from his shoulders.

"You know better than that," the mother warned. She turned back to the cart, spied the cookies, and slapped the girl's arm sharply. "I toldja, I toldja." The report of the slap was so loud that Edna turned reflexively to look at them. The girl looked away from her mother, absolutely sullen, absolutely shamed. When she caught Edna's eye for a moment, it made Edna's cheeks burn.

*Must be some new welfare people,* Edna thought. *That nuclear plant again.* Lowmarket had always had its share of relief cases, but until recently, everyone had known who they were. It had seemed like they were always the same families, from the same neighborhoods in town.

But the nuclear plant had changed things, because the prospect of new construction had brought laborers from all over the state in search of high-paying seasonal jobs. That had raised housing prices for everybody, pushing some families over the edge. Many more came than found work on the site, and then some never found a way back out.

Edna pushed on to finish getting groceries, aware that she would have to hurry to get dinner ready by noon. But still, when she reached Grace Zerrillo at the checkout counter, the welfare family was ahead of her again.

Edna was not surprised to see three packages of cookies in their cart, even if they were different brands from the kids' choices. And she also wasn't surprised that the woman was paying for the groceries with food stamps. But she was surprised at the nonchalance with which the woman handled the food stamps. Didn't she even know enough to be embarrassed?

Grace was poring over the items on the conveyor like an overzealous auditor, but not more painstakingly than Edna. *Store-bought cookies, SpaghettiOs,* she catalogued. *Potato chips—doesn't this woman cook? Wouldn't know beans if the bag was open.*

Then Edna noticed a bruise on the woman's left forearm, and two smaller ones on each side of her Adam's apple. And the children were not only sullen, they were fearful. They had the look of the Molshoc girls—hollow-eyed, bloodless, rabbit-scared, drained, heart-beating-too-fast, flinching, huddled, terrified.

She thought of the Marley kids back home in Vermont when she was growing up, spurned by the rest of the town because their father was a Catholic. Her family, like most of the community, had come from Puritan stock who had emigrated from the Massachusetts coast. They were true believers, more pure than those Puritans who had let the calling-off of the witch trials shake their faith.

"You can't use food stamps for cigarettes," Grace cautioned.

"I know. My husband gave me some cash for those," the woman sighed.

"I'll have to ring 'em up separate, then."

"Okay." She wearily pulled the cigarettes back behind the rest of the stuff, glaring at her kids to keep their hands off the gum and candy bars in the rack next to them.

Edna started to get nervous about the time. It was already twenty to twelve.

Grace seemed to be working even more slowly now, rotating each item in her hand like a baton twirler, apparently in search of conflicting prices. Every time she looked at Edna frowning, she believed it was in sympathy with her vigilance.

Finally the food stamps were presented and the change was returned. The woman proceeded to hand some of the cash back to Grace for the cigarettes.

"You can't do that," Grace announced.

"Can't do what?" the woman said.

"You can't pay for cigarettes with the change from food stamps," Grace persisted.

Edna sniffed and tapped her foot on the polished plank floor.

The woman sighed, paused, then sighed again. She had been through this before. She would have to dig her purse out from her pocketbook, put the food-stamp change away, then pull out some cash from another pouch of the purse. She looked at the two women who were making her do this, and wearily began the charade.

Edna was about to explode. "It's okay, Grace. She said she had her own money."

Grace was rebuffed. "But you can't use those for cigarettes," she repeated.

"Here's some other cash," the woman said.

The transaction completed, the woman began to leave, then turned to Grace.

"I just wanted you to know that I don't smoke."

"Cuttin' it kinda close, weren't ya, Edna?" Bob asked, as she burst into the house with the first two bags of groceries.

"Yes, it took longer than I thought."

"Thought you weren't gonna go to that new place in Onlius."

"I didn't, I went to Zerrillo's."

"Are you kiddin'? Is Herm gettin' even slower?"

"No. It took a long time at the checkout, is all," she offered. "I'll make something quick."

At twelve-eleven she delivered his tray to him in the recliner, loaded with a bowl of tomato soup, warmed-up potatoes, and a grilled ham-and-cheese sandwich on homemade bread. The coffee was fresh from the percolator, too hot for Bob, but she was fortunate enough to have two oatmeal cookies, no raisins, left for his dessert.

"Could you turn this up, that damn wind is howlin'," was his thank-you. She retreated into the kitchen to make herself something to eat.

Dinner at twelve noon was a ritual as sacred as getting groceries on Thursday morning. Renee was certain that it was her father's idea, just another dimension of his tyranny, but Gerry wasn't so sure. He could remember too many times when they were working in the fields or on some piece of equipment when dinnertime rolled around, and its making his father angry to be interrupted. But since breakfast and supper were ruled by morning and afternoon milkings, the twelve-noon dinner was just as important to him, when he wasn't busy.

Once when Bob was thirty-one and his father had gotten angry with him, he went off to work at a local feed mill. Gerry wasn't yet in school, and on her days off Renee loved having soup and sandwiches for lunch. Edna cut the sandwiches into neat little squares and made green tea for them to drink. Every day was like a picnic with royalty.

But Bob got into a fight with his foreman after he'd been there less than three months, and wanted out. His father had wanted to stay stubborn, but it was close to haying time, so he grudgingly agreed to Bob's coming back. For years after, Bob's excuse for returning to the farm was that Edna had not been putting a decent dinner on the table when he was gone.

The phone began to ring just as Edna's sandwich was done. On the fourth ring, she realized that Bob would not get up to answer it, so she turned the heat off and walked through the kitchen and dining room to pick it up.

"Hello."

It was Stormy, calling for Bob.

"Yeah, Edna, heard you called me this mornin'. What's Bob up to?"

"He wanted you to pick up that blue heifer he got from Molshoc."

"Well, when?"

"Well, I don't know, Stormy. He's right here, let me ask him." She turned to Bob, who was listening to the phone conversation but still planted in his chair. "It's Stormy. He wants to know about the blue cow."

"Jesus, yes. When can he take her to the auction?"

"Stormy, Bob wants to know when you can take the cow to the auction."

"T'morrow mornin' at the earliest."

"He says tomorrow morning at the earliest."

"Why isn't he goin' to the Ebens auction today?"

Edna looked at Bob as if to say, *Do you really want me to ask that?* Bob's return look said, *What are you waiting for? Ask him why he's not going today.*

"Uh, Bob wants to know, are you going to the Ebens auction this afternoon?"

"Yup, but I already made my run this morning. I'm heading up there right now." Stormy was beginning to sound a little annoyed.

"He says he's about to leave for Ebens now."

"Well, Jesus, Edna, ya didn't ask him the right question. Can he pick up the blue cow today?"

"I already asked him that. He said no."

"You didn't ask him that."

"But he said it was too late to pick up any more cows for Ebens."

"Jesus! And she'll prob'ly freshen before tomorrow so she won't sell worth a damn. You should've called before breakfast." Edna's hand felt warm and sweaty over the phone receiver. She was sure that Stormy was not happy waiting on an answer.

"Do you want him to come tomorrow?" she asked, hoping to break her husband out of his fit.

"Yes, if she hasn't freshened," Bob snapped.

"Stormy, he says to come tomorrow if she hasn't freshened yet. . . . Okay, bye." Edna hung up quickly.

"She ain't gonna last that long," Bob said, shaking his head in disgust.

Edna retreated to the kitchen. Her sandwich was too greasy from sitting in the pan, but she ate it anyway, because she could remember times she had really needed food to eat and there had been none.

"Edna, could you turn this thing up? The wind is howlin' again."

She walked back into the living room again, wondering, *Did he turn the TV down before I ran in to answer the phone?*

The television volume was much lower than before.

*He must have,* she thought. *I don't believe it.*

"My tray's ready, sweetie," Bob said, motioning for her to carry it back out to the kitchen.

"Thanks," she replied, feeling better now.

Her father used to call her sweetie.

All through dishes she pondered at how she could get Bob to ask Renee to come home during her college break. She was sure that Renee wouldn't even consider it unless her father asked, and she knew with just as much certainty that Bob could never be persuaded to ask. Because of the way they had fought the last time, she was not even sure that Bob wanted Renee to come home.

Edna knew that if she made the arrangements all by herself, it would have to be exactly what Bob would want, and he would have to be in a good mood when he heard it. Or she could let him know that she had decided this on her own, but be ready for the third degree that was sure to follow.

When Edna came to him with a problem, and let him know that the kids were too afraid to come to him directly, Bob invariably asked her detailed questions for which she had no answer, making her feel inadequate for not having thought of all the myriad ways in which her children could be trying to put something over on her, and by extension, him. She always felt chastened by these sessions.

So she didn't ask. They sat in the living room together all afternoon, she in her rocker and he in his recliner, she distracted by the *Ladies' Home Journal* and he poring over the auction listings in the *Onlius Daily Times*. Bob complained about the soap operas, never budging to turn off the TV.

A commercial came on for orange juice, depicting a family on vacation in Florida.

"Edna, look at that. Lotta people do that now, and they'd be just as well off at home keepin' the fire goin'."

Edna was silent.

"I said they'd be just as well off at home."

"Yes. M-hm," Edna assented without looking up from her magazine.

"Ya know what my father used to say," Bob snapped.

Edna was frozen. Bob hadn't mentioned his father in years. She didn't know what to do.

"F . . . Florida isn't for real people . . . not workin' people. That's what . . ." Bob's voice trailed off.

Edna wanted him to keep talking, but she knew he wouldn't. There was so much about Bob's father, Russell, that he needed to get out. It was like a poison that paralyzed instead of killing.

Bob lifted the newspaper back in front of his face. He rubbed the corners of his eyes with his thumb and forefinger, not taking off his glasses, acting as if he had said nothing.

*Some working people do go to Florida,* Edna thought. *Some even live there all the time.*

Bob couldn't say any of these things, but lately she'd been making a list of Russell's ideas that she thought were cockeyed. *You shouldn't love a dog, or pet him or play with him too much. Indians just live to take advantage of the government by not having to pay taxes.* She paused a moment, embarrassed at herself.

*I shouldn't do this. It's just not right. Here he's been dead now for over three years.*

*It's just not right for black people and white people to get married and have children.* She tried that idea out on herself and concluded that this one, indeed, was right. It was what her own father would have said.

She remembered the story her father had told about the woman he knew as a kid on Raymond Lake who had fallen in love with a colored man and before she knew it, had gotten pregnant. They got married and had a bunch more kids and she had to live with all the Negro people down on the end of the lake where the mill pipes emptied. Poppa said that their kids were really lonely, not good enough to stay with white kids, and they didn't fit in with the colored kids. She didn't care what Renee or Gerry would say, that made sense to her.

*It's just not right for women to work. They take jobs away from their men and their kids grow up bad, raised by baby-sitters or the TV.*

*It's just not right. It's just not right.* It suddenly made her angry to realize that was what Russell used to say. *Why did he have to do that to himself? So you could never let go, never forget about him? Why did he have to do that?*

"It's just not," Bob suddenly said.

"What?" Edna asked.

"Uh, nothing. I didn't say nothing." Bob hurried up out of his chair and disappeared. Edna heard the bathroom door slam closed. Bob stayed in the bathroom until after Gerry got home from school, then emerged red-eyed behind his glasses and went directly down to the barn, early, to start the chores.

The sky changed, from steel gray to black in an instant, the darkness amplifying the wind. It was snowing, too, bitter grains of half-ice peculiar to this end of the Great Lakes, where the crystalline snow got tossed and swirled around in the frigid arctic air before it came slashing at the plastic Edna had put up for storm windows in the kitchen.

Her legs were aching again, mostly in her ankles. She wished that she could go to the doctor to get it checked out, but Bob would find out and be pushy about her going and then complain about the cost. They had never been able to afford health insurance.

Edna was peeling and cutting up potatoes to boil for supper to go with the round steak and home-canned green beans.

She had just managed to finish baking eight loaves of bread and two pans of rolls, and while the oven was still warm she decided to make some cookies for dessert. The kitchen was filled with the smell of chocolate and peanut butter when Gerry and Bob came up from the barn.

"What's that?" Bob sniffed, then drew in a deeper breath.

"Cookies, for dessert," Edna said.

"Smells like chocolate to me," he grumbled, stepping to the kitchen sink to wash the first layer of the barn from his hands.

*That's right,* Edna thought. *Oh my Lord. Bob doesn't care for chocolate. These are Renee's favorites.* Her hopes for a Renee visit slumped. She waited for some more serious complaint from Bob.

"You don't even play all the time for your school team," he said in Gerry's direction. "What makes you think you can play somewhere else?"

Edna watched Gerry's embarrassment darken into anger. Bob was walking away toward the bathroom, his back turned to Gerry.

"You . . . you know why I don't play," Gerry shouted.

"I do! How the hell should I know?"

"Because I'm a farmer."

"That's no excuse. A lot of players have been farmers."

"Yeah, maybe, but not from here. You know that."

Bob turned his back again and stormed into the bathroom, clumsily kicking over the coffee can of stones that held the door open.

He slammed the door shut. Gerry paced in front of the refrigerator, temporarily cut off from his tormentor.

"You can rot in this town," he finally shouted at Bob through the door. "They'll never let me play here." There was no sound from the other side of the door. Gerry stared at the door, his face contorting with rage.

*He looks just like Bob when he's mad,* Edna thought. His cheeks and neck were a deep purplish red, eyes narrowed into fierce slits, lips twisting and pursing.

"You got that right," Bob grunted inaudibly. Gerry was trapped in that town, just as he and Edna were. There was no denying it. He steadied himself against the sink, trying to wash the salt and the redness out of the corners of his eyes.

The door answered Gerry. No sound came from it. It stayed closed.

"I'm goin' out, Ma," Gerry muttered. He turned away from the closed door, tearing at a fingernail with his teeth.

"No . . . you're not," Edna answered. He glared at her.

"Supper's ready. You've got to have something to eat."

He pulled his fingertips from his mouth and began chewing on his lower lip. "I'm not hungry." Without changing his shoes or washing up, he strode through the dining room, grabbed his school coat, and disappeared out the front door.

"What . . . where the hell'd he go?" Bob asked when he came out of the bathroom.

Edna was still suspended, standing frozen between the stove and the kitchen table, a frying-pan lid in her hand. Suddenly she didn't know what she had meant to do with it.

She had tried to watch television, she had tried to sew, she thought several times about calling Renee, and even had the phone receiver in her hand, twice. But she was afraid to call, could not talk to Renee about Gerry's walking out, and especially not about Bob's going out on a drunk.

TV never had held much interest for her, and now since Bob was so absorbed by it, she had come to hate it. Whatever attention she should be getting was directed toward the TV. It seemed his feelings could safely flow only through what he saw on the screen. What was worse, she suspected that he enjoyed watching the young girls in miniskirts that seemed to have invaded. Once she thought she had seen Bob smile knowingly back at Pete when he had called it the boob tube.

She knew she wouldn't be so bothered by it if they still shared a bed, but that time was long since gone. No decision was ever made that they would not sleep together, it had just started to happen off and on until being alone had become a habit. The damage that Gerry had done to her insides at birth had ended her child-bearing, and most of what was left of her interest in intimacy. The rest evaporated with Bob's utter lack of sympathy for her, when he took insult that they could have no more children.

Her second night back from the hospital was the first time they had slept apart since they were married. The last night they had been together was three years ago, after the calling hours for Bob's father, the night before the funeral. Bob lay on his side, curled into a ball, with his back to her all night. She held him gently, not letting on that she knew he was sobbing. By the morning his face was the expressionless mask that he had worn most of the time ever since.

The wind had picked up as the snow had subsided, but it was swirling into nasty drifts. She watched the tire tracks fill up in the driveway.

It began to snow again around nine-thirty, so hard that with the wind she was unable to see the barn across the two stretches of driveway. One fierce gust obscured even the milkhouse light, jolting Edna alert. "I'd better go down to kick up the hay," she whispered to the silence of the house.

She pulled on Renee's pac boots and her own worn winter coat, and fought her way against the wind to the barn. The hay was thin in front of the cows, so she broke open three bales for both mangers.

When she went down the barn floor to scrape the manure from behind the cows and shake up their bedding, she found Aretha ready to freshen, two tiny hooves already protruding from her.

"Oh my Lord." Edna leaned on the dung fork, unbelieving. Gerry should have known that this cow was going to freshen, and Bob certainly knew. She could not fathom how they could have left her alone to deal with this. For a moment she thought of going back up to the house, pretending that she had not seen that Aretha was ready.

Aretha was quiet, in shock from the knowledge that there was something very wrong with the calf inside her. She could feel that it was not ready to be born, that it was in fact almost dead, having struggled for over an hour to emerge after her water had broken. She had bellered and bellered, getting a half-dozen other cows to join in, but they were drowned out by the wind.

This calf had quickened very late, just a few days ago, and from the first instant that she knew it was inside her, Aretha also had known that this calf was troubled. There was no way she could know for certain whether it wanted to be born.

"I've got to help this cow." Edna heard her father's voice, driving away any thoughts of inaction. She reached her hand past the hooves to feel around for the calf's snout. She kept checking until she was sure that these were the rear hooves, and that the calf was going to come out backward.

She tied twine around the legs, just behind the hooves, and slid the dung fork handle through the loop of the twine. "Steady, girl, steady," Edna coaxed, trying to get the cow and calf to work together.

Edna's insides began to ache and throb. As she pulled on the fork handle, she felt the flesh of her womb strain and tear, the pressure of the breech birth forcing her to her knees. Edna began to pant against the pain.

The thing inside Aretha dug at her, grew nails, then claws, then talons. The waves of hurt hit harder, more often, until they merged into one great wave of fire burning her alive from the inside.

Edna settled into a rhythm with Aretha's shallow breathing and straining, inching the calf toward life. She was angry with the calf for not being ready to be born, for having weighted its mother down with hurt and worry. And even if it lived, and its mother survived, its mother would have no control over it. This child could live a day or to a ripe age, and there would be no guarantee that the sacrifice made for it would be recognized or returned.

Aretha fought against the fire, put wall after wall against it, only to feel the flame grow hotter. She finally was consumed, gave in to the flame without struggle, and found herself outside of it, watching the woman trying to coax her flesh to give birth.

"What's wrong with you? What's wrong with you?" Edna screamed at Aretha as she felt her body relax. "You can't give up! You can't!" She started hitting Aretha, and screaming at her. And before she could stop herself, she was sobbing. "You *can't* give up, you can't, you're the mother. You can't give up!"

Aretha slammed back inside her body, instantly feverish again from the pain. She strained and pushed harder and harder, but could not keep herself in the moment. She saw ghost cows and ghost calves and ghost humans passing in and out of view, doing things that she knew were important and somehow meant to help her now. But she had no idea what their message was, because she could not stay connected to the present long enough to understand.

"I can't help you if you don't help yourself!"

Edna felt so helpless that she was furious.

"What am I doing here, anyway? I hate this farm, I hate all the work, all the time. It's like his religion. You can never do enough, never feel done, never be all right with yourself. I hate being taken for granted." She couldn't stop herself, even though the cows seemed to be listening. "And I hate the cold, and the snow, and haying. I hate . . . I . . ." She started to choke on the sobs. All this time she was pulling on the handle of the fork, and her knuckles were white. The calf's hips and rump were almost out.

Aretha was lost in a vision of the future, delirious. She saw calves stillborn, aborted spontaneously, born as monsters with two heads, no legs, calves destroyed by the ruin of the air and the land. She saw all the elders slaughtered, no cows allowed to grow old, none ever let outside to graze or to feel sunshine, cows alive only to give milk or their flesh for humans to eat. Each vision was more frightening than the previous one. Supercows—the product of chemicals and growth hormones, until humans were afraid of milk, cheese, and butter from real cows. Then vats of bacteria digesting grain and grass, oozing out milk that had never touched a cow's stomach. Finally extinction, humans completely cut off from the rest of creation, and doing their best to accelerate the process. And just as this last image unfolded, the calf's shoulders and head broke free, bringing it into the nightmare world.

By the time Edna had finished pumping air into the daughter's lungs and brought her around to be cleaned off, Aretha had settled back into real time. Aretha lovingly licked and nuzzled her new baby, grateful that she had survived and that there was another chance to mother her creation. And that the age of barbarism was not yet come.

Edna did not leave the barn until after midnight, letting the blue calf suckle some milk from its mother's swollen bag once it was able, rather than using a milking machine she was not sure she could operate. It made her feel useful and needed, in a way that she had not felt for a very long time.

Once she was back up in the house, had tended the fires, called the dog in for the night, washed up, and put herself to bed, all of her body began to ache. It was one more reason for her to lie awake, besides waiting and praying for Bob to come back, listening for the squeak of the third stair to signal that Gerry was home safe, wondering whether Renee was spinning uncontrollably away from her, despairing that she was one of the last of her kind—a mother who lived through her children.

The next morning she was so resigned to depression that she didn't bother to protest when Bob told her to call Stormy to take the calf to auction. But she did think about Renee, for some reason, and then she cried.

## Chapter Eleven

# Thunder

(1971)

Thunder couldn't take it any longer. She was feeling bloated heavy, sick with the weight of the calf inside her and the tension all around. They had been drying her off for weeks now, so she wasn't bothered by milking, but these days everything was annoying her. Just being pushed over against the post for every milking so Merle would have the room to milk Bossy was getting to be too much.

And the Order seemed to be breaking down. John had learned to do his job only when he could not hear the humming sound that had forced him from Charlotte. They had mated successfully, but without the dance. Charlotte could not be convinced that the dance hadn't been the problem before.

Thunder couldn't care less about the dance, or Charlotte, or even John. She wanted the Order back. She needed it. It was the only way she had ever been part of anything, had had any chance for acceptance. If the Order was lost, she'd be gone with it. The more Thunder tried to figure out why things had gone wrong, the more they pointed to that no-tail blue cow. Thunder was so suspicious, she couldn't even get herself to call Aretha a sister.

Thunder was filling with disgust; each day's addition to the weight she was carrying around inside her was a fresh source.

Every day she felt more like killing something.

Inside her was dead uncalm, mass without energy. She was sure

that, even though she felt a greater burden with each sunrise, there was no life inside her.

"Okay, I'll take care of White Brat," Merle offered, as if he were accepting a mission behind enemy lines. White Brat was dangerous, but Merle knew that Thunder was becoming more unpredictable. He preferred to let Bob roll the dice.

Thunder had decided to step on Merle's foot this morning just as he had pushed her over toward the post. When she was nudged over without picking up Merle's alcohol odor in her nostrils, Farmer Bob's arrival sent her into instant rage. She began to premeditate.

Bossy wouldn't help her. All the sisters were becoming terribly disaffected, but Bossy had yet to demonstrate that she was ready to sway from her loyalty to Farmer Bob. That was all right; she was respected in the Order because everyone knew where she stood. But as an accomplice in Thunder's new self-appointed mission, Bossy could not be trusted.

She would have to do this alone.

*Now,* she thought. Once Farmer Bob got back out onto the barn floor, she probably would lose her chance. She rocked sharply to her right, catching her jutting hipbone into Farmer Bob's ribs, pushing him back into Bossy and toward the manger.

"Hey! Move over, you son of a bitch." Thunder's blood went molten, then ice. With her right front hoof she flailed at the back of Farmer Bob's leg, not quite reaching it, until he decided to bring his fist down on the top of her spine. She bellied him over against Bossy, then caught the side of his ankle with her front hoof.

*C'mon, bend down. Get your hand down there,* she commanded telepathically.

He did. In a single movement she trapped his right hand under her front hoof, shifted her weight onto her left rear hoof, and aimed a murderous right rear hoof at Farmer Bob's temple.

"Uhn. Ooh," she heard, in her own voice, her hoof still cocked in position. She was being kicked.

"Ow. Oww," she grimaced, letting Farmer Bob loose. Her rage evaporated in wonder. The calf was alive, it had just this moment quickened, barely in time to save Farmer Bob's life.

Thunder moved over against the post contentedly, as if she did not even notice Farmer Bob thumping her spine with his fist. When he

glared into her eye, her expression stopped him cold. It suggested forgiveness.

Bob almost appeared to understand. Without knowing why, he didn't comment, or even smirk, when White Brat caught Merle in the shin as he stepped out onto the barn floor. For the rest of milking he felt as if he were charmed.

Merle arrived back from breakfast early, in an uncharacteristically good mood. Bob was suspicious as soon as he saw the grin on his face.

"What the hell's up with you?"

"Nothin'. Ain't nothin' wrong with me," Merle drawled, relishing the obvious anxiety building in Bob. He fished a plug of Red Man from his shirt pocket and bit off a healthy chaw, leaning against the door of his Ford. Bob watched Merle working his jaws while the grin again spread magnificently across his face.

"C'mon, c'mon, what is it?" Bob urged. Merle spat a luxurious supply of juice onto the ground midway between Bob's feet and his own.

"Tom is comin'," Merle blurted, unable to sustain the suspense.

"Whaddaya mean, Tom's coming?" Bob grunted.

"He is, he told me."

"When?"

"He's comin' over today, with Doris an' Young Russ an' Jeanine, and the baby."

"Today? But we got hay to put in," Bob complained.

"Tom knows. Said he don't mind." Merle couldn't help himself from grinning. With Tom there, the balance would be shifted, away from Bob at the center of everything. He finally might get the chance to turn the tables on him.

Or maybe not.

"I sure hope, for his sake, he don't mean it's okay because he expects to sit under a shade tree watchin' me work," Bob grumbled.

"Whaddaya talkin' about? He said he's gonna help, an' Young Russ, too."

"Young Russ, huh? How old is he now?"

"Fifteen, or sixteen, I'm not sure. Big strappin' kid, though, Bob."

"Bet he's prob'ly got hay fever, though." Bob could not allow his mind to get around the idea that his brother would help him with haying. *And his kids helping, too. Hmmph. I'll just bet,* he thought.

"Look, all's I know is what he tol' me, they're comin' today and they know there's hay to be put in an' they're gonna help. Now what you want me to do?"

Bob took a step back and cocked his head sideways. *Jesus Christ. Merle askin' me what I want him to do? Somethin's really wrong here. What's gonna happen next, fairies comin' to do the milkin'?*

Merle was still studying him, awaiting a response. Bob caught an apparently humble look in his eyes. It scared him. It made him suspicious.

"Uh, I was thinkin' about whether it'd be okay to mow the Old Woods lot. Whaddaya think?" Bob baited.

Now it was Merle's turn to be suspicious. He chewed more slowly and spat a sickly stream of tobacco juice that caught and lingered on his chin stubble. He wiped it off thoughtfully.

"Might rain tomorra," he said to his work boots.

Bob waited, letting him play out more of the line. Merle couldn't bear to lift his eyes to meet Bob's.

"Yeah, it might," Bob offered.

"Then again," Merle began, looking past the bottom end of the driveway toward the cloudless western horizon, "might not."

"Well, what's it . . ." Bob jumped in. He almost lost control, jerking the line before the hook was in place to catch flesh. Merle turned to meet his gaze, calm. Collected.

He wanted to be right, he needed it. Tom was coming and Merle couldn't stand to be shown up and belittled with Tom there. *Please, God,* he prayed to himself, *show me how to know what to do.* He weighed the alternatives. If they cut hay and it rained, it would turn bad. If they didn't cut and it didn't rain, they would miss the chance to get more hay in before it could be spoiled.

Bob started to slack his jaw, the way he did when he was full of himself, thinking he had someone stumped. Merle felt like he'd been seeing that look all his life. He hated it.

"Think it's gonna rain soon. Already got a lotta hay down. Wouldn't cut any more," Merle answered. He felt the sky darken cloudlessly.

Bob saw it, too, but pretended he didn't. "Thought you might think so." For the briefest moment he contemplated letting Merle's decision stand.

Merle saw the hesitation; a warmth filled his chest. Something behind his eyes told him he was right.

"Can't get hay in unless it's down. Don't look like rain to me." Bob felt a sudden rush of adrenaline, then it dropped away from him. "Whyn'tcha rake the Alfalfa Hill, an' I'll mow."

"Okay. Want me to use the Farmall?"

"Yeah, all right. Go ahead." Merle usually despised the Farmall, the oldest tractor Bob had, his father's tractor. "Just be careful goin' down the hill. That clutch slips out, ya know."

Merle pursed his lips and shook his head. "Yeah, I think I know," he grumbled.

*Same old Merle. Back to his old self,* Bob thought with relief.

Tom and his family turned into the yard in their big Buick at eleven-thirty, just in time for Doris to help Edna finish getting dinner on the table. Jeanine sat in the shade of the double maples out front, watching the baby crawl around looking for ants to sit on.

"C'mon, Rusty. Let's see what yer Uncle Bob's up to," Tom said. He always felt obliged to lead his son around the farm to find something to engage him. Tom wanted him to know why it was a special place. He never had come close to succeeding. Tom wondered why he even bothered anymore. So did Rusty.

Gerry was almost finished raking the hay lot nearest Molshoc's. Rusty thought he wanted to go ride around the lot with him, but was too listless to say anything about it.

Bob had begun putting a load on the wagon so it would be put in the mow right after dinner, a sure sign there was a lot of hay down. As Tom and his son kept pace alongside the wagon, dust from the bales showered them each time the kicker slammed them against the rack. Rusty couldn't believe they were even there, but Tom was getting antsy to join in somehow. Finally he climbed up over the side, hefting the bales to see if the tension was right, feeling between the wads of the bales for signs they might be too wet or green. Bob looked back from the tractor and grinned, holding his forearm level with index finger pointing toward the ground, swirling it clockwise, questioning.

Tom eased himself over the front of the rack, jumped to the ground, and quick-walked to the baler chute. Two jerking turns on the tension handles and the bales would be perfect.

Bob admired Tom's grace with the machinery, so confident and assured. It seemed the wagon eased him back on. Catching the next four bales, Tom built a stack in front to hold the last bales once the load was full, and gave Bob the okay sign. This time he swung around to the side of the rack from the front and climbed easily to the ground in step with Rusty.

Tom and Rusty were on the knoll at the rear end of the hayfield, atop which they could see Gerry making the last figure-eight turns that finished up the raking. He unhitched the rake and headed straight across toward them near the gate.

"Hi, Uncle Tom. How you doin', Russ? Wanna help me hitch up the wagon?"

"Yeah, okay. You comin', Dad?" Rusty mumbled.

"Naw, go ahead. I'm stayin' here in case Bob needs some help." *Huh, Gerry seems okay to me,* Tom thought. *Wonder what Merle was talkin' about.*

He studied the scene from the vantage point on the knoll, unable to find fault. The New Holland was running like a charm, each bale perfectly knotted. He admired the technique Bob had developed for adjusting the kicker direction and speed, placing the bales so neatly that he could really fill up the wagon. *Beats pilin' 'em,* he thought. He looked farther past the baler, on up the hill that bordered Molshoc's and to the southeast, where Merle was raking the hay on the Alfalfa Hill. At the same moment Merle saw him from the tractor and began to wave broadly to catch his attention. Tom waved back, thought about going over to ride with him, then thought better of it.

Bob was rounding the near corner of the cutting when a bale shot up and skittered along the length of the topside rail of the wagon. He eased in the clutch of the tractor, leaning, trying to will it into the wagon. It teetered and rocked, and balanced impossibly on its end before it gave in to the inevitability of the day.

Tom was fairly dancing along with the bale, body-Englishing it into place. They caught each other's eyes, laughing out loud. Nothing could go wrong today.

Rusty and Gerry came back with the empty wagon, to switch with the full one on Bob's next turn.

"So they're okay, huh?" Bob asked Tom.

"Couldn't be better. Nice and square, dry as a bone. Be easy to pile an' walk on in the mow."

"Not that you'd know much about that," Bob jabbed reflexively.

Tom was silent, expressionless.

"I mean, uh, anymore. Hey, how's it goin?' " Bob covered clumsily. He tried his best to grin.

Tom finally relented. " 'Bout the same. Lenny's still in charge, still takin' most of the money for sittin' on his ass. It's still Adventnor Construction, I still do most o' the work." They fell silent again.

They stared at each other awkwardly for a moment. Rusty had hitched up the loaded wagon for Gerry, and they were headed back to the mow. Gerry was riding the clutch on the Ford, creeping along to give his Uncle Tom a ride.

" 'Bout time for dinner, Bob, ya know," Tom said.

"Yeah, I know, but we got so much hay down," Bob sighed.

"Well, go on up, then. I'll bale this load and eat later."

"Naw. You just got here, Tom."

"Aw, bullshit. I ate real late. Your ass has been bouncing around on that tractor seat since the dew's been off. C'mon," he grinned, "give the tractor a break."

"Why, you horseball. I'm bettin' we'll hafta spend the rest of the afternoon fixin' the baler after you get through with it, but go ahead." Bob slipped the power takeoff out of gear and jiggled the gearshift to neutral. "But soon's I'm done eatin', I'm comin' back to bale," he continued. "I know a hay hook with your name on it."

Tom shrugged good-naturedly and climbed up on the tractor. He took a deep breath, held it for a few seconds, and let it go. Then he gingerly eased in the clutch, shifted the power takeoff into gear, and pulled the gearshift into second. The baler hummed into its rocking motion just before the tractor started forward.

Bob watched the whole routine anxiously. When Tom got around the first turn uneventfully, he walked up the road to the house, looking forward to one of Edna's hot meals.

Thunder was different. The other cows all could see it. They thought it might be something special about her calf, though no one was sure.

And of course no one talked about it.

Thunder set out for the edge of the woods as soon as she was let out from morning milking. She knew from experience with her second calf that the Old Homestead was not a safe place, so she plunged deep into the woods near the river, on the extreme southern end of the meadow.

She was barely allowing herself a moment's rest as she climbed each ravine along the way. This calf seemed ready, it wanted to come quickly. And when it came, it wanted to be deep in the woods and to grow up wild. Thunder was more than happy to make that happen.

She reached the clearing used for the Gathering, and began to feel chills. There was a pungent sweetness in the air, a lightness that made breathing easier. She paused to drink it in and taste the energy there. Thunder did not know that it was from the Gathering, but she did feel overwhelmed. She knew there was something very strong here, stronger than herself, than the Order, perhaps even stronger than the humans.

By strict custom, any one sister was not to linger in the place of Gathering, but the voice soothed her. She needed for it to be all right, because she could not get herself to leave.

She still fretted superstitiously that she might be undermining the Order. But it was simply too beautiful, and she was too weak.

"Fine meal, Mother," Bob pronounced, all too conspicuously setting an example for everyone else at the table. Gerry was embarrassed that he would have to be reproached into complimenting the meal. It was wonderful.

Fresh cucumbers and string beans from the garden. Grilled hamburgers and round steak with poor man's gravy over boiled potatoes. The first harvest of blackcaps, with milk and sugar, for dessert. Tom's family was as impressed with the clarity and sweetness of the water from the spring-fed well as they were with the food.

Rusty especially liked the jelly rolls Edna had made. They had been intended to be an enticement for Renee to come home, but she had not taken the bait.

Edna appreciated Doris's help in the kitchen, and her trying to fill the void left by Renee's distance, but it was more than another pair of hands that she needed.

Renee had always been Edna's sense of balance. Bob could have his hopes and expectations for Gerry, but that would be all right only so long as Edna had Renee.

Gerry was more starved for the company that Rusty provided. It was so unusual to have anyone different help with the haying, or even come to visit.

"Doris, this is the best meal we've had here in such a long time. Thanks for showin' Edna the ropes," Bob kidded.

"Oh, Bob. You know that I really didn't do anything. Edna's such a wonderful cook," Doris said.

Edna's frown evaporated into a smile. *At least someone can see what you don't,* she thought toward Bob.

"Well, I bet she 'preciated the help, didn't ya, Edna?" Bob continued.

"Sure I did. Doris did the blackcaps and asked for the poor man's gravy. Actually," Edna added, "didn't you say that Tom asked for the gravy?"

"Uh, yeah. He did," Doris answered. "He talks a lot about how good your cooking is." She seemed embarrassed.

"Well, don't let him get you ta thinkin' bad about yourself," Edna heard herself say.

Everyone looked over at her, surprised.

"Whaddaya mean?" Bob said in that blustery way that showed he was fishing for assurance.

"Well, talkin' bad about someone's cookin' might make 'em feel bad about themselves, is all I'm sayin'."

"How do you know?" Bob persisted.

"Some men do that, ya know," Edna replied, with just the trace of a smile.

"Don't worry, Bob. She couldn't be talkin' about you," Merle offered. He looked across the table at Gerry and Rusty, winked extravagantly, and added, "Edna wouldn't let ya."

"Yeah, you think so, do ya." Bob suspected he was being picked on, and didn't like it.

"Day-do," the baby said.

"What's that, honey?" Doris leaned over toward Clairie. "What'd you say?"

"Day-do. *Day*-do."

"Oh, po-*ta*-toes. Did you hear that, Edna?"

"Sure I did. She's a good talker."

"How's baseball goin', Ger?" Rusty asked shyly.

"Okay, I guess. Just Babe Ruth now."

"Uh-hem. Hey, Merle. Gonna be done with that goddam gravy anytime today?" Bob asked, blustering for attention.

"Gay-be. Ga-da gay-be."

"Oh no, honey," Doris blushed. "Don't say that."

"*Gay*-be. Ga-da *gay*-be."

Rusty looked at Gerry for guidance. Gerry had heard the baby in the midst of a large gulp of milk, which he was desperately trying to swallow.

Rusty knew about the no-monkeying-around rule at his Uncle Bob's table, so he didn't make a sound. Instead, he caught Gerry's eye before folding a huge piece of Edna's marble cake into his mouth.

Tears were forming in the corners of Gerry's eyes, his jaws clamped closed. Jeanine saw Gerry's eyes start to bulge, and she crossed hers in return.

Bob wore the sternest expression he could muster. Doris was holding her breath, her eyes cast downward at her plate.

*"Ga-da gay-be,"* Clairie insisted, returning Merle's grin.

Gerry exploded, milk shooting out his nose. He coughed and laughed until he couldn't breathe. Rusty fell over; even Bob had to laugh. He started to say something else, but everybody was laughing so hard now that no one was listening.

It took Doris's attention to the baby's crying to get them to stop.

The screen door yawned open and Tom strode in.

"What's the joke?"

"Bob's teachin' the baby some new words," Merle said.

"Well, Jesus Christ, Tom," Bob started to say.

Everyone looked at the baby.

"Edna's gonna hafta start layin' down the law, Bob," Tom said.

"That's right," Merle said, "so ya better siddown 'n' eat before she decides ya shouldn't get any dinner."

"Then don't argue with her," Tom said, "at least until I'm done eatin'."

"Now you just might get something special for supper," Edna promised.

"Get back to work, boys. I'm earnin' my dessert," Tom announced.

"So how'd it go, anyway?" Bob asked suspiciously.

"How else could it go? Like a charm."

*God. He must not know what it's like here,* Gerry thought.

"Are you kiddin'?" Merle laughed. "If it weren't for bad luck, Bob wouldn't have none."

"That's right," Bob said.

"Get outta here. You were lucky. You got this place."

"Well, sometimes that don't feel lucky," Bob said quietly.

"Ain't no place that ever does, all the time," Tom said.

"Well, I know that. Jesus, just be quiet and eat your dinner. The boys can maybe put the first wagon in by themselves, if Merle unloads."

"Sounds good ta me," Tom said, around a mouthful of potatoes and gravy.

Merle, Gerry, and Rusty left to put the first load of hay in the mow. Gerry waited for Rusty to climb up the elevators before he turned them on. First the extension elevator in the mow rattled to life, and then came the throbbing hum of the stationary one. Merle kicked in the clutch. The paddles began to screech and lurch upward.

Rusty was sixteen, almost two years younger than Gerry. Perhaps that was why he looked up to Gerry, studied and mimicked his every move. He had no love for the farm, but his father did. So, despite himself, he had a desire to be part of it.

Bob had snickered at Merle's suggestion that Rusty could be a good summer hand. "What's he know about anything to do with farmin'?"

"Well, he's real strong, Doris says. He's got lotsa muscles," Merle offered.

"Like teats on a boar hog, if he ain't workin'. What's he use 'em for, anyway?"

Merle thought for a moment. "Geez, I dunno, Bob. But give 'im a chance, will ya? What could it hurt?"

"Got enough people around here that don't know what they're doin', or what they want. Can't have people gettin' in the way."

"Well, they're gonna be in the mow, an' you're out on the tractor. Don't worry about the pilin', we'll take care of it."

"All right," Bob had said reluctantly. But now that he was alone on the tractor steering the baler around the hayfield, his attention drifted back to worry about what was happening in the mow.

* * *

Tom had come down to help unload and chased Merle up into the mow, where Gerry and Rusty toyed with his poor piling skills. Gerry winked at Rusty, then let three or four bales pass him by, piling up at the end of the elevator where Merle was frantically trying to figure out how to fit the bales in without leaving a hole.

"C'mon now. Jesus. Take some bales, will ya?" Merle begged.

"Oh, all right," Gerry relented. "Come on up here and start a new tier. I'll finish filling that hole."

Merle watched Gerry grab six successive bales and jam them into place beneath the end of the elevator, providing a flooring upon which to walk when piling the next tier. He was envious of the confidence that was so evident in how Gerry worked.

Just then a bale dropped off the end, and bounced back up under the chain. Gerry sweep-kicked it out, then jammed it into the last space on that tier. Rusty thought it was like seeing Brooks Robinson backhanding a line drive in foul territory before firing it across to first—it was that natural, that beautiful.

*He must really get a kick outta doin' this,* Merle thought. *He's so good at it.*

*God, I hate this. This sucks out loud,* Gerry almost whispered, almost a mantra. *I wish I had some goddam way to get outta here.*

"Doris, will you help me with something? Oh, and Jeanine, I got a special job for you, if you'd like to help," Edna asked. The weather had been so warm and humid the last several days that everyone had been especially on edge. When Tom's family came to help, it had given her an idea about how to break through the oppressive heat and tension.

"Well, sure, I'll help," Doris said timidly. "Jeanine, honey?" she whined. "Could you be a good girl and give us a hand?"

"With what?" Jeanine shot back, getting primed to be surly.

"I need you to kill some bugs for me," Edna said. "Do you think you can do it?" She was gambling that the challenge to this thirteen-year-old would work as well as it used to on Renee, when she was that age.

"Killing bugs. How?" Jeanine asked.

"With a spray gun, from down at the barn."

"Kills Bugs Dead," Jeanine mimicked. "I can do that."

"Good. I'll get the spray gun for you. Doris, let's set up some fans, then go to the store for something for supper," Edna said.

Edna had decided that if there was a way she could complete making the day perfect, she would do it, so she had put Jeanine and Doris to work getting the bedrooms cooled and cleared of mosquitoes. And she had set about to gather all of the fixings for the best supper the men could hope to come home to.

Doris was unusually quiet. Not as if she had nothing to say, but as if she had too much and didn't know how to say her thoughts out loud.

She seemed anxious and irritated. The irritable part wasn't surprising to Edna, because she'd felt it all along as the central part of Doris's personality. In fact, while Bob had wondered what Tom had seen in her, because she was a city girl with no feeling for growing up on a farm, Edna had chalked it up to the balance that happens in many marriages. Tom was easygoing and needed the harder edge that Doris provided. Doris had grated on Bob's nerves earlier, especially very early in her marriage to Bob's brother.

And she had gotten on Edna's nerves, too, but now she seemed to have lost her sense of direction, that edge. *Maybe Jeanine's sucked it out of her,* Edna thought.

Jeanine used to be a sweet kid, but had entered puberty with a fury.

She couldn't figure out who Rusty was taking after. He seemed to be sullen most of the time, which was unlike anybody in his family. But the more sullen he became, it seemed the more angry Jeanine was, and the more withdrawn their mother.

Doris had sighed as they were mixing Kool-Aid for the men to drink when they came out of the mow. She sighed again when they went into town to get some special food for supper.

When they got to the garden and were pulling more string beans and picking leaf lettuce, she paused for a moment, put her hands on her hips, drew in a breath; then, the largest sigh of all.

*I wish she would just get it over with,* Edna thought. *Whatever it is she wants to get off her chest, I wish she'd just say it. She's driving me crazy.*

"Is there anything else you can think of that Tom or Rusty might like to have for supper?" Edna asked, hoping she could somehow break the silence.

"Tom doesn't know what he wants, Edna," Doris replied wearily.

"Well, we can fix him a couple of different things, if that's what he wants."

"No, no. That's not it, Edna. He doesn't know what he wants to do with me, the kids."

*Oh, Lord,* Edna thought, *so that's what the problem is. What can I possibly say?*

"Um, hmm," Edna said, trying to buy time.

Doris was studying her, angrily. *I should have known she'd never help me. It's because I don't fit in. I'm not a farmer,* she thought.

*What's wrong with Tom? She's never done anything to displease him, except try to give him some ambition. And the kids,* Edna thought. *I can't believe he's thinking about leaving them.*

Edna could not bear the avoidance of Doris's eyes. She looked over her shoulder, and up at her sister-in-law.

"I don't know what to say."

Doris felt about ready to explode.

"I'm sorry," Edna finished. She turned back to the row of lettuce, but couldn't get her hands to work. She rose and turned back around.

Doris had wanted to scream at Edna, for being so stoic, so aloof, so much the kind of person her husband thought he wanted to be with, to mother him.

Edna reached out to hold on to a stalk of corn. The rough edges of the leaves kept her upright, facing Doris, though still unable to meet her eyes. It restored the coldness she needed to face this, the coldness she had watched engulf her mother after her father had died.

"Bob's gone through that," she said. *And so have I.* This last was swallowed before it was voiced.

Doris's jaw was clamped shut. Her scalded heart was tearing through her ribs.

"I . . . can't . . . help . . . him," she struggled out.

Edna's awkwardness gave way. "You're right."

"So what am I supposed to do?" Doris demanded.

"Only what you can do," Edna said quietly. "Only what you have to do."

"What's that mean? How do I know what it is I'm supposed to do?"

"I can only tell you what happens with me. Whenever things are out of control, I work harder. It doesn't always give me the answer I want, but it makes me feel like I've done all that I could do."

"But what if that isn't enough?" Doris said, crying now.

"Then . . . then, it just isn't." Edna let loose her grasp of the cornstalk, and agonized her hand toward Doris's right shoulder. She started as Doris's heat surged through her fingers. Her eyes opened to their purpose.

*We can only try to give them what they think they need,* she thought. "Now . . . I . . . still want to give Bob and Gerry this day. No, I want to give 'em all this day," she said out loud, turning Doris back toward the house. "But there's no reason why we can't give ourselves this day, too, while we're at it."

Together they put in over thirteen hundred bales, clearing two and a half fields. Gerry, Tom, and Merle took turns unloading and driving the empty wagons to be exchanged with loaded ones. So much hay was being put in that they had to crank up the elevator three times and heave it in toward the barn. A light breeze from the west cut the heat and humidity as they piled.

Merle was listening all day to the screeching and clattering of the elevators, for any signs of trouble. He longed for the chance to show Tom what he could do with the machinery, but today it would not let him.

Gerry started milking after the eleventh load, and Rusty stayed to hang out in the barn and talk. Gerry knew that Thunder must be off freshening someplace as soon as he saw her empty stanchion.

"Hey, Rusty. Ya wanna go look for a cow for me? I think she's probably freshenin'."

"Ya mean she's havin' a calf?"

"Yeah."

"Then why isn't she up here in the barn, so you can help her have the calf?"

Gerry looked at him for a moment, to see if he was really that dumb. Rusty looked back with a straight face.

"Whaddaya mean? Cows go off 'n' hide when they're 'bout to freshen. They don't go check in at no hospitals."

"Well how am I supposed to know what the dumb things do?"

"They're animals, Russ. Animals. *They* don't even know what they're doin'."

"Right. So how am I s'posed to know?"

"Oh, I guess you're right. You wouldn' know anything, coming from the city."

"No, not about farm animals an' breedin'."

"Hey, watch it. I don't like that shit," Gerry said, eyes narrowing. "And neither do the cows. They get to worryin' that a guy like you'll wanna get himself broke in on one of 'em."

"Yeah, well . . . you . . . you won't catch me doin' nothin' you farm boys do," was the best Rusty could muster in reply.

"Just watch that, I mean it," Gerry said. "Hey, you gonna go look for the cow, or you thinkin' you'll find some city poodle for a girlfriend instead?"

"I'm goin', I'm goin'," Rusty answered. "Where'm I s'posed to look, anyway, your bedroom?"

"Naw, don't start that again. First look on the road side of the meadow, an' don't forget to look real careful, because the cows hide their calves an' they won't make a sound. Got it?"

"Yeah. But who's gonna unload the wagons?"

"Don't worry about that. They might be done soon, and my father will unload 'em. Just get goin'!"

Young Russ picked his way across the dried mud of the barnyard, through fresh splatters of manure, and climbed between the strands of the fence.

The last glimpse Gerry caught of him, he was skirting to the left around the Old Homestead, where Calvin had hidden three years before.

"Merle, whyn'tcha rake in the outside windrow while I help Bob put the twine in," Tom said.

"Don'tcha wanna change the wagons first?"

"Nah. You know Bob never changes 'em till they're full. Besides, if I pile this one, we can probably get it all on this load."

"Yeah, prob'ly." Merle fired up the Farmall to kick in the outside windrow on the Alfalfa Hill. He eased the tractor and rake counterclockwise around the hayfield, navigating along the stone wall under the tree line. Merle saw Grampa's woodchuck hole up on the hill inside of the windrow just before he squared for the turn. He steered well around it.

*Right over left, left over right,* Tom was struggling to remember.

If he tied a granny knot instead of a square one to connect the new bale of twine, it might break the spell of good luck with the baler. He pushed the knot together, then pulled it taut again. *There, that looks all right.*

Bob grinned at him. Three more passes in the middle and the outside windrow, and they would be all done.

Tom pulled himself up through the open side door of the wagon and began to toss the bales into more orderly piles. Bob cruised the tractor, baler, and wagon back and forth across the center of the hayfield, then swung onward to the last windrow. Merle had just managed to unhook the rake and hook up the last empty wagon. He watched from the far end of the lot as the baler and wagon rounded the corner up on the hill, when the front wagon wheel found the woodchuck hole and tipped over the whole load.

Bob was frozen in place on the tractor, horrified, as the wagon rack rocked far to the right, hesitated an instant, then rolled completely off the carriage onto its side.

*I can't believe I gave this up,* Tom had been thinking. *This farm coulda been mine. Then Russ 'n' Jeanine and Clairie woulda grown up safe, like I did. An' Doris woulda been happy takin' care of all of us. . . . The bastard, he thought. I wouldn't hafta have nothin' to do with Adventnor. I do mosta the work, anyway, he's just a front. A big-shot engineer. Construction work stinks. Here I coulda been my own boss all these years. The bastard.*

*This is perfect,* Bob had been thinking. *This is the reason why I stayed on. Don't seem like nothin' can go wrong today.*

*Just goes to show, there ain't nothin' we can't do, when we're all together,* Merle, the youngest brother, had thought.

He had the best vantage point, from the far end of the lot, of what happened. Tom had spied the woodchuck hole just before the wagon wheel found it, and had stepped back away from the door, giving the weight of his body to balance the load on the carriage. He leaned hard to the left as the rack tipped, then held steady through the hesitation.

The bales began to shift and roll, fifty pounds at a time, all toward the small hole in the earth. Against Tom's will, and Bob's, and Merle's.

Tom could feel a bale at his back as he launched toward the side door, running in his long, loping stride. He had ducked under the rough boards of the doorway just as the rack uncoupled itself from the carriage.

Merle felt as if he were watching a Harold Lloyd movie, seeing his brother running out the doorway and escaping the avalanche of bales while the hay rack smashed to the ground.

Bob jammed the power takeoff out of gear and shut the tractor off still in gear, to keep it from rolling down the hill. He could not see around the edge of the fallen rack. He was afraid to move.

Merle had the Farmall in road gear, bouncing up and down on the seat as he raced across the lot. Bob saw him grinning, laughing like a madman. He wanted to kill Merle then.

"Jesus, oh, Jesus," Bob wailed, after he got back to the overturned wagon. He started pulling bales away in every direction, yet finding no trace of Tom. "I knew it couldn't go all right. Jesus!"

"Looks okay to me. Nothin's broken. We can set that rack right back on the frame."

"Goddamm it, Merle! Tom was on the wagon! He's underneath the wagon!" Bob screamed.

"Whaddaya talkin' about?" he heard Tom say. "I'm okay."

"Then where the hell are ya?" Bob was frantic.

"Around here. C'mere."

Bob walked around the back of the spilled hay to find Tom inspecting the wagon carriage. Merle pulled up on the tractor, still laughing.

"Didn't bend the tongue, or a bit of the frame. Didn't even break a board on the rack's far as I can see. You are a lucky son of a bitch, Bob."

"You shoulda seen yourself, Tommy. Wish I had a picture. Looked like you was in one o' them old movies. Just stepped out through the door and kept on movin'," Merle laughed.

"An' you ain't got a scratch on ya, I suppose," Bob asked.

Tom shook his head and grinned.

"Then I ain't the only one with good luck. Jesus!"

Merle retold the story of the wagon tipping over five times as they loaded the fallen bales onto the empty wagon, each time with Bob more frantic and himself more omniscient about the outcome. They were able to heave the rack back in place upon the carriage and eased it out and around the woodchuck hole to finish the baling, this time with an empty wagon that was unlikely to tip over.

*Be nice if that goddam dog could get ridda some of these son-of-a-bitchin' woodchucks,* Bob thought.

He didn't know that Grampa already had been ambushed and killed by King and Scout, weeks before he even had started haying.

"Let's unload the rest of these after we eat," Bob had shouted over his shoulder to Tom as they drove the wagons up to the barn. *Then to-morrow,* he gloated to himself, *we'll put in that Old Woods lot that Merle was afraid to mow.*

"Sounds good to me."

Merle steered the full wagon up to the elevator and parked it. Even though they all could hear the vacuum pump still on, they walked up to the kitchen-porch steps. Tom turned around for a moment to survey the farm stretching away to the southern horizon, hauling in a breath of warm, humid air.

"Hey, what the hell's Rusty doin' out there?" he asked.

"Where?"

"By the Old Homestead. Wonder what's goin' on?"

"Aw, Jesus. Thunder probably didn't come up for milkin'. Guess I better go look for her. Merle, can you help Gerry finish up?"

"Yeah." *It figures,* Merle thought. Although he had been his mother's favorite, he never felt that he had seen the look of recognition in his brothers' eyes that said family.

"I'll go with ya," Tom offered. "She might not have had the calf."

"Okay, thanks." Bob stepped one work shoe into the kitchen. "Edna, we got a cow that's ready to freshen to go look for. Me 'n' Tom might be late for supper."

He thought he heard "Okay" or "Uh-huh," but he wasn't really listening. When he slammed the kitchen door closed, Edna surveyed the table of almost-ready food and thought, *All our work, going to waste.*

"So, you're looking for Thunder or her calf?" Bob asked when he got within shouting range of Rusty.

"Uh, both, I guess. The cow didn't come up to the barn."

"Where've you looked already?" Tom asked, focusing in.

Rusty dropped his eyes to a patch of orchard grass in front of him. "Over that way," he said, sweeping his right arm toward the woods in the eastern end of the meadow.

"Did you walk through all of the Old Homestead?"

"Yeah, I think so."

Tom and Bob looked at each other in silence. They'd known before they started out that Thunder was probably in the southwest woods, but each had been hoping they would not have to go in after her.

"Uh, you can go back up an' help Gerry finish milkin', if you like," Bob said.

"Okay," Rusty mumbled, disinterestedly.

"Well, let's start up by Little Rapids," Tom said, pointing toward the northernmost strip of river-edge woods in the pasture.

"Yup," Bob replied, in unspoken agreement that they would cover all the other possible hiding places before checking near the power line, which he could not know was also the place of Gathering.

They combed through the trees along the river edge southward, about thirty feet apart most of the time, lost in their own thoughts.

*This is the way it ought to be,* Tom thought to himself. *If I had my own place, some land, I'd be okay.* Tom's resentment of his job had been growing for so long, his family had forgotten what he was like when he was happy.

*Wish I had this much help every day,* Bob thought, and then he remembered Renee's abandonment of the farm and Gerry's dreams of escape.

*Looks like I'm headed in the opposite direction, though.*

The woods narrowed near the swimming hole so that they closed in next to each other. The silence was becoming unbearable, but neither could pierce the tension of the other's thoughts.

The baby Clairie had been an accident, trapping both Tom and Doris in a marriage that had lost its life. Tom refused to look at it that way, always blaming it on his job and his boss, and on living in a suburb of Syracuse.

*Those people who talk about good money bein' all you need are just foolin' themselves,* he thought.

Farther south, they reached the fishing hole. Half of the circle of stones were still in place for the fire, like jack-o'-lantern teeth.

Tom broke the silence. "Remember when you caught that big ol' bullhead?" he chuckled.

"Yeah. Ya mean the one that horned me up so bad?"

"Yeah. He was a sonuvabitch gettin' off the hook."

"Tell me about it. An' you wanted me to throw him back."

" 'Cause he was so old."

"Didn't make no difference."

"Somethin' lives that long, it's a shame it has to die."

"Mebbe so, but I had enough work an' blood in him."

"Yeah, I guess."

They fell silent again, for a moment.

"But ya know," Tom continued, "you never would let anybody tell you what to do. Not even Mother and Dad."

Bob blushed slightly, embarrassed and proud. "Yeah, somebody hadda give 'em grief."

"Yup."

"And you always did everything right."

"Whaddaya mean? Don't ya remember riding the yearling heifers?"

"Hell, yeah. That was fun, wasn't it?"

"Yeah, until Dad caught us."

"About time you got caught for somethin'. Seemed like I allus was holdin' the bag."

"Whu-ut? Not for anything you didn't deserve."

"Yeah, bullshit. You were real good at givin' me credit for ideas of yours when they got us in trouble."

Tom grinned. "Well, maybe just a little bit."

"At last, you'll admit somethin'. I thought I'd never live to see the day."

"Oh, you're so full of shit," Tom joked back.

"Jesus, Bob," he gasped. "Look at her. She's half dead."

They had just stumbled into a clearing, where Thunder had delivered her calf. She was also delivering the uterus it had grown in.

"Ohmigod, ohmigod," Tom kept repeating.

"Don't stand there, gimme a hand," Bob shouted, already hefting the portion of Thunder's womb that had detached. "An' be careful not to get your fingernails into her insides, 'cause it'll give her an infection, sure as shit."

Thunder was in shock. She had been on her feet through the whole delivery and had stood stock still when she began to cast her wethers. Their only chance for saving her life depended upon her staying in shock, standing absolutely still.

"Tom, you gotta hold this while I try to put it back inside her.

Damn," Bob said softly, "I wish we'd had Rusty come with us, or Merle."

"So do I, right now." Tom was stung by the thought that Bob didn't think his city brother could handle this situation. "You just get goin'," he shot back.

"There's no way to get this to stay in place," Bob worried. "We'll just hafta hope it sticks."

"What . . ." Tom puffed, straining under the weight. "What in *hell* coulda caused this, anyway?"

"Can'tcha see her cleanin's didn't come out right?"

"Yeah . . . I can see that . . . but *why* didn't they come out right?

"Jesus, who knows? I never had a cow do this before."

"Then how come," Tom panted, "you know what it is?"

"Grenny Teller," Bob puffed back, then wiped the sweat from his forehead with the back of his hand. "He tol' me there's a lotta farmers havin' troubles with their cows freshenin' . . . and havin' stillborns . . . not carryin' to term . . . lotta shit." For a moment the weight of it all made Bob dizzy. Then he focused on Tom's face, red from straining to hold up Thunder's insides, and got back to work.

"But . . . why . . . is . . . it . . . happenin'?" Tom gasped.

"I don't *know!* Jesus!" Bob turned his head away, to let sweat roll around his eyebrows, past his eyes. "Can'tcha hear the goddam lines humming? It's the power lines . . . or this nuclear stuff . . . it's no good. . . ."

Tom cocked his head to listen, could hear nothing. "Whaddaya mean . . . humming?"

"The wires . . . the power lines . . . Jesus."

"I . . . can't . . . hear . . . nothin'."

Bob started to mutter a reply, then waited, listening, holding his breath. There wasn't a sound from the power lines.

"Neither can I . . . right now . . . maybe it's just . . . this spot."

Together they lifted the last of her wethers into Thunder. Bob held the mouth of her womb closed with his hands.

"I don't know what ta do now, Tom."

"Can she move, d'ya think?"

"I don't wanna try it. Can you go up an' have Edna call Doc Powell? Ask him if he can come out here to take a look at her."

"Sure. You gonna stay here till he comes?"

"Yeah. Hey, is the calf all right?"

"Yup. Breathin' okay, waitin' to get licked off."

"Then push it around in front of her, maybe that'll help."

Tom squeezed the calf's tailbone to get it on its feet, and backed it around in front of Thunder.

"She isn't doin' nothing yet," Tom said.

"That's okay. Just get goin'. Maybe she'll come around later."

"All right."

By the time he reached the edge of the clearing, Tom could hear the humming and snapping of the wires.

"Do you suppose they couldn't find her?" Charlotte asked Young Smitty. She was snatching up the occasional bites of clover when she could, but was really more excited to find out about what had happened to Thunder.

"I doubt it. Farmer Bob wasn't in the barn at all during milking. And that other boy, that friend of Gerry's, was supposed to be looking for her."

"He don't look like he could find his way around a fence post," White Brat scoffed. "They're safe if he was the only one on the job."

"What's that down by the woods?" Smitty asked.

A strange truck was emerging from the trees, bounding in the ruts of the logging road. It was unfamiliar, yet not completely strange. By the time it got to the gate past the Old Homestead, White Brat had recognized it as Doc Powell's.

"She's sick, Smitty, she's sick," Charlotte said. "I just knew something was wrong."

"Yeah, somethin' musta gone bad," White Brat agreed.

"You sound like that's good," Charlotte said accusingly.

"Whaddaya mean?" White Brat shot back, in mock hurt.

"You sounded like you think it's good if something is wrong with Thunder."

"I did not."

"It sounded that way to me, too," Young Smitty added. "So what have you got against her? Huh? Tell us!" Charlotte persisted.

"I ain't got nothin' against her. It ain't personal."

"Then what is the problem?"

White Brat moved off away from the rest of them, who were all working their way toward the woods.

Charlotte and Young Smitty were forced to follow.

"What is your problem?" Charlotte persisted. "I wanted to go see what happened."

White Brat checked their distance from the rest of the herd, judging it to be safe. "I don't like the way she's so pushy."

Charlotte couldn't suppress a laugh.

"What do you mean?"

"Ya know what I mean. Pushy. Bossin' people around."

Charlotte giggled again. Trying as hard as she could, Young Smitty could not chase the smile away from her eyes.

"Uh . . . how can I say this?" Charlotte began.

"Some of the sisters say that, uh . . . that, uh . . . you're a little that way," Young Smitty offered.

White Brat looked at both of them, full in the face, frustrated and pained.

"Don't you think I know that?" she said softly. "Do you think I'm stupid?"

"No, no, not at all," Charlotte replied. "Then, what's wrong with Thunder?"

"It's not her," White Brat said, in a lowered voice. "It's the Order."

She was staring into Young Smitty's eyes. She half expected her to turn her in, because Smitty was so important in the Order.

But Smitty was absolutely quiet.

"What are you saying?" Charlotte almost shouted.

"I'm saying that the Order is not helping us anymore," White Brat said, slowly and evenly.

"And what makes you say that? I don't believe it's true."

"Well, what good is it? What does it do for us?" White Brat demanded.

"It gives us a way of knowing where we stand. Especially when new cows come in, we know where we stand."

"Yeah, and then we're stuck there, forever."

"Not forever. You can move up."

"Only through the Order. Only by doin' stuff for them."

"Well, that makes sense, doesn't it?"

"Not if the Order is just as bad as Farmer Bob."

"What?"

"Don'tcha see? It divides us, just like he does. The Order sets up ranks and all that other garbage. We've got more certainty, but the Order doesn't stop anybody from bein' sent away. Not if that's what Farmer Bob wants. That's why I hate him."

"But it's better for the new cows. When they come, the Order gives them a way to get used to things here."

"Yeah, the Order's way."

"But we need it," Smitty said quietly. "We need the Order."

"For what?" White Brat shot back.

Smitty and Charlotte looked at each other.

"It helped them while John was . . . uh . . . not himself," Aretha offered. She gradually had grazed closer without their noticing.

"What do you know about it, Stubtail?" White Brat said, with the special meanness she reserved for Aretha.

"It did help them for a while, like when that Peanut sister disappeared," Aretha continued shyly. "But only for a while."

"Get the hell outta here," White Brat snarled.

"Wait a minute. What's she trying to say?" Smitty said. She and Charlotte had to glare White Brat into silence.

"Well, I . . . I . . . think that she's right. It's . . . it's not helping anymore."

White Brat was growing more angry. She was bitterly hateful of Aretha, from the moment that Aretha had tried to help her, to share her pain. Her meanness had become such a part of her that she could no longer distinguish between compassion and pity.

"So you agree with her?" Charlotte asked, incredulously.

"Yes, I do." Aretha's eyes seemed especially clear, her expression focused with incredible intensity.

"Then I guess I do, too," Smitty said. "But only if you'll accept her," she said, looking from White Brat to Aretha.

"You'll need me," Aretha said to White Brat.

"We'll all need each other."

Doc Powell had said that there was nothing more he could do for Thunder once he had sewed her up. She had licked off her calf, and was even grazing a little in this clearing. The shock was wearing off.

"It's a miracle, Bob. She looks like she might pull through," the vet had said. "She'll be better off if you leave her out with the calf tonight."

"Jesus, Doc, then how we gonna find the calf after it's been out overnight?"

"Just get her up to the barn tomorrow, when she's a little stronger. The cow won't even make it through the night if you try to move her now."

*Yes,* thought Thunder. *We'll have a Gathering.*

Moments after the humans left, the first sisters appeared at the edge of the clearing.

"There's got to be a Gathering," Thunder said. "My calf is in the wild." The more sisters who arrived, the more forcefully she repeated it.

*This is how we can renew the Order,* she thought.

Dutchess entered the place of Gathering with eager magnificence. The word had been traveling backward through the herd that the calf was still in the woods.

"We've got to have a Gathering," Thunder insisted. "My child has not been taken by the humans."

"So you were able to hide the calf from them?" Dutchess asked.

"Uh . . . no . . . I birthed her here."

"In the Gathering place?"

"Y-yeah. I couldn't get no further." Thunder was losing her strength and confidence rapidly.

"But the humans didn't find you?" Dutchess was extremely stern.

"No, no, yes, they did. They was here."

"The humans were here? And they let you stay? With the calf?" Dutchess asked suspiciously.

"Yeah." Thunder began to lower her head, in fear and shame.

"Then there ought to be a Gathering," Young Smitty interrupted. She and White Brat, Aretha, and Charlotte had just arrived, the last of the herd to reach the clearing.

"But the child is not really fresh. It has been touched by humans. They may have left it here on purpose," Dutchess protested.

"I think my mother would have wanted a Gathering," Young Smitty insisted. She knew she couldn't pull rank on Dutchess, but the fact that her mother had conducted the last Gathering would help.

"We should have a Gathering," Forty agreed. She had been eyeing Thunder's calf closely, and sensed something familiar.

"The doctrine is clear in this case," Dutchess said. "She was not supposed to be here, and the calf is not truly wild. I'm afraid . . ."

"I almost died," Thunder said quietly.

"What?" Dutchess said.

"I almost died," Thunder said, now more firmly.

"That settles it. She may have had a vision," Smitty trumped.

Dutchess surveyed the anxious faces around her, weighed the risk of enforcing the literal interpretation of the doctrine, and decided that she could not.

"With the first sign of moon," she said, officiously.

There seemed to be absolutely no air when the sliver of moon appeared through the gray overcast sky. No wind. No movement of any creature. A sustained pause of all life.

None of the sisters had moved far from the clearing since Dutchess had called for the Gathering, so they all were assembled in the circle in just a moment.

Forty was positioned to the left of Dutchess, in the place reserved for the mother of the last child of the Gathering. She could not take her eyes off the heifer calf in the center of the group, next to Thunder. Something about the eyes and the way the calf was sitting seemed familiar, but she could not place it.

"Mmmmmmmmmm." The low hum started to build, the voices of all the sisters reaching to meet each other. Dutchess was calling for the return of the Days of One.

The calf sat up on its back haunches, eyes shining, eager for the attention, as if it had been there before.

"We ask that this one remain wild . . ." Dutchess intoned. Forty began feeling the Gathering as a relived experience, right down to her connection with the calf.

". . . We ask that this child be the one to bring humans back. . . ."

Young Smitty and Charlotte waited until Dutchess was ready to begin the final prayer before interrupting.

"We need to hear one more sister before we're done," Smitty spoke up.

"What are you saying?" Dutchess huffed. "No one else speaks."

"We want to hear the blue sister speak," Charlotte said.

"No," Thunder commanded. "This is a Gathering, and my child

is the one who is chosen. You can just be quiet, or leave."

"We don't hafta listen to you," White Brat cut her off. "This is a Gathering. We all belong. This is got nothin' to do with the Order."

"But you are disrupting this Circle," Dutchess insisted. "You must stop. This is for Thunder, and her calf. Still in the wild. Don't forget, you wanted this Gathering."

"Yes, and we want another voice. Not for the Order, but for all of us."

"It's Calvin! It's my calf! Come back!" Forty started yelling.

"But your calf was sent away, long ago," Charlotte corrected.

"Yes, of course, but not the one you think. Not the last one, but the one born three grass seasons ago. The bull. The one at the last Gathering."

"No, you don't. This is my calf. I almost died," Thunder snapped.

"Yes, this one is your calf," Forty said. "But it was mine, at the last Gathering. This calf is the one, the same one."

"It's not gonna work," Thunder continued. "You're not gonna destroy the Order."

"To hell with the Order," White Brat shot back, nose to nose with Thunder.

"You have no right to interrupt this Gathering," Dutchess repeated.

"Yes, she does."

This was a new voice, not until then part of the argument. "What Farmer Bob had done to her was wrong. When John was, uh, sick, what Farmer Bob did was wrong." It was Bossy. No one had ever heard her question Farmer Bob before; everyone was hanging on her words.

"Let the sister speak," Bossy said, then was silent.

Aretha opened her mouth, but she was so terrified that at first nothing came forth. Then she saw a white bull in her mind and turned to Bossy. "Your father did care about you, more than anyone else."

Thunder tried to protest again.

"It is no use, child. The time has come for her to speak," Dutchess said, in a new, soothing tone. Then, for the whole congregation she spoke. "There is a legend of one that knows not only who we are, but who we have been, and who we are supposed to be. It is the Seer. We shall listen, for she may be the one." Dutchess nodded at Aretha, who at that moment regained her voice.

"The old understanding is past, it is forgotten," Aretha said, in a voice not entirely her own. "The humans have lost, as we have, the knowledge of who they are. So many many grandchildren's grandchildren ago, we all walked wild in the woods and meadows. But we, we traded our freedom for the security that humans offered. It is not their fault we bargained for security, and got insecurity." Her voice lowered, faltered, almost breaking. "We ate the grain and the hay, that was what we received in exchange for the fences. We accepted it then, and gave away our grace. We have forgotten our names."

The hush became deeper, as the heaviness of the air increased. It was as if the darkness of the sky became darker with her words.

"We cannot teach the humans, because they no longer listen. They do not see us as we are, cowkind.

"Now we can only try to hold the faith for both our kinds. That is the way back to the One."

There was a prolonged pause. Then Dutchess gave the closing prayer, and without prompting, they merged their voices into the "Mmmmmmmmmm." It was still building when John joined them in the clearing, completing the destruction of the Order. The wind came, and the thunder, rolling around and around them where they huddled together all night through the storm.

Edna already had shut down the fans and closed most of the windows before the nonstop crackling from the sky awakened Bob.

"Goddammit," he said to himself. "Merle was right."

He lay awake through the storm wondering why he ever was so foolish as to believe that things really could go his way.

## Chapter Twelve

# Bob

(1971)

Why can't I ever get any goddam peace?" Bob swore at himself, tossing and turning in bed.

He had not slept in three days, or at least he had not slept well. The familiar list of worries surfaced: the newly freshened cow coming down with milk fever; getting through the rest of haying season with the old equipment; the eight hundred bales of rotted hay from the Old Woods lot under a tarp, hay that he'd have to feed in the fall when the cows were still out on grass—eight hundred bales that he might be short in March or April; this new test for leukocytes in the milk; the boy not wanting to stay on the farm after school; their spraying pesticide along the power-line pasture.

But none of this was new. What was different, what was haunting him?

The calf from Thunder had been the start of it. His heart knew this, but his brain would not listen. Why had he not sent the calf off to auction? Why was he keeping it when the veal market was so bad?

It wasn't that Gerry much cared for the calf, even though he was raising it, because Gerry had lost all interest in the farm. Bob didn't want to think about what the real reason was, could never let anyone know, because it was crazy.

The eyes were familiar, reminding him so strongly of someone that he could not sell the calf until he found out who it was. And even though there was no way to make sense of it to Gerry or Edna or Renee, whom he had always told about the need to be practical and businesslike regarding calves, he knew that he was supposed to keep this one.

He climbed out of bed, already tired at the beginning of the day. The sky was early light, blood-red. "Shit," Bob said. *Sailors take warning.*

They had endured nearly two weeks of rain since the storm, and Bob was anxious to bale the two fields mowed for today. He worried if he would have enough help; Merle had been drinking again lately and sometimes didn't show up. The baler timing was off. Some of those circles were showing up, right in the middle of the hay. Nobody could explain it, but it was getting a bunch of the cows really agitated, the older ones especially. And from the time it was first born, Thunder's calf used to bleat and bleat, until Forty would come and beller back. Then it would settle down.

That goddam dog ran out the door when Gerry left to bring the cows up for milking. While it actually looked like he was helping to bring them in, Bob preferred to believe that he somehow must be messing them up.

Merle didn't show for milking. Bob was dreading that, because when Merle was there, Gerry was usually pretty quiet. When he wasn't, Gerry wanted to talk about playing semipro ball or the war. Since his birthday last month, Gerry got on about the war all the time.

"So you're tellin' me you think it's right?" he demanded.

"Jesus, do we have ta go through that again? I told ya, I'll get ya a farm deferment if ya want me to." This was Bob's trump card, played early to shut down the argument before it could start.

Gerry gritted his teeth in silent response, while Bossy winced as Farmer Bob was jerking the last bit of milk from her udder. She was angry enough with Farmer Bob to want to kick him, having just the week before pledged to transfer her affection from him to Gerry. But now he was done with her and had turned around to put the machine on Thunder, who had a terribly sunburned udder.

Bob was still annoyed with Gerry, so annoyed that he was rough with Thunder, normally a dangerous thing to do. However, Thunder had undergone a transformation since giving birth to her calf, especially because it was being raised and the other cows were treating her differently, like someone special. She flinched and squirmed, but would not kick at him.

The cows were waiting for something to happen, because Farmer Bob had been so short-tempered that something was sure to break. When Thunder was done, they quietly listened for the next cow's reaction. Gerry finished milking Charlotte at the same time and was slowly gathering the machine to step out across the gutter to begin on the next pair.

Billie was the next cow to be milked, the most disagreeable, mean cow in the barn. Gerry's father was also being methodical, hoping to wait out his son.

"I'll milk the Molshoc cow," Bob volunteered as he strode across the floor.

*Aw gee, thanks, Dad,* Gerry thought. *Leave Billie for me to milk. Why don't you just send me to Vietnam?* He climbed in between Billie and Dutchess, who wasn't inclined to move over much to give him room to dodge Billie's kicks. Gerry attempted to wipe some dirt gently from Billie's teats before putting the machine on, but she aimed a jab at his chin. Gerry ducked back, and Billie's hoof caught his toe and sent him hopping on one foot. "Stinkin' animal, rotten son of a bi—" Gerry choked down the rest of the curse, still unable to disobey his mother's dictum, at least not in front of her or his father.

"Go ahead and put the rope on her," Bob said. Gerry slipped through the stanchion, grabbed a length of rope off a nail on the wall, and cinched it tight just in front of her haunches. She kept trying to kick but could only rock back and forth, mincing around as the teat cups squeezed her sunburned nipples. Each pulse stiffened her resolve to get back at Gerry somehow when she had the chance. He seemed to sense it, though, not taking the rope off her until milking was done so he could undo it while shielded by the post on her left side.

Bob tried to relax while milking Aretha, but about halfway through she turned around and fixed an unnerving gaze on him. Then she mooed gently, in a way that reminded him of Peanut, and looked away. As she was let out of her stanchion she kept looking back over her shoulder at him.

When he thought about it while rinsing out the milking machines he had a mild panic. *Jesus, I've gotta get a grip. This is ridiculous.* He thought again about selling Thunder's calf, but that would have to wait until tomorrow when the auction was on.

"Renee, we need a hand this afternoon when you're done with work. We got a lotta hay down." Bob's eyes were fixed on the sink faucets just behind Gerry, as if there were something very important about them.

"No, I don't think so . . . Da . . . uh, no," she replied firmly. "I'm meeting some friends right after work about a dem—an event we're setting up next week."

A yeaı ago this past spring Onlius State had closed early, before final exams, after the rioting at Kent State, but Renee had stayed in town and organized protests until late May. She had been involved in protests ever since. All of Edna's entreaties were met with "It's what I have to do, Mother."

It worried Edna sick, and made Bob furious that she wasn't helping out on the farm. Now Gerry was growing bolder in his opposition to the war at the same time that he was rankled about being stuck on the farm with his father.

"Well, ya know we need the help. Merle hasn't been showing up, an' your cousins have got hay fever now that they know what real work is like."

"Maybe you could meet with your friends tonight, after we're done," Edna offered, her eyes pleading for some recognition from Renee. For months now Renee had been avoiding her, and could only seem to look directly at her father, who always refused to return her look.

"We've already agreed on meeting at five-thirty, as soon as I can get over there from work."

"Well, bring 'em over here. You can talk on the wagon, unloadin', or up in the mow with me," Gerry said.

"I don't wanna bunch of people gettin' in the way who don't know what they're doin'," Bob shot over at Gerry.

"Look, this is really important. It's what I have to do," Renee said resolutely, in the direction of the toaster.

"Two fields down and it's goin' to rain sometime this afternoon, sure as shit. The baler's not tyin' right and we're shorthanded. Helpin' is what you have to do."

"I don't want to argue with you about this," Renee said evenly.

"That's right. You're not gonna. Just git back here after work an' help. That's what puts food in your mouth, clothes on your back, an' a roof over your head."

"But I—"

"And it sends you to college."

"Well, it doesn't have to," Renee said to her plate.

"Whaddaya mean?" Bob shouted. There were flecks of spittle in the corners of his mouth.

"I mean that I have a place to stay, and with my job now I can get by on my own," she said defiantly, straight into Bob's eyes.

"After all I did for you, and now you could go off an' move in with that bastard banker's son. *Jee-sus.*"

Renee was white-hot with anger. Edna was in disbelief. Renee had not been seeing Hugh for months, not for over a year.

"I am *not* going to live with any *banker's* son," she screamed. "And I am not going to stay where I'm taken for granted just for being a woman."

"Renee, Renee, wait. Don't say that. You don't mean that," Edna pleaded.

"Mother, you, you're part of the problem. *Don't you see that?* You let him get away with it." She started to break down into tears, but stiffened herself by getting up and storming out of the kitchen.

"I'll come and get my things later, when I'm ready," she said as she walked out the front door.

Gerry's mouth felt dry and bitter as he watched his father tear off a chunk of toast and chew, as if that were all he had on his mind.

Merle coasted into the driveway not more than two minutes after Renee had left, grinning from secret knowledge that Bob was having a bad day. He had gotten more attention from their parents all his life, but now that they were gone, the only thing that made Merle happy was when Bob was having trouble. That was why going on a three-day drunk when Bob needed his help was what he just had to do sometimes.

He'd heard last night at Groh's that Edna had been seen getting baler parts over at Zelzac's, so Merle had determined to show his brother up by fixing the baler once and for all. In five minutes he had taken one side of the knotter apart.

"What the hell are you doing?" Bob exploded.

"Well, Jee-zus Christ, I'm fixin' yer baler for ya."

"Who asked you ta do that? Where didja hear there was anything wrong with my baler?"

"At Groh's. Curley told me you was havin' problems yesterday, so I came over to fix it." Merle grinned solicitously.

"Goddammit. If I needed your help fixin' somethin', I'd hafta sell the place."

"Why you ungrateful bastard. I'da had this all fixed if you'd given me five more minutes."

"There's nothing wrong with the sonuvabitchin' knotter. Now you probably screwed it up good. Jesus!"

"I'm a mechanic. I've worked on more equipment than you'll ever see—"

"Yeah, you're some mechanic! Didn't even know what was wrong with this and took a perfectly good piece o' machinery apart for no reason."

"I'm a mechanic. I worked on everythin' at New Process."

"Then why'd they ever let ya go on disability, if you was such a goddam good mechanic? They couldn't wait for ya to leave. Jesus, I coulda used your help puttin' hay in, but where were ya? Gettin' drunk with your no-good friends."

"My friends are all right. They know I'm a mechanic."

Merle was still tired from the last three days, and his mind had not yet cleared from all the beer. During his twenty-five years in the factory, the measure of a man's worth was how many different machines he could keep in operation. Merle had operated several over that time, none of them in outstanding fashion.

"Well, if you wanna help, then come back ta put hay in. Whyn'tcha go get some coffee and get somethin' ta eat? Come back around eleven-thirty if ya wanta help."

"If ya don't want the help I'm offerin'," Merle slurred as he walked away, "mebbe I won't be back."

Gerry had been told to grease the rake and start kicking over the hay in the lot bordering Molshoc's, after he finished cleaning the barn. All the while he was doing chores he swung back and forth between anger and confusion.

*He said he always hated being drafted into the army. He hated the officers, hated the work, the filth, the killing, everything. So he wants me to either go to Vietnam or stay here and rot on the farm, helping him. But Renee doesn't hafta stay, she can go and demonstrate against the war, or bullshit with her friends about how they should go and protest the war. Then Merle finally shows up to help fix the baler when it's broke down and we've got a ton of hay to put in, and he sends him home. And I can't take one day off to go to a tryout. Or Woodstock.*

*You gotta be home for milking,* he heard in his father's voice. As he idled around the field in second gear turning over the thick hay, the resentment cycled through his head, a tape loop of repressed rage.

Turning the corner on the far end of the field, Gerry caught a glint of light from a car on the road and figured it must be the mailman. So when he reached the near corner of the field he shut the Farmall off and bounded over the windrows toward the mailbox.

Gerry loved getting the mail. Even though he rarely received anything, he always daydreamed of winning a lottery he never even had entered, and it couldn't happen if anyone else got to the mailbox first.

But when he was almost upon it something stopped him; there was something wrong that he could not put a name to. He walked past the mailbox, past the driveway and the vegetable garden, down the back road.

Barely above his own heartbeat the source of the fear focused into a whimpering. He ran to the ditch past the corner gatepost and found King in the roadside grass. Blood was trickling from his nose and mouth, the light nearly extinguished from his eyes. His chest had been crushed by the car he was chasing. He only had the strength to whimper softly, but he tried to open his mouth a little more to let Gerry know that he recognized him. More blood issued forth.

Gerry was too shocked for tears; numbness was radiating outward from his heart. He desperately wanted not to have to do what he knew had to be done. He found a thick stick from beneath a nearby maple, choked back a sob, and clubbed King just behind his ear.

The second blow ended the whimpering and drained the life from Gerry. He sagged to one knee next to his dog and cried.

"What the *hell* are you doin'?" Gerry hadn't heard the kitchen screen door slam as Bob had come back out from the house. "Why aren'tcha rakin' over that Molshoc piece?"

"I was . . . King's dead. . . . I stopped to get the mail." Bob looked from his son to the crumpled dog, silent.

After a moment Bob said quietly, "Better bury him in the grove, when ya finish rakin' that lot." Then he turned to go back to work on the baler.

"You don't even care," Gerry hurled at him.

"There's nothin' I can do about it. It's not that I don't care. There's just nothin' . . ."

"But you know . . . you know it's the last connection to Gramp."

Bob's eyes dropped to the dog, his first instant of understanding of its special bond with his son.

"Listen," Bob confided. "He was a dog, an' no good at what he was supposed ta do. We've got a lot ta do today. Better get back to it." He turned away to go to work on the baler.

Gerry went back to the rake, but not until after he had buried King in the same grove where his grandfather had buried so many of the woodchucks King had brought home from his hunting.

"Have some more potatoes, Ger," Edna said. She was shaken and could only cover it by pushing food.

"No thanks, Ma, not hungry."

Merle reached for the dish of warmed-up potatoes and scraped a healthy second portion onto his plate. He served himself up another hamburger with onions, then motioned Edna to reach him another cup of coffee. She poured it to overflowing, not paying attention to his cup. For some reason she could not take her eyes off her son.

Bob was beginning to be embarrassed by Edna's odd behavior. This was all out of proportion to the dog's being hit by a car. Something else must be wrong.

Merle slobbered ketchup over from his hamburger to the potatoes. Bob frowned at Merle's plate and shook his head. "Ya don't need to put anything else on those potatoes, buddy, they're fine just the way they are."

"I like 'em sometimes with ketchup. It's makin' me feel better," Merle said. "They're good potatoes, Edna, b'lieve me. Ma was the only one could make 'em better."

Bob wanted to argue with him, but thought better of it. With Gerry and Edna looking like zombies, anything might send them off the deep end. He searched his mind for a neutral topic.

"Edna, we get any mail?"

Gerry's eyes narrowed fiercely.

"That's it. That's who hadta of hit 'im. The mailman."

Edna had blanched instantly. Bob was now annoyed that she was so bothered by the dog. Merle was fishing a couple of Edna's molasses cookies out of the jar to have with his coffee.

"Well, Edna?" She tried to avoid his look, to get him to drop the subject. When Bob began tapping his fork on the edge of his plate, she knew it was no use trying to ignore him.

"Uh, no . . . we didn't get anything."

"Nothing? Why'd he even stop then?"

"I mean nothing important, not for us."

"I didn't get anything either?" Gerry asked.

"Uhm-uh."

"What?" Bob demanded. "Did he or not?"

"Yes," she whispered. She got up from the table and went to the bureau in the dining room, where all the household papers were kept. She returned with a small white envelope, which she handed to Gerry.

"Well, what is it?" Bob asked, as Gerry tore it open to read. His expression turned hard.

"What is it?" Bob grew louder. Edna's mouth was too dry to form words.

"Gerry, you look like you seen a ghost," Merle offered.

*"What is it?"*

Gerry looked his father full in the face. "I've been drafted."

Bob stared at the knotter and the threading arm like a newly discovered hieroglyphic. The more he tried to concentrate, the less he was able to focus. Just as he was about to decipher the sequence of the breakdown, the picture dissolved before his eyes. He blinked, tried to reset it, but could not hold it. Merle was right next to him, looking over his shoulder, pressuring him even more.

"Jesus Christ, Merle, give me some room. You're standin' in my light."

"The sun's over there on the other side of the baler, Bob."

"Well, you try figurin' this bastard out, I'm sick of it. Had this sonuvabitchin' piece of junk sold to Molshoc until his wife hung herself. Now I'm stuck with it." Bob stormed off, presumably to check up on Gerry, leaving Merle to puzzle out the baler.

He crossed the road and watched Gerry raking. He tried to focus on the hay turning over, work getting done, but from this distance things seemed to be moving too slowly. Gerry was very methodical and was distracted today, so he was working even more slowly.

*He'll never get done the rate he's goin'.* He felt himself filling with fury, and unconsciously began to trot across the field.

"Oh, man, what is it now?" Gerry said to himself, instinctively nudging the throttle down in case he was going too fast. "Suppose I better stop to see what's wrong."

"What's the matter?" he yelled to his father after he shut the tractor off and climbed down.

"Whaddaya doin'?" Bob yelled back.

"Tryin' to find out what's wrong."

"You're goin' too slow. Don't ya know how to rake faster?"

Gerry's face burned. He turned to walk back to the tractor.

"I'm talkin' to you! Don't turn your back on me!"

"I'm goin' to finish rakin' this piece over!" Gerry realized he had been raking hay since he was ten years old, and he couldn't believe he was getting yelled at now.

"Well, why don'tcha do that, goddammit, and hurry up about it."

"I was doin' that."

"You were draggin' your ass around this field. *Jee-zus!* You couldn'ta gone any slower, couldja?"

"What do you *want* from me? Can you tell me that? I'm doin' the best I can do! *Jee-ee-zus!*"

Bob was backed up for a second.

"Well, just get—"

"*Don't* tell me what to *do!*" Gerry exploded. "I'm not listenin' ta you anymore, ya hear me?"

"The *hell* you say!"

Gerry started up the tractor and opened up the throttle wide. He slammed the gearshift into third and popped the clutch, turning his head away when he saw his father still yelling and waving his arms in the air. He did his best to focus on the windrows of hay in front of him.

*One thing at a time,* he thought, as he began to plot his way out.

*Oh Christ,* thought Bob. *He'll wreck that thing at that speed.* He watched the tractor and rake bouncing around the field and realized it was out of his control. He turned back toward the house with the intent to go back to the baler, and as he walked quickly, images from his past began to swim through his head.

He saw himself as a twelve-year-old, driving a rake behind a team of horses while his father was working at the feed mill in town to make ends meet. He saw his mother pushing him off her lap, embarrassed, when he was five. He saw his brothers, Merle and Tom, going fishing, when he had to stay home and help kill and dress chickens. He saw the smoke on the northern horizon from Eddie's barn, the only memory he had of the last moments of his best friend's life. He saw the art-school recruiter driving away in his big Ford, and himself leaving to go into the army, eventually crossing Omaha Beach.

Suddenly he realized he had been standing in the barn, alone for unknown time, in the spot where Forty's strange calf had been tied up. Once he was aware of it he began to move away, but not before he caught the new calf, Thunder's calf, looking at him with the same strange calm intelligence. It seemed to want to speak to him. He hurried off, with no clear sense of destination.

Bob fled the barn, but then had nowhere to turn. On his left, Merle was waiting to see him break. On his right, his only son was desperate to get away from the farm, and from him. Pain stabbed at his chest. He was stuck in the center of the oval driveway, the strange calf behind him and fear of letting Edna see him like this stopping him from going forward.

But when he looked up at the porch it was longer and lower, made all of wood, his mother's porch. And he could see her standing on the top step, looking in his direction, but past him, through him, as if she was looking for Tom or Merle behind him. Her face transformed to Edna's, reminding him how upset Edna was about Renee's leaving, and Gerry's being drafted. He couldn't face her in this trouble.

The pains grew stronger, he sagged to his knees. *Don't let Merle see me,* he begged, or Edna, or Gerry, or his mother. He couldn't calm his mind. The forbidden memory came back. He fell on his side, covering himself in Edna's peonies. Then his father's last trip to the woods wound, slow-motion, through his mind. Bob couldn't change it, speed it up, slow it down, or stop it.

*He had been embarrassed too many times. This would have to be the last time. If he was not good for anybody, could not do what he wanted to do, needed to do, then he would not stay. He went into the kitchen and from the closet behind the door took his twelve-gauge shotgun and a handful of shotgun shells. This war with Bob had gone on long enough. If Bob believed he was no longer useful, then there was no sense in continuing.*

Bob watched his father slowly opening the gate to let himself through, bracing the butt of the shotgun against the gatepost.

"He's only goin' huntin', Edna, don't worry about him."

Gerry was watching a World Series game on TV, not interested in tramping through the woods this afternoon with his grandfather and King.

Bob rose from the flowerbed to tread on his father's path. As he was pulled toward the river, like someone being called, the scene of Russell's death unfolded from deep within his memory.

They had heard his shotgun fired once, then only silence for hours. King had come up from the woods alone, not unusual, but very agitated and nervous.

When he had not returned by milking, Bob sent Gerry to look for him.

Bob crossed the lane and followed along the stone wall until he reached the ravine. He was only semiconscious of where he was walking. But the pains were just as strong, and his sense of being trapped just as desperate.

Gerry had found his grandfather dead, shot in the chest, his stilled heart half torn away. He was slumped forward from a sitting position, under a beautiful beech tree which had been split up its trunk by lightning decades ago, but had not fallen. It was surrounded by younger hemlock and pines that kept it braced upright. The yellow beech leaves had been blown gently around Russell's legs, giving him the look of an unfinished Halloween dummy.

Gerry had brought the county sheriffs almost to the spot where he'd found him. Bob would not let him go all the way back to the scene. Despite the scene and everything Gerry told them about how Russell carried his gun, they called it a hunting accident. The town paper carried it that way, the minister Edna found to do the eulogy consoled them all about "the accident." But Gerry and Renee heard the whispers at school, and so did Edna at Zerrillo's, and Bob at the milk plant.

Bob stumbled in a woodchuck hole on the far side of the ravine, climbed to his feet, and kept moving toward the river. He was almost to the woods along the river, near where Peanut had forded it on her running-away attempt, a short stretch north on a cowpath from the clearing used for the Gathering.

He turned to walk down the path, across the ravine where it emptied into the river. It was the beech tree calling him just beyond the crackling, humming wires of the power line.

Russell had been exhausted by the last days of haying. Then he'd been unable even to drive the pickup truck around after the combine to collect the bags of oats. He was sick with fever and pain racking his guts. The gospel of work that he had been raised with, and taught, was attacking him now, from the inside.

He was so depressed about not being able to work that he had started sneaking looks at the family Bible, mostly the Old Testament.

Although it was of little comfort, every day he grew more religious, and less spiritual.

Bob's trance had deepened beyond consciousness, sleepwalking toward death. The scrub maples and alders gave way to a clearing, where his pace quickened. Before he reached the far side, the blue cow from Molshoc's farm crossed his trail. She stopped in the middle of the cowpath, blocking his way. He began to circle around her, but she moved with him, turning always to look in his eyes.

"C'mon, ya dumb animal, let me get by," Bob yelled, his voice almost breaking. She would not let go. He took a step to the right and she cantered in front of him. *He's not calling you to go to him,* Aretha thought toward him. *You don't need to go there. What you need is right here.* Then she twitched the stub of her tail, and a fly somehow was knocked off her flank. He saw the energy of her phantom tail. She was still whole.

Bob blinked, tried to clear his vision. Aretha squared to face him directly, looking straight into his eyes. Charlotte appeared, and Thunder, and Young Smitty walking gracefully and purposefully toward him. Forty joined them, with White Brat and Billie, each approaching him as they would an initiate in the Order, capturing his attention, compelling him to recognize them.

Bob felt weak. Whenever he tried to move to one side past the cows, more appeared gently to block his path. In moments they had surrounded him in a loose circle, filling the Gathering place.

The crush of his father's suicide was suffocating. He had held on to it for too long, letting it overwhelm him. Bob was wrapped so tightly within himself that no one had been able to get to him and no one had been able to count on him, for almost four years. His father's death had taken away his last chance to prove himself worthy. It was beyond Edna's or Gerry's or Renee's powers to fill the void blasted through Russell's son.

But the cows danced for him, a combination of prancing and slow cantering that rippled and surged around the circle. The air seemed to get sharper, more crisp, helping to ease Bob's breathing.

He could not get around Aretha, could not get out of her sight, so he stopped, looked back into her eyes, and suddenly knew that she was sacred. For just one moment, he knew the name of everything.

He began to see what she could see. Souls swirled in the air, just above the heads of the cows assembled in the clearing. Near Young Smitty were her mother and grandmother. Bossy was flanked by her mother, Marianne, and White John.

Forty and Thunder were connected by rainbow links to a ghost calf, the one that had seemed to try to talk to him in the barn.

The cows were enchanted that he could see them. They bounded to show him they were not really tame at all, urging him to play. Bob touched Brownie's flank, then scratched Bossy behind the ear.

He was alert but with an added dimension. Textures were more intense, aromas carrying him to distant parts of his memory.

Designs whose meaning he did not know flashed into his brain, as they appeared in sculptures, on rock walls and mountaintops, embedded in standing fields of crops. Without knowing why, he felt the calming presence of Peanut, mooing the same messages in the new language of the vision dance.

His father and mother waited just beyond the edge of the circle, luminous. A warm light melted through his chest and stretched out to them, looping back to fill him again.

The light deepened as if filtered through a canopy, and the cows seemed to disappear. The trees were thicker, their bark shaggier. It was before the clearing existed, before cows were even known in this part of the world. He saw it in winter-deep snow disturbed only by tracks of deer, rabbit, wolf, bear. It thawed before his eyes. He heard the river, swollen, rushing its snowmelt to the lake.

Bob was transfixed. His heart opened for the pain to flow through and out, leaving a feeling of grace. And, finally, the wisdom that neither pain nor joy, life nor death comes only once.

The warmth of the summer settled over him. Charlotte, Aretha, and Forty cut through his vision. The maples surrounding the clearing were thin again, newer, their bark smooth and gray.

He checked Aretha's eyes, caught the violet tint; then beyond, just a normal, dumb curiosity. He knew the moment was past.

That evening Bossy felt the great care that Bob took while cleaning her bag before milking. And all of them noticed when Renee came down to the barn. *Ooh, Princess is here,* echoed from thought to thought when she crossed the threshold between the milkhouse and the barn. Bob's face lit up, even though he was still upset about Gerry.

Merle was a little late, came into the barn sheepish on the inside and glaring on the outside. Bob said "Hulloo" pleasantly. Merle waited for the barrage. When he saw Renee standing down on the barn floor as if she owned it, he got suspicious. By the end of milking, Merle's nerves were raw.

Not so for Edna. She had started the evening routine as soon as Bob left for the barn, had chatted interestedly with Renee about college cafeteria food as she was putting her work shoes on, then tried to return to it. Instead, she cried. Hot, bitter tears streamed uncontrollably down her cheeks so hard and fast that she could not see what she was doing. She finally collapsed onto the bed in the spare room that Gerry usually slept on in the summer, and let go of them. She soon fell asleep and dreamed of her father, sitting with her in the kitchen of their old house in Vermont. He told her she would be okay, said goodbye, and strolled out the door to find her mother. Brilliant sunlight flooded the windows and open door, blinding her momentarily. When the door closed, she saw herself, a woman approaching fifty.

After Bob came up for supper and asked for just a bowl of shredded wheat, she knew something powerful had changed but still was angry with him. Even when Bob told the story about his father riding the tractor like an Apache on the warpath, she could not let go of her anger, of the question *Why did it take you so long?*

Because Gerry had been gone for hours. During supper Renee spoke out.

"He's going to try to get out, you know."

"Yeah, I expect he is," Bob whispered.

"And he can, without the farm deferment."

"He can? How?"

"As a conscientious objector. It's not easy, but it could work."

Bob looked at her. "Did you learn that at college?"

"Yeah, that's one of the things." She braced herself for the attack.

"That's a good thing," he said to his cereal. He couldn't lift his eyes to meet hers.

Edna could not even begin to forgive him when he came in her room to talk about how glad he was that Renee was staying and of how much he missed his father and mother. She held him as he cried, face to face, before he fell asleep. Then she lay awake, listening for the creak of the third step.

But Gerry was still sitting alone in his car, afraid to move, biting his nails, watching the lights reflecting on the St. Lawrence, trying to figure out how to get to them, unable to understand why his dad always had to act more like a boss than a father; wondering if he could get across the river, to Canada.

# About the Author

RAY PETERSEN teaches political science and lives in a lakelocked village in northern New York State, one slapshot away from the Canadian border. This is his first novel.

Tension between scientific
& spiritual

VIETNAM ERA

HUMAN FAMILY

COW FAMILY